HIGH INFIDELITY

At forty-four, loyal English wife Lara Winters discovers that Brock, her husband of 21 years, has been cheating on her. Devastated, desperate, she flees her home in London and heads for the farthest place she can imagine, from her old, blinkered life. She escapes to Byron Bay, Australia. On her first day in the laid-back town, Lara almost runs over the red-haired, slightly raddled Ruby in the car park. Relieved to be still alive, the warm-hearted Aussie leases Lara a small cottage on her semi-rural property where Lara's adventures of self-discovery begin ...

SPECIAL MESSAGE TO READERS

THE ULVERSCROFT FOUNDATION
(registered UK charity number 264873)

was established in 1972 to provide funds for research, diagnosis and treatment of eye diseases. Examples of major projects funded by the Ulverscroft Foundation are:-

- The Children's Eye Unit at Moorfelds Eye Hospital, London
- The Ulverscroft Children's Eye Unit at Great Ormond Street Hospital for Sick Children
- Funding research into eye diseases and treatment at the Department of Ophthalmology, University of Leicester
- The Ulverscroft Vision Research Group, Institute of Child Health
- Twin operating theatres at the Western Ophthalmic Hospital, London
- The Chair of Ophthalmology at the Royal Australian College of Ophthalmologists

You can help further the work of the Foundation by making a donation or leaving a legacy. Every contribution is gratefully received. If you would like to help support the Foundation or require further information, please contact:

THE ULVERSCROFT FOUNDATION
The Green, Bradgate Road, Anstey
Leicester LE7 7FU, England
Tel: (0116) 236 4325

website: www.ulverscroft-foundation.org.uk

SHELLEY DAVIDOW

---◆---

HIGH INFIDELITY

Complete and Unabridged

AURORA
Leicester

First published in 2019 by
Journeys to Words Publishing

First Aurora Edition
published 2021
by arrangement with
Journeys to Words Publishing

*A catalogue record for this book is available
from the British Library.*

ISBN 978–1–78782–715–8

Published by
Ulverscroft Limited
A̶ ̶ ̶ ̶ ̶ Leicestershire

und in Great Britain by
l., Padstow, Cornwall

nted on acid-free paper

1

Outside, London wept at Lara's late afternoon departure. The ground couldn't hold any more water and visibility stayed at a cold, grey minimum. Her dull-eyed reflection stared back from the A380 window. 'You did one thing right,' she said to her sullen-looking double. 'You raised two amazing kids. On your own if the truth be told. And you can feel good about that.'

No use. She didn't feel good — about anything.

Lara used to be terrified of flying. It took Valium to get her from London to Hamburg. She was convinced that every bump signaled both engines seizing and stalling after being hit by birds. But this time as she boarded the Singapore Airlines A380 at Heathrow she felt calm. So what if we crash, she thought. As they took off, Lara relished the engines roaring like monsters beneath her. At that moment, she knew she could, for the first time in her life, manage a bungee jump without thinking if someone cared to offer her the chance. This new mood had everything to do with no longer caring about her old life. Fears that she'd long held all vanished. She was also sure she could abseil forty metres into an airless cave with a pool beneath crawling with leeches. As the airbus hauled its massive hull into the sky, her heart didn't even skip a beat. She watched tiny grey houses, roads, cars, shards of her life, disappear below the clouds. When the plane hit turbulence over France, she held the shaking hand of the older lady next to her offering comforting words. 'Don't worry,' Lara said. 'I promise there are things worse than dying in a plane crash.'

Lara did, however, make a small request to the universe at that moment: if this plane falls out of the sky, please don't let it be in a remote Eurasian desert but somewhere tropical, with blue waters and shiny rainbow fish.

2

Australia was the Dark Continent. She couldn't see it, but Lara knew it lay beneath now. She'd been excessively map-watching rather than movie-watching for the entire flight. Below, no lights, no sign of human habitation for the past four and a half hours, flying at nearly a thousand kilometres an hour. Outside the window, Orion hung sideways and new constellations appeared, one of which Lara stared at, recognising it from books and films. The Southern Cross announced she'd made it into new territory, a hemisphere untainted — a Brock-free zone. From now on, she would claim every experience as exclusively hers. Lara had no idea what that meant, but she relished the thought.

She arrived in Brisbane in the early morning, still in one piece and felt not a jot of jetlag. Perhaps the overnight in Singapore, lying in the airport hotel spa and scrubbing her skin until it almost came off, helped her get some sleep. At any rate, she noted she'd still made sense to the friendly Aussie personnel at the Thrifty Car Rental place, and she had managed to find her way to a slightly mouldy Best Western Hotel near the airport. Even the rush-hour cars streaming into the sun-drenched city's CBD seemed mostly familiar, European and Japanese. Thank goodness they drive on the correct side of the road here, she thought. The left side. She would get by almost as if she was on home turf with the help of her GPS. Humidity wrapped itself around her. The air felt heavy and thick with the smell of undergrowth and damp and the perfume of foreign blossoms.

★　★　★

When Lara opened her eyes, it was morning, a full twenty-four hours after arrival. She thought someone was shining a spotlight onto her face but it was only the southern hemisphere sun pouring through a gap in the curtains. Someone should have told her about the light. And the birds. The sheer joy in the atmosphere was an affront if you were feeling glum, she thought, or if you were tempted to sink into depression. Outside on the balcony, rainbow lorikeets screeched their welcome. Sulphur-crested cockatoos screamed from a Poinciana tree sounding, she thought, like furious humans battling laryngitis. She looked at the red leaves on the tree against the birds' snowy feathers. Never in her life had she seen such brilliance nor heard such a raucous dawn chorus. Beyond the hotel, the Brisbane River snaked by on its languorous journey to the sea. She squinted as she stood in a pink nightshirt watching the traffic trawl down Kingsford-Smith Drive. Finally, she thought. She'd made it. The Great Escape. From Brock. From betrayal. From a life far too ordinary.

★　★　★

At the checkout desk the young man asked if she was on holiday or returning home.

'I'm on my way home,' she said straight up. If home was where the heart was, and hers lay jigsawed in a million pieces under her clothes, then this might as

4

well be it for now, she thought.

'Welcome home, then, Mrs Sinclair.'

'Oh, it's Ms, if you don't mind.'

'Ms Sinclair,' he corrected with a bow of his head. She stood staring at him for a moment as she continued to rearrange her life. Let this be the last time anyone called her by Brock's surname. Ever, she thought. She was taking herself back. Lara Anne Winters again,

L.A.W. from now on. A law unto herself.

'Enjoy your day,' she said, and swept out of the hotel to her Thrifty Toyota in the car park.

★ ★ ★

The Pacific Motorway wound south, out of Brisbane. Lara didn't see the sea until she'd been driving for almost an hour, and when she did, she got distracted and drove onto bumps on the side of the road designed to make a horrendous noise in order to wake sleepy drivers who might not be holding to the designated straight and narrow.

'Fine, fine!' she said, pulling herself back into the centre of the motorway.

The view that met her took her breath away. Why wasn't everyone in London living here already? Who would be able to sustain a two-hour to-work-and-back tube commute on a London November afternoon or a February morning, after knowing about this? Under an almost equatorial sun the sea spread out, a blue carpet that reflected billions of flecks of light. Beyond the dune foliage, a stretch of sunlit sand went for miles. The ocean breathed in, and as it exhaled, waves tumbled towards the shore. Oblivious to all the trouble in the world, nature seemed wild and happy. She tasted salt and realised tears were sliding down her cheeks. Lies. Deceit. Lost youth. Clichés — her marriage an unfolding soap opera that was only too real. The worst thing was that she hadn't seen it coming — a well-disguised metaphorical tsunami. She felt like an idiot. How many things over the last twenty years should have alerted her to his infidelities? She had been brilliant at denial, though she suspected it was more an inherent flaw — her unjustifiable belief in the goodness of most people, including Brock, which prevented her from comprehending that things as she saw them, were not as they seemed. She felt like a colossal fool. Lara hadn't even questioned his response after finding brightly coloured condoms in his desk drawer. When Brock said he'd bought them as a joke for a friend, she'd believed him. She gripped the wheel and wished, for a moment it was his neck, or at least the part of it that allowed blood to flow to his brain.

After a few miles of sea and sand to the left, a dark thought struck Lara. She contemplated what would happen if she found an optimum point somewhere ahead and drove off a cliff into the sea. It might be weeks before anyone knew she'd vanished, if they ever did. She imagined her rotting and bloated corpse showing up one day in some fisherman's net, covered in barnacles and clusters of coral maybe months from now. The poor man would hold his nose in disgust and think, oh my God, the ugliest drowned woman in the world. And what a stink! Then he'd vomit off the side of his boat.

She held the wheel so tightly her nails dug into her palms.

Brock had left thirteen messages on her mobile phone in the two days prior to her departure. Message 1: he asked her to *please* call him. Message 2: he was concerned about her mental health. Message 3: he wanted her to please understand that he just needed to be himself, finally, and not suppress his impulses. The next few were insulting variations on the general theme of 'you selfish cow, return my calls'. She stopped listening after the sixth.

Brock, in the greasy style of one accustomed to sliding out of anything uncomfortable or confrontational, had assuaged his guilt by paying her out pronto. Director of his own architectural firm, he had transferred a respectable sum of money – no questions – into her bank account. She had not interpreted this as an act of generosity. He just wanted no contest when he wiped the marriage slate clean. Bastard. She knew deep down that the cliché that she deserved better was true — if she could only figure out what 'better' looked like.

Lara's thoughts about driving off a cliff came to an abrupt conclusion.

No. If only to spite Brock, she *wouldn't* drive into the sea.

It would be a meaningless end for a betrayed, slightly greying, forty-four-year-old. She kept her hand steady on the wheel and drove the next hour to Byron Bay.

3

Byron Bay, to the eye of a tired new arrival, looked like an afterparty from a bygone era, which no one had noticed was over. Rainbow coloured tie-dye shirts on dreadlocked men and women; no shoes on any feet; a middle-aged woman wearing a gigantic writhing python around her neck; feral-looking children sitting in a tree on the side of the main street. Lara rolled down her window as she headed to the beach car park. A young man on his phone said in a drawl to his friend, 'nothin' mate. I'm doin' nothin'. So fucken bored, ay, just wanna die.' Lara smiled. Even in this alleged paradise where Elle Macpherson, Chris Hemsworth and Olivia Newton-John chose to live, some folks apparently wanted to die of boredom! They should try South London on a tube in Autumn after the clocks were turned back an hour and the gloom of failing sunlight lasted from ten in the morning until three-thirty in the afternoon. Lara sighed and parked the car metres from the beach.

The crescent of beachfront smelled like sunscreen and popcorn. The ultimate romantic holiday aroma, she thought. The Pacific shimmered in afternoon sun. Lara looked south at the headland where a white lighthouse rose into the cloudless sky. She felt sand warm her toes as she walked the shoreline and inhaled breaths of unfamiliar, saline air. This place, she thought, exists every day — looks like this, smells like this, feels like this. In contrast, the northern hemisphere demanded that much of the year be spent

8

beneath onion layers of heavy clothing, low light and bad tempers.

Lara had imagined it would be easy to find a hotel, but that proved not to be true. She'd left it rather late after her walk, and one after another, the no vacancy signs out the front of both glamorous resorts and dingy hotels sent her on her way. No room at the inn for this weary traveller. She drove around and eventually stopped at a local pharmacy to purchase a few essentials: leg wax, toothpaste, and hair conditioner. Lara took stock of her situation at a juice bar. She ordered something that looked like pulverised and freshly mown grass and which promised to boost her immune system and make her young again.

A man in a G-string, his skin as tanned as a piece of leather, strolled past her. The sulphur-crested cockatoo on his arm looked her right in the eye. 'Go to hell!' it squawked.

'Go to hell yourself,' she said and bent down to take a long sip of liquid lawn. She smiled. The cockatoo-owner frowned.

Feeling slightly nauseous after her drink, Lara went back to her car. She decided that whatever happened, she would need some basics for survival. Down the street, she spied a Woolworths and headed into the car park. She went into the store and bought ingredients for a finger-supper speculating that she could possibly, actually end up spending the night in her car. She would try one last place, after which she felt tears and general collapse into self-pity might be unavoidable.

Lara got into the car and tiredly backed out of her parking spot. Suddenly an ear-splitting horn blasted behind her, and she turned, heart kicking into a rapid-fire assault against her ribcage as she slammed on brakes. A Hyundai had materialised at the rear. Lara rolled down her window, shaking, tears rising in her throat. This was an insane place. What if the offended driver pulled out a gun?

'Honey,' said a round-faced woman with shining red hair who leaned out of her window. 'Are you try-inta kill me?'

'Oh gosh! Oh I am so, so sorry! I honestly did not see you! Blind spot. Jetlag. My error. Please forgive me. I'm so, so tired and I have been looking for a decent hotel for hours and they're all fully booked and …'

'Hang on there, darl. Let me just park okay?'

Lara dropped her head onto her arms on the steering wheel. Tears fell. Her nose ran. The plastic got sticky. The red-haired lady came over and Lara looked up. The lady pulled a stack of tissues out of her handbag with stubby fingers. 'Here, no need to cry, okay? Look, darl, you didn't hit me, so stop look-ing so miserable.' Lara didn't know what to say. Was she being deceived by vision warped with the tears that trembled on the edge of her eyelids? This woman was a hippy relic from Glastonbury way back in the mists of time.

'Now, you mentioned you didn't have a place to stay?'

Lara blinked, took the wad of tissues, nodded her head and blew her nose forcefully.

The woman put her elbows on the window frame and smiled. 'My name's Ruby and I think I might just be able to help you.'

★　★　★

10

Lara followed Ruby's rusting heap of a car out of Byron Bay for a few kilometres down a winding road to a small suburb that nestled amidst trees and riotous undergrowth.

After travelling down more narrow and rustic roads, Ruby's Hyundai pulled into the drive of a sprawling property. Tall gums, bunyas and bangalow palms surrounded a Queenslander that had seen more stately times. Lara followed her new friend around the back and parked beside a high-set one-bedroomed cottage across from the house, looking out over hectares of national forest.

'It's for rent. Mates' rates. Yours if you want it,' Ruby said moments after Lara had climbed out of her car.

Oh, I want it, Lara thought. After her sad visions of spending the night in her Thrifty rental and likely being accosted by thugs and drunkards or bitten by some head-sized venomous spider, she was overwhelmed by gratitude for her sweet-smiling saviour and the magnificent surroundings. Never in her life had a near car accident been such a good thing.

'Darl, what about dinner? Do you want to have a bite to eat with me?'

'Ruby, you're too kind. I think I might just eat the cheese and crackers I bought and retire. It's been a hectic day.'

'No worries,' Ruby said. 'But don't be shy, mind, and come and get me if you need anything. Tissues, a shoulder, whatever. Bed's made. Clean towels always there at the ready. You have an accent. From the UK?'

Lara looked at the high-set cottage. 'Yep,' she said.

'I see,' said Ruby. 'Let me guess. You're here for a reason. Something's happened?'

'Exactly,' Lara said, amused at Ruby's attempt at

11

psychic reading and caught off guard by her direct-
ness.

'Darl, I'll let you get some rest and leave you to it.
I'll come by in the morning. Don't cry alone, y'hear?'

'Yes ma'am,' Lara said. 'Thanks for the rescue. I
could see myself spending the night in my car.'

'Nah,' Ruby said. 'That's not how the universe
works, darl. You need to have some trust.'

Ruby stepped forward, wrapped her ample arms
around Lara in a she-bear hug and said, 'welcome to
Byron. If you've come here for healing, you'll find it,
darl. See ya later.'

How did she know?

As Ruby strode off across the lawn to her house,
Lara waved with two fingers. 'Bye,' she said. 'Thank
you for everything.'

'No worries,' Ruby called.

If angels ever appeared in human form, Ruby was
one of them, Lara thought, drunk with gratitude.

The steps to the high-set cottage creaked under
the weight of Lara plus suitcase, but the haven in the
trees was worth the climb. The cottage had a wide
wrap-around deck. Inside the French doors, was an
idyllic one-bedroomed, high-ceilinged home. Wow,
Lara thought. This will do. She dragged her suitcase
into the bedroom and, standing at the end of the bed,
dropped onto it, sinking her face into soft pillows.
Beneath her nose, she found a bar of pink, rose-
scented soap in the shape of a heart. Thank you Ruby,
she thought, Goddess of Small Things That Matter.

Midnight came and went and Lara wasn't even close
to dropping off. She climbed out of bed and went out
onto the deck to gaze into the night. A foreign night.
A new continent. A new hemisphere. A new life.

That's what she wanted, right? And, were all Australians as generous as Ruby, she wondered? Was there something wrong with her that she had just followed a complete stranger into the bush? Bloody hell, Lara thought, where was her suspicion, her self-protective instinct, or didn't she even have one? Ruby could have been an axe-murderer. Thus far things seemed to be working in her favour, but she did question her profound lack of mistrust. Ruby hadn't even mentioned rent money yet. Lara found this rather refreshing.

These were chatter thoughts, not the ones keeping Lara awake. She was wondering what in God's name she was going to do with her life as of tomorrow, or rather, today. The moon rose. Behind her, Jupiter winked. The Milky Way, a splash of white across the sky, had shifted towards the horizon over the past three hours. She waited for the elusive God of Travel Exhaustion to prompt her to bed, but he wouldn't. Her ears rang with the pulse of Australian crickets. Two bats exploded out from under the eaves of the cottage and she had to duck as they beat the air just above her on their way to distant night hunting.

What a place. The wooden deck chair pressed into the backs of Lara's legs. The wrap-around veranda enabled her to peer into the back room of her new landlady's house. A light went on. A shadow passed in front of the bay window, and a short while later, the light went off again. At least, she thought, she wasn't completely alone.

The luminous hands of her watch marked another hour. She should have tossed the bloody thing out of the window on the way down here, allowed some hitchhiker the good fortune of finding it on the side of the road. The watch had been Brock's gift on her last birthday. Good Lord, was that less than a year ago? That was when his office assistant — allegedly a lesbian — had first become a topic of conversation over the dinner table. He was working with her on two projects, found her fascinating, felt intrigued by her love for other women, was vaguely repulsed by her, he said. Ah, yes. Repulsed by her. That sentence fragment had only been for Lara's benefit. Why would she ever see a lesbian as a threat to twenty years of marriage? Anyone else would have seen that coming. But not Lara. She was, apparently, the world's biggest idiot. She remembered decades ago, how her science teacher had tapped his head when pupils failed to give him the correct answers. 'Osmium. Pure Osmium,' he'd say, referring to the densest metal. Osmium, Lara, she thought to herself, pressing her fingers into her temples. As far as Brock's antics were concerned. Pure Osmium.

She looked at her watch again. One in the morning. Even the watch was a joke at her expense. Time's up, it said, before he or she did. And so, her worst relationship nightmare had come to pass. Here she was hitting forty-four, alone, in a one-roomed rented cottage in Australia on the east coast, without a single plan in her head. Just over a month ago, she had thought she was the happily married wife of Brock Sinclair, shopping at Sainsbury's in her old jeans whilst trying to decide which yoghurt to buy.

The moon rose higher, a cruel celestial body that pulled all bodies of water, including hers, and mapped the tides, the monthly clock, measuring a woman's age, from fertility to sterility, in its ongoing passage through the skies. Lara's dark thoughts ran with her into the heart of things, and she couldn't look away.

Her children, Simon and Rose, now nineteen and twenty, immersed in their own lives, no longer needed her in the way that they had. Simon had worked his way into the music industry and his band was gaining popularity. She chatted with him on the phone each week but they saw each other less often because he was so busy. He'd taken the news of his parents' separation with equanimity. 'You guys were practically living separate lives anyway,' he'd said. He thought it was a good idea that his mother jaunt off to the far ends of the earth. 'It's what I'd do,' he'd said. Rose,- passionate about art, had recently landed a curator position at a small gallery while she studied. She'd been less nonchalant about the news. 'What a fuckwit dad is,' she'd said. 'Don't worry, Mum. Just see it as, he's having his second childhood early, and get on with your life.' Lara had felt comforted by her daughter's words. When she'd told her about Australia, Rose had encouraged the trip. It was obvious to Lara then, that her children were making their way in the world and that there was nothing of necessity tying her to England. Her soon-to-be ex-husband, Brock had passed her over for a pseudo-lesbian lover a decade younger and had made her feel as worthless as a carton of long-expired milk. There was also the reality of the lost years of believing in a fiction he created for her. Ugh. The biggest problem about betrayal, she thought, was how it made you a minor character in your own life – without you even bloody knowing it.

Lara realised she had been holding her breath, for God knows how long. She let it out in a long, sonorous sigh. She was going to metamorphose overnight into a bitter, sour, jilted left-over with a downturned mouth if she wasn't careful. While she had been sitting at home hoping he was okay because he was so god-damn late, he'd been with the so-called 'lesbian'. He'd come home at midnight and pour out his duplicitous heart, telling her how overworked he was, how over-whelmed and tired. God, how often had she clucked in sympathy and gone over to him to rub his neck? Now, she thought, she would wring it if given half a chance. The worst thing was that the bloody lesbi-an's friends and all the other staff would have known about it for ages. She got it now. This was why, at office events, the office staff had looked at her with a mixture of pity and guilt and thinly veiled contempt. UGH!

Later, so much later, a line of dawn appeared far in the east, over the sea. Lara hadn't ever heard a real kookaburra. Raucous cackles from the trees at the edge of the thick, overgrown garden, followed by a raw echo from several equally loud comrades assaulted her ears. Sounds like monkeys in the jungle, she thought. Only then did the God of Sleep arrive and she trudged inside, curled up under the covers, and pulled both pillows over her head.

Lara dreamed that she stood on the deck of the cottage holding a picnic basket full of sand. When she put the basket down to dig through the sand for her picnic items, she unearthed a white-bellied viper. The snake buried itself again, and she hurled the entire basket over the balcony. As it hit the ground, it tipped over and the viper slithered from the sand, vanish-ing into the bushes. Half-awake suddenly, she got it: Brock was a viper in her life-basket. Snake man be gone, she thought as she drifted back off to sleep. She thought she heard children shrieking, but then real-ised the noise came from enthusiastic birds singing joyful morning songs. She shook away the shadow of the viper, and sat up, swung her legs over the bed, pushing lavender sheets aside. In the kitchen, a kettle and a box of tea stood on the counter as if Ruby had been expecting her before the near collision in the car park. Fate. Karma. Kismet.

Lara unpacked. Her former life lay wrapped in every item of clothing she'd shoved into her suitcase. The smells of their bedroom, the laundry, the living room, her *life*, whirled up like ghosts out of the suitcase. Had she really actually physically packed these undies with their hanging, unraveling elastic? This stained cotton dress she'd bought in Greece eight years ago? This smelly old jacket, which had withstood her thirties so well and now looked misshapen, much like her body? Winter in the UK was so dark that the jacket, which she'd imagined to be black was actually midnight blue. She should have travelled with hand luggage only. All this would have to go. She kicked the clothes into a pile and went to rummage around in the cupboard under the sink and pulled out a black rubbish bag. She scooped all her clothes into it. There they went, like bunches of rotting autumn leaves.

17

4

'Good morning my dear.' Ruby — new landlady, saviour, Goddess Gaia, stood at the door in a green and white cotton dress, which hugged her earthy figure. She'd swept her red hair into a bun and outlined her eyes with thick eyeliner. 'Hope your night was all right. Just wanted to check the electricity was on and you'd stopped crying.'

'Oh, gosh. Was I really bad?'

'Nah, darl, just kidding. You were fine. But you did use up all my tissues in five minutes in the Woolies car park.'

'I am so sorry. Can I repay you with a cup of tea?'

'Love a cuppa, and any excuse will do,' Ruby said.

Lara went to the kitchenette and put on the kettle. The cosy living area caught the morning sun through its big windows. A skylight gleamed in the roof.

'You look a bit wretched, if I might say.'

'Just tired. Didn't sleep much. All the travel has finally caught up with me. Travelling to the exact opposite end of the world without going through the middle of it in a straight line takes its toll I guess,' Lara said.

'Yes, yes, of course. Look, darl, I don't mean to intrude. I'm just going out for the day and wanted to say that if you need anything for this place I have a ton of stuff in the garage, extra furniture, a desk, whatever. Feel free to have a peek but I warn you, it's a bit of a mess in there.'

'Thanks, Ruby. That's kind. I might take you up on

18

the desk idea. If there's a chair to go with it.'

'Oh, bound to be. There's a whole range of chairs, from the truly daggy to the almost upmarket. Just help yourself.' Ruby's eyes almost vanished in myriads of lines and wrinkles when she smiled. 'Rob hasn't picked up his stuff and it's been ten years. I guess that makes it all legally mine.'

'Lovely. I'll check that all out. Rob's your ex?'

'Thank goodness, yes.'

'Were you married?'

'Oh yeah, darl, for a quarter of a century. But marriage is overrated, and so are men.'

'You got that right,' Lara said. 'Milk and sugar?'

'Lots of both,' she said. 'The best thing is,' she said, as if she and Lara were midway through a much longer conversation, 'I sleep better, eat what I like, and do what the hell I like, and, guess what? I have luscious lustful sex with whomever I like, and I'm never disappointed, 'cos everything I do is on my terms.'

'That's nice,' Lara said, swallowing her tea too hot. 'I'd like to get the full episode on that one.'

'I promise, in time. What happened to you?' Ruby asked.

'Long story.'

'Don't think so,' she said, and eyed Lara. 'Your face tells me. Heartbreak? Betrayal? I can feel it in my bones.'

'I'm that transparent?'

'Sorry, darl. A familiar story. And yeah, I knew it just by looking at you. The hunched posture, you know, and the downcast I-feel-like-a-worthless-piece-of-shit eyes. Nevermind. We'll get you right.'

'More tea?'

'God bless. Thank you. Listen, I know that right now

you might find it hard to believe, but this end-of-re-lationship disaster could actually be the best thing that's ever happened to you.'

'Ruby that's generously optimistic, but I do seri-ously doubt that.'

'You'll see,' she said, and took a big slurp.

'I'll make sure I have a look in your garage.'

'Good onya. What else are you doing today?'

'No plans.'

'Maybe you could do the lighthouse walk. Get some perspective on things.'

'Okay, I'll do that, thanks. Oh, Ruby?'

'Yes dear?'

'Thanks for rescuing me. I feel quite terrible that I was about to drive into you.'

'No worries, darl. Around here, most folks believe that some things are just meant to be. Well, that tea was lovely. Better get going, so shut me up. I'm outta here. Be back for part two, okay?'

'I'll see you later. Thanks.'

After Ruby left, the image of her landlady's eyes, her wrinkles and the dark spots on her skin, lingered in Lara's mind. She was being uncharitable, she mused, particularly after all Ruby had done for her but good-ness, she thought, is this what fifty years under the Australian sun can do to you, or is Ruby's face just the face of someone weathered by betrayal, by yet another cheating bastard? In six years' time, Lara wondered, would she too, acquire neck skin that looked like crocodile leather? And why would any man want to run tender hands across flesh that had the texture of a handbag? Not that this was the goal of existence, but it bore thinking about. Anyway, aging gracefully was a cruel oxymoron, she thought, with the emphasis on moron. As she began to wither and wrinkle and lose things (husband, house, youth) she sensed an unavoidable and sad end of self-looming ahead of her. This was not a particularly exciting thought.

* * *

Something close to a death wish compelled Lara to examine herself in the mirror. She hadn't looked at her naked self for months, because she knew that, unlike Brock, mirrors seldom lied. But now was the time for a reckoning. Anyway, she reasoned, she couldn't feel any worse about herself than she already did, so she decided to face it head-on. If you have a handbag face, she thought, what are you going to do about it? You can fight back with surgeries and facelifts until your smile wraps itself all the way around your bloody head, or you can suck it up and decide to get on with life. Age, that proverbial thief, creeps up on you, she thought — it steals youth from beneath your very eyes, one sag at a time. And it's time, Lara thought, to front up to the facts.

Lara stripped off and braced herself. She turned to the mirror. Her long-suppressed twenty-five-year-old groaned as it looked out at its older reflection. So, this is the woman he no longer desired or wanted in any way. She gazed at her body with an attempt at detachment. Somewhere along the line, maybe between thirty-three and forty, her arms had morphed into ovals. Her under-chin skin crinkled when she turned to look sideways at herself. A turkey neck lurked in the not-too-distant future. New lines must have arrived just last night, cutting into her top lip, drawn by a universe with a nasty sense of humour.

Without makeup, the ragged roadmap of her life etched her face.

She looked down at her thighs (always too big, now sloppy as bread dough), her breasts (still holding out against gravity) and her stomach (giving in to it). Part of Lara's soul broke away. This package, she thought. It's all I've got. A sad, but undeniable fact.

Love, Lara knew, was a trick of the hormones to keep the species going. She hadn't believed that when she was younger. She'd been starry-eyed and, like millions of others, had bought the myth — the idea that love was a connection, a collision of self with other, lasting forever, companions on a life journey, for better for worse, sharing toothpaste, till death did you part. What a load of utter crap, she thought now. It was obvious: evolution was everything. Therefore Brock, done with his evolutionary job, could ignore the used mother of his children and get inside the pants of as many hot young things as he could find. He was having a predictable existential crisis based on an evolutionary compulsion to keep mating and procreating and demonstrating youth and virility until death took him out. Lara had no shred of sympathy for his position. She wondered whether she, rejected and fearing death, should now also rush down a similar path? Should she try and find somebody who would show her she wasn't completely dead and invisible yet?

No, she thought. I can't. That would be a pathetic trajectory. I'd end up properly thoroughly obliterated if I tried that. I need to not need anyone. No man. Ever. Again.

Lara needed a new self, and the place to start, she thought, was here and now, with a good defuzzing of her legs. If she wanted to wear shorts — and she did — she realised she'd have to brave the no-name brand depilatory wax strips from the pharmacy on Jonson Street, where she'd stopped before almost wiping out Ruby at Woolworths. She couldn't count how many years it had been since she'd waxed her legs, let alone let them out into the light. Though she never enjoyed leg waxing ever, she enjoyed hairy legs out in the fresh air even less. They interfered with her aerodynamics, she believed. Cyclists, she thought, would attest to this.

Lara sat down on the bathroom floor, peeled a single wax strip, and discovered, in the minutes that followed, that all wax strips were not created equal. After thirteen strips and plenty of pain and bad language, she blinked back tears and gave up. Then she perused her half-waxed legs. It wasn't that a whole bunch of strangers on the beach in Byron Bay would cast their eyes over her patchy wax job. On the contrary. If she were twenty, tall blonde and gorgeous, people might notice, but right now, she could have legs as hairy as a gorilla's and no one would stare.

Life simply wasn't fair. What did that old philosopher Thomas Hobbes once say about life being nasty, brutish and short? Granted, he was talking about society in a state of war, but love and war, Lara thought, had some uncomfortable similarities — all was fair, right, in love and war?

23

5

Far out in the Pacific, against the hazy line of the horizon and the layers of mountains and hills at the other end of the bay, she saw it. At first a fountain of water shot skyward, and then the blue-black hulk of a whale appeared, its shiny body followed by an enormous tail. Soon after that, a baby whale followed. The pair broke free of their dark blue world and arced through the sky.

'Wow!' she blurted out loud, and turned to look at the sun-drunk occupants of Byron Bay's Main Beach. A young couple with a toddler a few metres away looked at her.

'That was clearly for you,' the man said, and smiled, giving Lara a thumbs-up as he wrapped his arms around his partner and child. A rush of dark green envy for their lives, stretching out unmarked in front of them overcame Lara. Would he betray this young woman one day? Had he already? What secrets did he have that he wasn't sharing with her? Maybe this guy had none. Anyway, he looked perfect. It was possible, of course, that the young man would in fact become a jerk one day, driven by some unevolved Neanderthal urge to explore a series of fertile valleys when his current partner started drying up. Looking at his full sensitive mouth, though, Lara doubted it. This man loved this woman. No other woman would ever eclipse her. They would come back here in fifty years' time and celebrate their golden anniversary. He would tell her he loved her more now than back on that day long ago when some crazy middle-aged woman over-reacted at the sight of a whale breaching. Yes, faithful souls did exist. Lara knew it. She just hadn't been lucky enough to find a matching one.

After a brief moment, the man turned back to his partner and holding their child between them, kissed his beloved long and full on her lips. Lara looked away. Brock had never ever done that, she realised. Not once. Ever.

Time to go.

★ ★ ★

She hadn't run for at least a decade, though once she'd loved it. It had saved her, even in the worst of London's weather. Starting out again was like turning the key in a car that had been left in a garage for years. The parts didn't quite remember what they had to do to get rolling. Eventually, muscle memory returned. She set out across the beach towards the lighthouse at a slow jog. Dragging her heavy backside behind her was like rolling white bread dough along sand. It was hard damn work to keep it all together. Plastered with sunscreen, wearing a large-brimmed khaki sunhat low over her eyes and a small canvas backpack with water and a few odds and ends, Lara picked up her pace along the beach making for a wide, rust-coloured lagoon. Her thighs slapped each other in joking high fives, back and forth until she had to widen her gait to avoid chaffing. The sun shattered into a multitude of copies of itself along the wet shoreline. Her sunglasses weren't dark enough to keep out the glare. Light danced under her feet and she splashed through the shallows. Blood pounded in her face, sweat poured into her eyes making them sting with dissolved sunscreen. She moved her unfit, deceived, discarded self into the wild world. She threw her legs out in front of each other. These things still work, she thought. Wow, legs, you can do it. Boobs, hang tight, please.

'I'm taking you back,' she said to all her wobbling parts. 'You're all I've got. So, get with it now. Stop fighting me.'

Out past the surfers (they did look so much like delicious seals in their shiny wetsuits, she thought — if she were a shark, she'd be so tempted), a man stood on a kayak paddling. He looked like the ocean-cleaner, sweeping for eternity, ridding the sea surface of oils, dust, debris and water-resistant sunscreen. Lara watched him until her neck hurt, until the green hills below the lighthouse came into view and she stopped. She dropped her pounding head between her knees as everything turned to a blur. She threw her backpack down, and without another thought, ran straight into a breaking wave and fell into it. The salty, warm water broke over her, and she lay on her back, pulled and pushed by the tide. When she felt saturated in Australian Pacific sea brine, she hauled herself out of the water, picked up the backpack and continued walking.

Lara felt forty-four going on ninety-seven. She also felt eleven. As she reached into her memory of past selves, she remembered a holiday with her parents in South Africa in Durban. That had been the first time she'd swum in warm sea water. Now she realised she felt like the laughing cheeky kid she'd once been, long before Brock, and before the Great Betrayal. She wanted to be that girl again, the one who climbed trees, rolled down hills, told bad jokes and stole gasping fish from fishermen's buckets to throw them back into the sea. She liked that self. She wanted her back.

She headed towards the lighthouse. The climb led through rainforest. She saw her first wallaby at the side of the paved walkway. He watched her with black, unworried eyes. Corellas shrieked from the trees. By the time she stopped for a drink of water, she'd forgotten about her slapping thighs. She could see across the Pacific carpet to the edge of the world. Mountains rose out of the haze in the distance, and she made out volcanic peaks that had to be ancient. Below her, the sea crashed onto rocks and battered them. Foam spread out like halos, and the sea turned turquoise in the shallows near the beach.

At the top of the mountain, outside the lighthouse gift shop, Lara bought a large hazelnut ice-cream complete with chocolate topping. She looked out over the miles of Tallow Beach (according to a sign) and ate the whole creamy thing without pause. She even let stuff dribble down her chin, licked chocolate off her fingers one by one, and wiped her mouth on her arm when the serviette would no longer hold more melted hazelnut mess. There was no one to say, Lara, please, that's gross. No one to please anymore. She didn't give a damn how she looked when she ate. This was Lara, messy and real, thank you very much.

★ ★ ★

Despite her attempt to protect her mid-winter British skin from sunburn, Lara failed. It took much longer to walk back than she'd anticipated. When she finally hobbled into Byron Bay and sat down at Thai Lucy's, she felt the skin on her face tight with sun. She realised she'd just taken one giant step towards attaining leather-handbag face. She picked up a free copy of *The Echo*, and scanned the classifieds as the sun went down. 'Tom yum with seafood?' The waitress asked. 'Oh, thanks, yes.' The fourth time she'd spoken all day, after the conversation with Ruby, the 'Wow' she'd given the whale, and the order she'd just placed.

'Tantric massage,' she read under personal services. 'Deep masculine honouring', 'Male Escorts Available', 'Female Sensual Massage'. Really? What? Never. Not her. She didn't even read such ads.Her eyes skimmed over them.'This is for all the lonely women, thinking that life has passed them by. Let me tantrically honour you for who you are. Rates, hourly or weekly, call Mario. First consultation free. No Obligation.'

Was this serious? Nice name, anyway, Mario. The tom yum soup tasted like heaven. Maybe she'd grown new taste buds, she thought. She ate slowly while evening came. A band started up at the restaurant up the street, playing covers of recent hits.

For the past year, after fifteen years of full-time teaching, Lara had been a housewife. At first, she'd fantasised about finally taking up art and guitar again, but Brock and she had begun redecorating the house. Now that she thought about it, he'd already been scheming to sell it. By her stomach-churning calculations, he was already being unfaithful with the lesbian. Anyway, the redecoration process had taken all her time and creative energy.

Her teaching days had been spent with groups of rascally four-foot high noise makers whose parents left child rearing to their educators. At least her job had kept her up to date on the latest trends in music, movies and memes. She knew the song playing in the restaurant down the street and tapped her spoon on her bowl to the rhythm, causing the couple one table along to stare just a little disapprovingly at the woman next to them. She ignored them.

On the way home, Lara stopped at the back end of a local charity. She stuffed the black plastic bag full of the clothes she'd discarded that morning on top of a full-to-bursting clothing recycle bin. Ghosts of her former self flopped out of the bag. Two flapping sleeves looked like they were waving goodbye.

By the time she got home, the Byron Shire lay under a blanket of night. Her car was almost out of petrol, she didn't have any clothes for the next day except the salt-caked ones she was wearing, and she hadn't collected the desk and chair from Ruby's garage.

No matter. Lara stood for a moment inside her cottage without turning on the light, taking in the stillness. This life, and that life. Which one would she honestly choose now? The loneliness of hardly speaking all day hurt so much less than the loneliness of a faithless husband creeping home to her night after night. She wished she could find a voodoo penis that she could use to wither his unfaithful member into something resembling dried papaya. Wrong country, she thought, and sighed.

If she had to choose? Tonight? This life, and that was the truth.

6

At 3.00 am Lara woke with a Grand Theory of Everything. She wondered whether heartache could eat your stomach lining? Maybe she had an ulcer. At any rate, she realised she'd finally figured it out, and this was it: in life, Lara decided, there are two rooms. Room Two is the room for those men and women who want to sleep around. Anyone entering this room understands that there is no commitment. People can do whatever they want and sleep with whomever they want and it's in the proverbial open. This is the room for the polyandrists, polygamists, polyamorists and free-love renegades from society who can have all the sexually-intimate-with-many-people fun they desire. Room One, however, is reserved for those who want one partner. Anyone entering this room knows that other people in there are looking for a romantic and sexual relationship with one person. And that, Lara thought, is the agreement. In Room One, the aspect ratio is 1:1, and constant. Not 1:2, not even for a second.

Lara's theory, she decided, should be made into a universal law: everyone has a choice to begin with. After which, no Room Two Person has any business being in Room One. This is about ethics, Lara thought, not God, or biology, or survival of the species, or anything. The only requirement is honesty. People who bring the dynamics of Room Two into Room One do not deserve to breathe air, she thought. She had no one in particular in mind.

Lara had given up being a morning person. The sun had risen high into the sky when she padded down the stairs in an old t-shirt that hung to her knees. As she walked across the damp grass, white blossoms clung to her toes. Her feet looked like a garden. She'd slept for nine hours, breaking her adult world record.

She looked up at the glass sliding doors that lead, she knew, into Ruby's lounge and found her way to the garage. Shifting an old chair out of the way, she went in through the unlocked door and stared for a moment, allowing her eyes to adjust to dim light and millions of cobwebs. The desk wasn't hard to see. It was beautiful, oak,in need of a little dusting, but a nice piece of furniture. She stepped over a lawnmower and gave the desk a tug. It was heavy, that was for sure. She tugged some more, feeling competent, but lost her balance and went crashing backwards over the mower.

'What in the Lord's name are you doing, my dear?'

Lara looked up from an inelegant position on the garage floor and saw Ruby's large frame blocking out the morning light.

'I, uh, just wanted to get the desk. Thought I might start writing — you know.'

'You okay?'

'Sure. Just a bit clumsy.'

'Here, take my hand.'

Lara gratefully accepted help up and dusted off her aching back, front and hands.

'You still in one piece?'

'Probably,' she said.'Didn't mean to disturb you.'

'I get up at the crack of dawn.' Ruby wore a flimsy

31

nightdress, despite the advanced hour. Her reddish curly hair stood up at odd angles and Lara watched her shove the lawnmower to the side and grasp the oak desk with both hands. She pulled it towards her and slid it across the floor and out the door. Lara watched with mouth-open admiration.

'I'll walk backwards. You hoist the other side now.'

Lara did as instructed. She thought, as they wobbled across the morning grass carrying the desk like insects struggling under a large breadcrumb, that they would have made a ridiculous sight; two women in saggy nightwear, huffing and puffing under the weight of their load. Sun rays warmed Lara's face as Ruby began to mount the stairs of the deck backwards.

'It's bloody heavy,' Lara tried to point out, legs quaking.

'It's oak,' Ruby said. 'Shit, it is heavy. But we can do it. One. Step. At. A. Time.'

'Yes. If it kills me.'

They stopped for breath, the desk balanced on the steps, Ruby's face purple with exertion. 'Since there aren't any handsome, single, sensitive men with big muscles in the near vicinity, we gotta do it.'

'Hup two three four ...'

'Just another heave-ho and we're up,' Ruby said. 'Crikey! So who needs men? We're as good as.'

'Better,' Lara added as they reached the deck and set their load down. Sweat ran rivers down Ruby's temples. 'You really shouldn't have,' Lara said. 'I could've done it.'

Ruby burst our laughing. 'Darl, if I wouldn't have come to the rescue you'd have killed yourself on the lawnmower.'

Lara laughed and lifted her shoulder to wipe sweat

off her cheek. 'I can do the rest.'

'No, let's get it inside together.' They lifted the desk again and half-slid, half-carried it across the deck and through the door. Ruby pushed it across the floor until it stood under the window, catching the light. 'Perfect,' she said. 'Now the place looks like some little haven. A retreat. I'll need to find you a rug. And another nice lamp. I have some good stuff in there, it's just buried under the weight of a million spider webs.'

'It's perfect now, thank you. Would you like a cup of tea?'

'Well, that sounds too good to pass up,' Ruby said, and sat down on the end of the bed, sweat running down her temples, her nightdress underarms dark with perspiration.

Lara walked over and filled the kettle. She pushed damp and unruly hair out of her eyes and while she busied herself with making tea, keeping her back to her, the older woman watched.

'So, darl, what happened? Time for episode two. Your sad story.'

'Oh, my husband and I ... we split up.'

Ruby made a farting noise with her lips.

'What?'

'Come on! Don't bullshit me. That sounds so civilised. What really went down? You can tell me. I have been fucked over so royally I can detect the aroma of betrayal like shit on a shovel.'

'Okay. It's true. My hus ... the man I was married to for almost twenty-one years lied to me and cheated on me and has happily moved on. He went at it several times that I didn't know of, and once that I did. And now he's found the love he's been wanting all his life. Apparently, she's capable of some spectacular bedroom feats. How many sugars in your tea, again, Ruby?'

'The works, dear. Two sugars, milk, nice and strong. What your ex-person doesn't realise yet is, a cunt is just a cunt. It doesn't talk, or console, or listen. It can't read your mind, discuss fucking Shakespeare or laugh at your jokes.'

'It seems though,' Lara said, though she couldn't help laughing, 'That I have been discarded as the owner of older, less spectacular, um, body parts ... I feel crushed.'

'Darl, call a spade a spade, or a cunt a cunt, I don't care. You have kids?'

'Two. Grown-up.'

'And you gave birth to them naturally?'

'I did.'

'And does that not make your cunt spectacular? Give me a break. There's not enough red carpet in the universe to roll out for women, darl, who pass small humans through miniscule holes and then recover and go on with life as if they haven't been torn in two. You are spectacular.'

'Thanks Ruby. I never thought of it like that. I just feel, you know, can't compete,' Lara said. 'With the youth and uh ... elasticity of my successor.'

'And why should you?' Ruby offered kindly. 'What kind of an idiot walks away from a lovely creature like you anyway?'

'Oh, you're too kind.'

'No, but it's true.'

'Thanks, but she was apparently very talented ... a double adapter ...'

'Oh darl, she must have been so much more exciting.'

'Yeah. Supposedly she was lesbian. But not exclusively. Whatever. It hurts.'

'Of course it hurts. The worst pain. But let it not define you. You will one day forget it, I promise.'

'How do you know?'

'Heartbreak, betrayal and me? We're like this.' She wove three fingers together.

'Tell me,' Lara said. 'It would help me to know that one day I might not feel like shit.'

'Ha! You should swear more, that's the first thing. Do you know it helps with pain? Proven, okay? Anyway, how much time you got?'

'No limit,' Lara said.

'Okay. Since you asked. I was pregnant with Hayley when Rob first had an affair. I went into hospital because I was bleeding like a dying pig, about to miscarry, and when I came out, there was mascara on my fucking pillow! And it wasn't my mascara, that's for sure. He hadn't even been bothered to change the sheets!'

Lara almost poured tea on her foot.

'Watch it!' Ruby exclaimed.

'He had someone in your bed while you were in hospital … miscarrying his baby?'

'You bet. I almost lost that little girl, and there he was …'

'Oh Ruby. That story takes the cake,' Lara said. 'Gross. Makes me sick.'

Ruby unravelled a loose thread on her nightgown. 'Yep. That's probably where things started going wrong. Anyway, all water under the bridge now. But back then, well, he didn't leave me and I didn't leave him. I did pound the shit out of him one afternoon.

35

I was pregnant and hormonal and beyond caring. I kicked him in the balls and punched his fat stomach in a fit of gratuitous violence. But then I had no options, you see. I knew I couldn't hack the child rearing thing on my own and I took him back. He tried to be a good father to Hayley, I'll give him that, but he was and is an arsehole of the most classic, cheating kind. When I finally gave him the boot, I wondered what had taken me so bloody long.'

'What was the final straw?'

'He ran off with Hayley's best friend's mum. I suspected they'd been at it for years, though what she even saw in him is beyond me. He's an ugly son-of-a-bitch. But Hayley and Rene, her daughter, were always together and so I got to see the two cheaters together often enough. I suddenly saw the light and figured out what was happening. I thought, man, what am I doing with this idiot? If he'd go, I'd have more money, more time, no stress, my own bed. And then he afforded me the perfect opportunity. I said I was going away for two days to visit a friend in Brisbane because I suspected what was up. He seemed very keen and helped me organise a picnic lunch for the road and was generally Mr Nice. I drove off on Saturday morning. But, I only went into town and had a long delicious breakfast. Four hours later, I sneaked back. Lo and behold, a white VW was parked in the drive. I turned off my car, and crept in. I found a gift from the gods in the form of an old wooden spatula lying on the table. Rest is history, darl. I heard sounds of sweaty lovemaking, coming from my bedroom. I opened the door and caught them! As his naked arse was conveniently raised over Hayley's best friend's mother, I whacked him so hard the spatula broke.'

Lara laughed until her stomach hurt. 'Ruby. I wish I could be more like you.'

'Nah, you don't. And there's nothin' to it darl. I just pointed to the door, and they scrambled out, naked bits hanging in the breeze as they lugged pieces of clothing and shoes and yes, my bed sheet to her car. That was the last time I saw Rob.'

'Here's your tea.'

'Lovely.'

They went out onto the deck and sat looking down at Ruby's house and out over the treetops.

'I'll let you in on a secret,' Ruby said. 'The best sex I've ever had is the unattached kind. Sometimes paid for, sometimes a gift, but so much more exciting. And Byron Bay's a haven, darl, for that kind of, uh, deep healing. You gotta love some of those workers for their gifts to humanity. Look at my life now. Look what I have.' Ruby made a wide gesture, including her house, her garden, and beyond that, the whole Pacific Ocean.

Lara sipped tea, tucking her feet under her on the wooden chair.

'God bless tea,' Ruby said, eyes closed, as she took a sip.

'This is probably a good time to talk about rent,' Lara said. 'How would you like me to pay?'

'Cash. Once a week, maybe on a Monday? You stay as long as you like. If you need to move, just give me a week's notice.'

'That's wonderful. I'm really so grateful.'

'You should be nothing of the sort. I'm glad you're here. In fact, just take up some space, I'd say. You'll forgive me if I'm blunt, but at my age, fifty-five soon, mincing words isn't in my repertoire anymore. You need to stop feeling like you come second, or last.

You're number one in your life, darl. You have a right to exist, to be you, to rent this place, and to be loved, okay? You close your eyes and give that bastard of an ex-spouse of yours a furious kick in the arse. Let him have it.'

Lara didn't mind being lectured by Ruby.

'One more thing, darl. Stop obsessing about that lover of his as if she defines you. She doesn't. Put her stupid cunt outta your mind. You gotta take back all that invisible self-worth stuff you've lost. You'll see. Once it's back, you'll never lose it again. I do recommend a tantric sex god for medicinal purposes. Check the ads in *The Echo*.'

'I did. I don't have the guts.'

'C'mon. You don't need guts. Just get someone to come over and deliver a massage at home … a relaxing treat. You specify what you want, man or woman, and what kind of massage you're looking for. I once got the wrong end of the deal. Some hot babe arrived wanting to give me the full treatment. Her name was Jo, so how was I supposed to infer that she was a she? Did not in any way want to hurt her feelings, but I had to ask her to leave.'

'Oh, right.'

'Check that stuff out. Really. Just be clear as day about what you want.'

'Thanks. I'll, um, yep. I'll have another look.'

7

By the time Lara drove into Byron Bay the next day, her Thrifty car gasped for petrol. She filled up and drove through town, parking at the beach. Armed with newspaper and phone, she walked past a bearded man with a llama on a leash. As you do, she thought, every ordinary day. She found a coffee place exuding the irresistible aroma of dark roast and sat down to observe far too many happy couples of all ages, passing by, as if love and romance existed for everyone else in this world; as if some of them actually had the real thing. It had to be possible, obviously, because surely, surely, those women weren't all being cheated on? Why, why, why did she have to end up with such a lousy end of the bargain? Her heart ached. The smell of coffee and sea breeze and sunscreen assaulted her nostrils, just as pangs of regret, nostalgia, envy and a dash of pure resentment for everyone not in her painful position fizzled in her veins.

Lara took out *The Echo* as she sipped a Latte Soy Dandy, an Australian special, an LSD, dandelion fake coffee with soymilk. She looked at the classifieds again. What the hell, she thought? What did she have left to lose? She pulled out her phone and dialled the number under 'Mario.'

It only rang twice.

'Hello, this is Mario.'

'Hi Mario, my name's Lara. I saw your ad in *The Echo.*'

'Lara! Hi.' Sexy voice. Hint of an Italian accent.

'What can I do for you?'

'Oh, I don't know. I was just intrigued by your ad. I don't really know what you do, but maybe you can tell me a bit about your services.' She felt herself blushing.

'Of course,' he laughed. 'You tell me what you want, and I give you what you want. Or, if you don't know what you want, I might be able to show you what you want. I'm a tantric sex worker, but also do deep tissue massage. We can discuss what you might need. I am in the healing arts.'

'Are you really sixty bucks an hour?'

'Sixty bucks an hour, yes. Plus, a free consult beforehand.'

'I don't know Mario,' she said, stirring her drink with a long spoon. 'How does a stranger trust you?'

What if he was secretly a predator with cannibalistic tendencies? What if he had a few ex-clients chopped up in his deep freeze?

He laughed. 'Well, I suppose, if we meet, and you don't feel comfortable, you never have to call me again.'

'What if I just want a massage?'

'It's yours.'

'And if I don't want to be touched … all over?'

He laughed. 'Anything you want, all your wishes. Granted.'

Had anyone ever said that to her, even for money? Was this sad, she wondered, drinking her Latte with a spoon?

'Fine. Okay, so where and how do you meet … prospective, uh, clients?'

'You in Byron?'

'Close by.'

40

'You busy at six tonight?'

'Mm, let me check my schedule,' she said licking her spoon again. 'Yep. No other appointments. Six looks good.'

'Let's meet outside the fish and chips shop at Main Beach. I'm in my thirties, tall with dark hair. I'll be wearing a blue and white striped shirt. There's no charge for our meeting, and if you decide not to call me afterwards, that'll be fine.'

You, Mario, sound too good to be true. She almost said it.

'I have messy brownish, blondish hair, and I'll wear something white,' she said.

And that was that. If Brock could walkout on two decades of marriage for a fake lesbian, Lara could call a young, six-foot-two Italian stranger named Mario in Byron Bay, who would come over and offer his devoted touch and if she wanted, his sexy tantric attention for the bargain price of sixty dollars an hour.

* * *

She had six hours to herself before her appointment with Mario, and enough shops, hairdressers, and beauticians available to attempt to have the bits of herself that seemed to have fallen apart, rearranged and stuck back together. She opted for first having her hair trimmed and highlighted and then spent the next hour lying, suffocating beneath a green clay mask, which promised to eliminate ten years from her life and face. The result was a burning, blotchy countenance, which dangerously resembled the one she'd received for free from the afternoon sunburn she'd worn so well. She ran out of time and didn't man-

41

age to have her legs professionally re-waxed. She did, though, find a soft, white, clingy, cotton-knit dress. Lara felt as nervous as she'd been on her first date at age thirteen with Jonathan Dean whose large front teeth had crashed into hers when he tried to snog her in the back row of a movie she couldn't remember.

She reminded herself this wasn't a date. She didn't have to impress anyone. She was paying him to make her feel good. There was some liberation in that thought, she decided, and then wondered about the hair highlights, the face-mask and the clingy dress. It was impossible not to want to try and be attractive, no matter how much she hated that thought. Goddamn it, she thought. She wished she could just not give a shit. Ever again. A tall and impossible order given her circumstances, she thought.

The sun dipped westward. She passed the llama plus man on the beach again and the guy said 'G'day,' as if a llama on a leash was as common as a poodle. Rainbow lorikeets flew overhead and screeched at the pink sky.

The rate of change in her life had given her jet-lag. Perhaps the shock of everything was resulting in mild, though temporary, insanity. Anyway, Lara thought, both shock and insanity were justifiable excuses for any strange behaviour at the moment.

The short walk up the street from the car park to the fish and chips shop at Main Beach almost finished Lara off. The humidity made her newly-styled hair wild, and her body felt tired, saggy, despite her recent attempts to turn back the clock. What madness was this anyway, she wondered? She almost panicked. Maybe she should cancel with Mario. She could just text him now and avoid further idiotic behaviour.

Just as she stared out at the shimmering mercurial sea, and as sunburnt surfers began strolling back to their vans with boards slung under muscular arms like sheaves of paper, she heard someone behind her say her name and she turned.

His careless, shoulder-length brown hair caught her attention immediately. A wide smile spread across his face.

'Hi,' he said. 'You must be Lara.' His olive skin gleamed dark against the striped shirt – the result, no doubt, of many hours spent under this almost-equatorial sun sans ozone layer.

'Mario?'

'The one,' he said.

Nice, she thought. Byron hills in the background. 'Happy to meet you.'

'Wanna go for a stroll?'

'Sounds good,' she said.

'This way,' he said, and they fell in step, heading towards the sea. 'You're English.'

'And you're Australian? Or Italian?'

'Born in Tasmania to Italian immigrants. I spent my teens in Italy.'

'Why did you come here?'

'Weather. I'm a sun child. And I like the energy here.'

'I get that. It's gorgeous.'

She walked next to him, trying to keep up with his giant strides. 'I'm sorry,' he said, slowing down as he noted her lack-of-fitness breathing. 'Tell me something about you, Lara.'

'There's not much to tell,' she said. 'I'm actually worried that I might be wasting your time.'

'No meeting with any human being is a waste of

time,' he said. He offered his hand. She looked at him. 'Go on,' he said, 'If you don't like it, drop it. I won't take offence.'

She hesitated for a moment. Then took his hand. It felt warm and solid and she sank into a moment of rented happiness.

'Don't worry,' he said. 'It's gonna feel kind of awkward at first. I mean, most women feel a bit daunted if they've never done this before. Just be okay about saying anything. This is about your needs. I do get paid, but you can think of me as a kind of energy healer. I'm here for you.'

'Uh-huh. And, so is that what makes you different from a regular prostitute?'

He laughed. 'Right. I offer sexual, sensual healing – whatever form that takes.'

The twilight intensified. Colours seeped across the sky. Venus appeared. Lara enjoyed the touch of Mario's hand and felt calmed by his attentive presence. Just looking at him was better than a day spa treatment.

'So, Mario,' she said. 'I've never done anything like this and I'm really curious,' she said. 'You don't have to answer this, but do you, I mean, I'm assuming you do have normal relationships with women, or men? How does that work?'

'I'm a ladies' man,' he said. 'Mostly.' He grinned. 'And yeah, it's kinda like any other job,' he said. 'I have relationships. Like other healers, I have boundaries between work life and personal life. But yeah, I love what I do.'

'I'd like to know, you know, whether your girlfriends mind, whether there are jealousies. I mean, how would that be for them, being with you?'

'Well, you know, there are challenges in every relationship.'

'Sure,' she said, not sounding at all convinced even to her own ears.

'It's true though. Ultimately, it's about openness, honesty and trust. And for me, of course, it's my own knowledge of the difference between my work and my private life. If I'm dating someone, I share my day, my stories. If there's understanding between partners, it works.'

What did this bronze beach god at least twelve years her junior know about the stormy sea of human lives and loves, she wondered?

'I don't know, Mario. I mean, it sounds too good to be true. You're sort of like a cross between Adonis and Superman and, pardon me for saying this, but I'm certain it's only *before* life properly kicks your arse inside out, that you can be this sure of yourself and the world. You know, once I believed I could do anything, be anyone, pick anyone I wanted. I felt invincible, immortal. Like you seem to feel. But that person vanished.'

'Tell me about that.'

'It's probably impossible for you to understand. You have no idea what it feels like to walk around in a body treated like discarded debris. I'm sorry, listen, this probably isn't the thing for me.'

'You want to go back?'

'Yes please.'

'No worries.'

To her embarrassment, tears spilled down her cheeks. Her nose ran like a leaking toilet and she had nowhere to wipe it. Mario reached into his jeans pocket and pulled out a neatly folded handkerchief. 'Here

45

you go,' he said. 'You can keep it.'

'Thanks,' she sniffed, taking it. She blew her nose hard and loud.

'You all right?'

She nodded. Then shook her head. Her knees buckled. Mario put an arm around her and walked, half-carrying her to a grassy dune where they sat down. She felt her eyes and nose streaming into her mouth and she didn't care. This was the real Lara: a complete snot-nosed, sobbing mess. She held the handkerchief to her face.

'Better out than in,' he said, 'all your tears.' He squeezed her shoulders. 'Tell me everything.'

Lara rambled in partly incoherent sobs about Room One and Room Two. And Brock, and the lesbian. And the lies. She couldn't stop herself, though she knew she would feel terrible afterwards and regret the out-pouring. It had to happen sometime, and Mario just held her and let her rant. She shared her Room One and Room Two insights with him and told him why she believed there should be universal rules about these things.

'I fucking hate him.' she cried. 'And I hate her.' She could hear her voice raised too high above the crashing sea. 'They're liars and cheaters and I hate them and all our friends except Joanne. I hate my life and myself for being such an idiot. He's made a mockery of everything I am. What kind of a psychopath is he? He could have told me, right at the beginning, years ago, the first time he went off betraying me and then I could have walked out while I was still young. I would've had the chance to meet someone who had the same values, and started over. Instead I tried to keep loving him, making the best of him, even when he got gross and paunchy and unattractive and sported middle-aged jowls. I should have known when he kept talking about the lesbian: 'She tells me all her problems,' he said. 'And she's sooo interesting ...' Lara choked on her tears. 'She is a piece of fucking work! She makes love to all these other women, she doesn't need any man, it's so attractive to him, her experiment in loving the self, yes, fascinating isn't it, and he tells me about her inner glow, from eating raw food for two years, and how we should go raw, he's really *inspired* by her. And how brilliant she is. Everything she does is *brilliant*. She is just a narcissistic fuckwit. And it's bull shit anyway. Her *inner glow* is because she's showing him her secret interior, and I'm not talking about her flat. He's just lapping it, her, up, literally, full of himself, suddenly losing weight and dyeing his hair and sporting new clothes that look like a teenagers' and no, he's not spending from seven to midnight working on a new design while I sit at home and fold laundry ...' She paused to swallow. 'I wish he would just ... just ...' She couldn't find the breath to continue or say the word *die*.

'I'm sorry,' Mario said. 'That sounds pretty bad.'

'Have you ever felt totally heartbroken, Mario? Like the only reason you haven't killed yourself yet is because it wouldn't matter to anyone except you?'

'I'm sorry. I can't say I have, Lara.'

'Of course not!' she said to the dying light of day. 'You, Mario, live in bloody Room Two! You and Brock and the lesbian and the other half-girls he slept with.'

'No. Actually, I'm the only one in Room Two,' he said. 'Brock and the lesbian and the others are imposters and invaders in your Room One. They're pretenders. If I were the king of that kingdom they'd be banished forever to Room Zero, where no one gets to screw anyone ever again.'

'Really?' she sniffed. She liked his narrative.

'Absolutely, yeah! Like you said. It's about honesty. Or lack of it. That's the root of all pain; you're totally onto it. And though I've never been you, I know heart-break and betrayal is torture. Feeling like someone's constructing a reality for you is pretty gross, isn't it? Brock and the lesbian will probably self-destruct because they lack the key ingredient for sustainability.'

'Which is?'

'Honesty and compassion. You can't sustain any human relationship without those.'

'You're a fine one to talk, Mario.'

'I am. I never lie to anyone. I have my clients, and I have girlfriends, and everyone knows where they stand.'

'But how much do you know about rejection and jealousy and aging and self-loathing and neck wrinkles?'

'Not too much, I have to say …'

'My point, you see? You can't help me. You just go around sleeping with gorgeous models and … I shouldn't be here wasting your time. I'm sorry.' She put her face in her hands, and shook her head.

A butcher bird sang a clear, bell-like song beyond the waves and Mario nodded. 'Hey, Lara, look, don't be too hard on me yet, okay? So, no, I haven't suffered much in that way myself. But I do know broken hearts. And sure, I've made love to gorgeous models, but also to a seventy-five-year-old in a wheelchair who hadn't had anyone touch her for decades, and to a woman with a neurological disorder that paralysed her from the neck down. Honestly, I can't say I loved being with the models any more than the old woman or the ill woman. I held them and cried with them and laughed with them and added their stories to my life story.'

'You are too bloody good to be true and you've done nothing to deserve my bad behaviour. And you don't have to be nice to me, or agree with me. I'm not even paying you yet,' she said, wiping her nose on her arm.

He laughed, patted her shoulder. 'Why don't we go get a drink, maybe some food. It's summer and your lips are going blue and you look freezing. Your choice of beverage. I'll pay. Okay?'

'Okay,' she said. 'Thank you.'

He pulled her to her feet. 'No worries, mate. Let's go.'

As they walked through the twilight back into Byron she wondered what the brain was supposed to do with the past, with all those memories that kept coming up like mind vomit. Where could the mind info dump? Where might it throw the thought that you'd be forever tied to a cheating lying bastard for the simple fact that he was the father of your two children? Where was the shredder for the images of every vein on his hand, every hair on his head, every pore on his face, the entire geography of his body? How did you erase the hard drive?

And what if the thought of having to learn someone else's body and soul geography after twenty years was just as upsetting?

★ ★ ★

They reached a road into town. The sea stretched to the end of the world. At the end of the world, the stars emerged out of the water and they stopped.

'I'll tell you something. Your ex, I bet he will eventually come running back to you.'

'He will not.'

'He will. Because he hasn't really changed at all. He's still a Trojan horse in Room One. He'll be sick of his transgressive fling, he'll realise what he had was better, but by then you'll be far beyond his reach.'

'How can you know that?'

'Because I spend a lot of time with women. They tell me stuff. It's the law of averages. It's more likely than not to happen.'

They climbed stairs and walked down the road. The air smelled of Thai food and steak and burnt caramel.

'Got a proposal for you, Lara.'

'Which is?'

They sat down at a falafel place. Mario ordered a platter of everything, and a hot chocolate.

'Spend some time with me in Room Two. Get yourself back. I can help you.'

'You're a good bloody salesman.'

'It's not about the money. I do a hell of a lot of charity work, believe me, and if you can't afford me, I won't charge you.'

'Oh great, I've always wanted to be a charity case.'

'You're seeing things through a self-annihilating lens. How about a three-hour session tomorrow night — free, no strings. If you never want to see me again, adios. If you want me, regular rates, okay?'

★ ★ ★

By 2.00 am, Lara was digesting an entire bottle of red, drunk on her own in her lovely tree cottage. In that state, she was seriously considering Mario-the-tantric-gigolo-healer's proposal, mostly because her sober responsible self would never have. She did have to weigh a few things up. What if it messed with her head? Would this be in any way worse than pouring out one's soul to a clinical psychologist? How, she wondered, did talking and analysing and understanding the ruined heart compare with putting the ruined body and soul in the hands of a sensual Italianate tantric stud called Mario for three hours? The answer would emerge, she thought, of its own accord.

8

Evening. Twenty-four hours after meeting him, Lara stood on the deck of her cottage on stilts neither awkward nor anxious. She looked up. Never in all her life had she seen stars like this. A meteor shot across the sky and burned out somewhere above the house.

'Wow!' Mario called out, slamming his car door. 'See that?'

'I did. Without the atmosphere, we'd be dead, right?'

'Most likely,' he said. 'Like the dinosaurs. Is this your rental place?'

'Yes,' she said.

'Very nice,' he said, just a black shadow in front of tall gum trees. 'Just getting my gear, okay? I won't be a minute.'

'Gear?'

'Massage oils. Towels. CD player. And by the way, do you have a preference for any particular kind of music?'

'No. After I got married, I forgot what I liked,' she called down. 'Bring whatever you want.'

The heat had built up inside the wooden house all day, so she had flung open the windows and turned on the yellow bedside lamp. She'd run on the beach in the morning, swum in the afternoon and had texted her kids, Rose and Simon and best friend Joanne just to assure them she felt better than when she left.

She could, of course, have gone for a relaxing therapeutic massage in a nice granola-inspired boutique on Jonson Street. That would have been the safe, sensible thing to do, and something her former self would have gone for. But New Lara had no history. She was a wildcard. So, no hot-stone massage. Instead, Mario's footsteps up the stairs shook the house.

'Whew!' He ducked to fit in the front door and looked around. 'Awesome place,' he said, plopping down towels, a soft pink blanket and a bag of oils with purple labels. He rubbed his hands together and surveyed Lara's dwelling.

'Love it,' he said. 'You okay?'

'I'm great. Better than before.'

Mario found the power outlet and plugged in his CD player. Then he rummaged around in his bag and came up with a CD. 'I hope you like it. It's from Mozambique. Very mellow. If you don't like it, tell me.'

Soft tones drifted across the room.

★ ★ ★

No one had, as far as Lara could remember, ever given her a full body massage, either for love, or money. At first, she was consumed with embarrassment. She tried to wriggle away from his hands until he laughed. 'Relax, will you? Stop trying to escape! Just lie still.'

'It's maybe a British thing,' she said, as she lay on her stomach in her underwear on a towel on her bed, her buried face in the pillow feeling red-hot.

'What?' he said.

'Cringing at the thought of a stranger's hands traversing my body and finding embarrassing things.'

'What embarrassing things?'

It was hard, no, impossible for her not to worry

53

that he might secretly feel smug, young and superior as he touched the loosening skin on her back. And everything else.

'Lumpy cellulite pockets that cling to my thighs? Wings under my arms? What about the way my face squashes sideways onto the pillow and folds in on itself?'

'Get over all that vicious self-judgement crap,' he said. 'Relax.'

'I feel like a lump of bread dough,' she mumbled.

'Well, relax into the bread dough feeling then. Lie there and let me knead you, okay?' He sounded like he was smiling.

'I thought you didn't need anyone,' she said.

'I'm kneading you now — if you don't mind.'

'Hmm. That actually feels nice. I'd never have guessed that being dough could be a good thing.'

Warm, oiled hands grasped her feet and the smell of neroli and rose filled the room.

Mario ran a thumb up her calf. 'You're holding a lot of stress in every muscle in your body,' he said. He held her feet tight and threaded his fingers between her toes.

Something in Lara let go. So what if he had a billion girlfriends and twenty-five million attractive clients? He'd seen every kind of body, like a doctor, and this one was hardly worth taking special note of. She didn't know Mario, she thought, but here he was, young, and attractive, devoting these hours to her wellbeing. How bad could that be? Plus, the only words she needed were yes and no. She could do that.

Mario's hands moved slowly from her calves to her thighs. 'If you're uncomfortable at any time, just say.'

'Okay.' Her thoughts tumbled as she tried to

catch them. How could twenty years of married life just wither into a small wrinkled thing of ... hatred, she wondered? In ten years' time, would she still be pathetically condemned to love/detest the man who had broken her heart? She dreaded that. People get over these things. Look at Ruby, she thought. She got through it. But she was the tougher and braver sort.

Could Lara be like that? She forced herself to concentrate on Mario's hands. She felt his long fingers on her outer thighs. Hmm, relaxing. After a few minutes, her inner thighs sensed the gentle pressure of his thumbs slick with warm oil. Her mind floated off to faraway places as she thought: what if I decided never to return to earth?

★ ★ ★

Lara woke with a jolt. Sunlight streamed onto the bed and birds sang songs bursting with joy through her open windows. She blinked. She was in bed, in her underwear, covered with a sheet, a blanket carefully placed over her feet. Mario, and all his gear were long gone.

'Oh no!' she said to the morning as she swung her legs over the side of the bed. Had she slept right through an erotic encounter, she wondered? Did they ... do anything? Teenage questions she never, ever thought she'd have to answer again tumbled around in her head.

A knock on her door brought her to full wakefulness. 'Who is it?' she asked, groggy.

'Who else but the the muffin lady?'

'Come in.'

'Thank God you're still alive,' Ruby said, pushing

the door open and standing there in red-headed glory. 'I thought you might be dead, darl. It's nine am, and I didn't hear you come in last night.'

'Morning,' she said. The smell of fresh baking filled the room.

Ruby put a plate of steaming muffins on the kitchen counter and wrinkled her nose.

'Smells like an aromatherapy experiment in here,' she said. 'Nice. Mind if I put the kettle on?'

'No, no, go ahead.' Lara yawned.

'So, where were you yesterday evening? I came round at five to invite you to a sausage sizzle on Mount Chincogan. Friends of mine have a nice little place there. We ate reefer cakes all night, so you can just imagine how lively that turned out to be.'

'Reefer cakes?'

'Dope. Baked into different goodies. I was stoned out of my head. Probably still am. I'm soooo hungry.'

'Oh, goodness me. Well, I was out until about six. I ran about six kilometres in the morning, and, oh, I followed your advice, you know, called a guy who'd advertised in The Echo and he came over last night and gave me a sensual massage, after which I fell fast asleep. That's the aromatherapy experiment you're smelling.'

'Ooh. Really? Tell me. Did the earth move?' Ruby said excitedly.

'No, but I reckon my cellulite did.'

'Well, whatd'ya know? You did it,' Ruby said, and slammed cupboard doors getting out teacups, small plates, evidently feeling very at home, since this was her home. 'Was he divine?'

'He was alright. Young, sexy, and also he has the whole universe figured out.'

'What did he do with you?'

'I, um, don't think anything. Though maybe I had wild sex and I've forgotten the whole experience already.'

Ruby clasped her hands together. 'Oh, darl, I'm sure you would have remembered if you did!'

'I hope so. But I was so tired. He gave me a massage. His hands were very sensual.'

'And then?'

'Then I woke up and you banged on my door.'

'You got his number?'

'Over there,' Lara said, pointing to the newspaper on the table.

'Maybe worth a call,' she said absentmindedly. Then she picked up the paper and read the ad. 'I've seen this before. Mario. Tantric Mario. His ad's in here every week. It just never leapt out at me for some reason. How's my muffin?' she asked, as Lara nodded and swallowed her mouthful.

'Thanks. Delicious. You don't have to look after me, you know, or worry about me. I'm really fine. These are great!'

'Now. About today ... which is Saturday in case you haven't noticed. There's a market in The Channon. It's a forty-minute drive from here through the hills, and it's a nice vibe ... lots of fresh produce, healthy treats, music. I'm inviting you, if you're interested.'

'Okay. Why not? Just give me fifteen minutes after this cuppa and I'll be ready.' They sipped slowly, and Ruby noticed Lara noticing the beautiful black and white photograph on the bathroom door; a young woman standing naked on a railway station platform, from the back, her long waist-length hair caught by a sudden gust of wind, perhaps from an

57

approaching train.

'Like it?' she asked.

'Yeah. It tells a story. It's lovely.'

'It's me.'

Lara almost choked on her tea. Ruby read the shock in her face.

'Thirty years ago. Before kids, before everything. I was a ten, back then. You can never imagine what life can do to you, can you? Don't get all pathetic looking on me. I'm not that bad, now, am I?'

Lara put down the cup of tea. 'You're fantastic,' she said.

When Lara looked at her landlady's face, she suddenly saw, beneath Ruby's weathered skin and tough exterior, the outline of sensual lips, the wide-set eyes and high cheekbones, a goddess buried under protective habits and extra weight necessary to push away the effects of a heartless world. Time is cruel, Lara thought.

'I'll tell you 'bout it one day,' Ruby said, taking the last gulp of her tea. 'I was a star. A ten out of ten. See you in fifteen on my verandah.'

9

The fact that people actually knew where The Channon lay, struck Lara as miraculous. Somewhere, at least an hour from anywhere, tucked away in the valleys and hills of the Byron Shire, down winding roads, which seemed to lead to nowhere in particular, lay a grassy field. Colourful stalls selling everything from flattened passion fruit in a round page that you could tear at with your teeth until they broke, to dresses and fruit and squealing puppies, embroidered the edges of the field.

Ruby and Lara took their time strolling around. She didn't think about England once in five hours. She was entirely distracted. Here, a man could be bald, and in compensation, grow a two-foot beard, plait it and tie it with a red ribbon. In fact, in this setting, the waxed parts of Lara's legs felt out of place. Here, she reckoned, she could grow armpit hair as long as Rapunzel's, tie it with ribbons, and no one would stop smiling kindly at her. She'd evidently stumbled into the the actual world of Tolkien's *Lord of the Rings*, complete with hobbits and other odd characters.

'Like it?' Ruby handed her a flattened passion fruit thing and she bit into it.

'I think I love it,' she said. A marimba band played mellow music from the dark shade beneath a Poinciana tree.

'Let's go see what the Gypsy Fortune Teller has to say to you.'

'Oh no, really, honestly, no.'

'Oh yes. It's on me.'

'That is a complete waste.'

'No it isn't,' Ruby said, dragging Lara by the elbow to a small tent where incense burned ominously inside. 'This is the Divine Deborah, and she's pretty good. Let's see if you have a bright future ahead of you.'

'I'm not saying anything to her,' she whispered hurriedly into Ruby's ear. 'Not even giving her my name,' she hissed, as Ruby shoved her into the tent.

Divine Deborah sat Lara on a chair, and drew her own chair around the table, so they faced each other. Then, to Lara's surprise she wrapped her calves around Lara's ankles and took her hands. She had fine grey hair, blue eyes, and a thousand lines crisscrossing her face.

'Now luvvy,' she said to Lara in a husky voice. 'I'm just gonna tell you how I work. My father and grandfather and great-grandfather all did this, so to me this is just life. I tune in, and I'll tell you what my guides tell me, okay?'

Yeah, right. Ruby settled on a soft, red, velvet chair and drew a deep satisfied breath.

'Don't worry about your children,' Divine Deb said. 'You're worried about them and you don't have to. They're fine.'

I'm not worried about my children. She almost said it aloud. The score was in her favour. One wrong already.

'You've got a beautiful, beautiful soul. Very strong, ooh, lots of guides around you here. They're telling me, you mustn't worry about the future. Everything that has happened is for the good. You wanted it to happen, before you were born. This was your plan.'

True. For everyone. Lara smiled at her, happy with her foregone conclusion.

'He wasn't the right one for you, luvvy. Even though it's hard to believe now, he was the wrong one for happily-ever-after. Just a necessary phase, see? But he wasn't the one moving on, it was you. Your destiny.'

Now Lara gave Ruby the eyeball. *What*?

'Any questions, honeybun?'

Divine Deb looked into her soul with crystal-ball eyes and Lara looked right back at her and shook her head, still saying nothing. Okay, one out of three. She knew she'd been unlucky in love. How often would that be the case for middle-aged women on their own seeking fortune tellers at a market? No doubt hundreds of women looking for divine answers to their lonely lives dived into Deb's tent on a regular basis.

'My guides tell me that there is someone. Not quite around the near corner, a bit further. He's waiting for you. He's the one. Tall, rich, handsome. Grey hair. Glasses. You'll know him when you see him.' She trailed off and closed her eyes.

Afterwards, Ruby was ecstatic. 'Isn't she wonderful?' she beamed. 'Isn't it amazing what she can do?'

'I'm sure she'd be a fun friend to have,' Lara said. 'Let's go find lunch. I'm starving.'

★ ★ ★

A couple of hours later they found their way to the small town of Mullumbimby, twenty minutes from Byron Bay, and sat in the steamy afternoon beneath a sky that threatened rain. They ate fish and chips and salad and sipped cold beer. Lara imagined people might arrive here, tourists from Europe, and be transfixed. They would abandon jobs, houses, ambitions and just sit here in the shade of old trees basking in sunlight until they grew old, or starved to death for lack of work. Here, everyone seemed permanently on holiday, or pissed, or stoned.

'You drank that beer too fast,' Ruby scolded. 'That fortune teller really hit a nerve.'

'Oh, rubbish.' Lara waved her hand, dismissing the comment, her body soft and relaxed. The air smelled of rain not yet fallen. Children played in a sandpit designed to keep them occupied while their parents grew more and more inebriated, and Lara fell under a spell of retroactive envy. Imagine little Simon and Rose growing up here in paradise – no big winter jackets, no endless snotty noses, no seventeen-hour winter nights. It was unfair, to say the least. She marveled at how far away England seemed, and how distance and now time in a new place with new people gave her a little more room, a little more perspective on exactly how depressing her life had been with Brock. Ruby slowly sipped the froth on the top of her third beer.

Lara's phone buzzed.

Hope you slept well. Give me a call when you get this.

'Ruby, just making a quick call, okay?'

Ruby didn't hear. Her eyes were fixed on a skinny man with a ponytail standing at the bar.

Lara hit the call back button. Mario answered before the phone even rang.

'It's me,' she said when he picked up. 'I promise you I always close my eyes and snore when I'm really enjoying myself.'

He laughed.

'Did I really just pass out on you?'

'Yeah.'

'I'm sorry.'

'Not at all. Hey, it's a compliment to have someone be so responsive to my touch.'

'Maybe it wasn't your touch.'

'Huh?'

'Maybe I was just dog tired.'

'Nah. You succumbed to the magic of Mario's fingers …'

'Stop being so goddamn conceited, Tantric Bloody Mario.'

'But it's true.' He laughed again.

'Anyway, so, um, how … um … much, how far, the touch, did you …?'

'Oh geez,' he said and smiled. 'After everything I told you. What's the last thing you remember?'

'Thumbs on thighs.'

'That was it.'

'Really?'

'Yeah. Pulled the sheet over you like you were dead, put a blanket over your feet, turned off the music, left.'

'Okay. Whew. Thanks. It was nice.'

'Now that you know you haven't been taken advantage of, can I ask you a question?'

'You just did. You mean another one?'

'Yes.'

'Okay.'

'Are you busy early tomorrow morning, say at five?'

'I will probably be snoring.'

'Would you put aside snoring in order to come on an adventure with me?'

'What kind of an adventure? A sixty dollar an hour one?'

'If you're happy with where I take you. But free if

63

you hate it.'

'Why not,' she said. 'But do you really mean five? As in, I should be dressed and outside at five am?'

'Yep. You'll see why.'

'Okay. Sure. I'll see you then.' She hung up.

Ruby had ordered another beer.

'Hey, Ruby,' Lara said softly, looking at her blotchy countenance. 'Are you sure that's not too much?'

'Course. It's nothing,' she slurred. 'I'm fine. See that god with the ponytail?'

'Who, that skinny guy?'

'Yep. Seen him around the place lots. He's known as a nudist. Love to see his willy in the nilly.' She laughed raucously. 'We can go as soon as I've downed this baby.'

'Maybe I should drive home.'

'Darl, I'm an old pro at this,' she said. 'Listen. Don't worry, okay? How d'ya think I healed all the cracks in my broken heart, eh? They are chock full of the best beers and chardonnay, sealed over with the melting mellowness of marijuana. That's the truth, darl.'

Ruby's speech deteriorated further and her eyelids hung heavy.

'Hand me the keys, Rubes. No way I'm letting you drive home like that.'

She fumbled in her purse. Found them. Dropped them. Burped. Laughed. Lara knew that if she hadn't said anything, Ruby would have driven home. As it was, Lara walked her to the car and had to hold her upright, and Ruby wasn't exactly light.

'Now about that railway photo,' she said.

'Yes, tell me,' Lara said, using her phone as a GPS to guide them back to Ruby's house. 'How old were you?'

'Twenty-fucken-one,' Ruby said sadly, shaking her head. 'The whole world was at my feet. Fuck it. Ah well, that's what we all think then, isn't it? I was modelling here and there, earning a living pretty much, surfing, living the life, winning competitions … and I even did some nudie shots on the side, made some extra money. Hence the railway shot. Imagine that. It was fun. Then I met him, you know, the usual story. I fell for him hard. He was one of the photographers, so yeah, he got the full close-up deal and said he fell in love with my body before he even noticed my face. He was also the drummer in a rock band. Great rhythm he had. I think that's what got me in trouble. So, I got pregnant, got married, modelling dreams came crashing to a halt and of course, no more glam work. I put on thirty kilos, got gestational diabetes, just to make the picture more revolting, and good old Rob, he didn't miss a beat … was off following his dick into every orifice that had legs around it … the mascara on the pillow affair was the first one … and after all that, through the years, I just got lost behind my blubber. I gave up. And he just got uglier and uglier, until he turned into the toad I booted out of my bedroom. I'm happier now, than before, when he was with me, but, that girl just seems like a dream I had of myself once.'

Lara helped Ruby into her house but stopped short of helping her into bed. 'Don't have any more to drink, Rubes,' she said. 'Go to sleep and you'll be good in the morning, though you're probably going to feel awful. I won't be here, okay, but call me if you need me – I'll be unavailable until lunchtime.'

'Ooo, unavailable. Doing what, darl?'

'Going adventuring with Mario. He's picking me

up at the crack of dawn. He says it's a surprise.'

'Ooo,' she said again.

'Sleep tight, Rubes,' she said. 'I'll see you tomorrow or the next day.'

10

The dawn sky stretched overhead, a canopy sprinkled with a billion jewels. In London, let's face it, she
thought, you'd be lucky to see a couple of twinkles
in the sky, but only right overhead because the city
lights turned the rest of the sky orange. So it took
Lara a while to understand what the dawn sky over
Byron Bay offered that took her breath away. Here,
the stars went right down to the ground. Smells of
foreign plants rose from damp bushes. Her hair went
permanently wild in the humidity and she stood on
her deck, watching the end of the street, which lay
like a long black snake, dead silent. She hoped Ruby
had gone straight to sleep and hadn't actually drunk
herself to death.

Finally, headlights appeared. An ancient Saab crept
up the road and slid to a halt outside the iron gate.
Lara pulled her long-sleeved shirt on and took the
steps two at a time.

'You're up early.' Mario grinned as she opened the
door and slid in next to him.

'This better be good,' she said, and slammed the
door. He drove away, careful not to rev his engine.
Mario smiled in the half-dark. 'You were wonderful
the other night,' he joked.

'So, where are we going?'

They drove north on the Pacific motorway. After
a while, they turned off and she read the sign that
flashed into his headlights: Tyagarah. She tried to
pronounce it.

'Tee ah gah rah?' Lara said slowly, like a drunkard.

'Tyagarah. Rhymes with Niagara.'

'Right,' she said. 'I see. What's in Tyagara?'

'Surprise.' Dawn had begun to spread its thin red line on the eastern horizon. Behind them, the silhouette of Mount Warning stretched up into the sky.

They turned down a small road following a sign that said *airstrip*. At the end of the road, they came to a tiny airport. A few biplanes and gliders and other light aircraft sat parked on the grassy edge of a runway. Kangaroos and joeys lay in the cool shade of the wings. 'Do they live here?' she asked.

'They do,' he said. 'And move away only reluctantly. When an engine gets too loud.'

'I love it,' she said. 'What are we doing here?'

'It's the best time of day,' Mario said. 'Winds are at a minimum and not too many other madmen are up in the air to spoil our solitude.

'In the air? Did I hear you say, *in the air*?'

'You did,' he said, and smiled. He parked the car next to a small hangar and pulled up the brake. It was light enough for them to see now. 'This is the other thing I do.'

'What?' she asked dumbly.

'I teach people how not to kill themselves in small, experimental aircraft.'

'Mario. We're going to go flying? In that?'

'That's the plan,' he said. 'Now's your chance to break the surly bonds of earth and fly like a bird. The bird being my beloved delta winged ultralight — over in that quadrant — with the blue and yellow wing. We'll head out in a northerly direction and you'll have the best view of the Byron Shire.' He opened the door and got out. Then he bent down and looked in

68

at her. 'Ready?'

'Look, you should know that at any point in the past I would never, ever, ever have been seen dead climbing into that ... that lawnmower with a hang-glider attached. But right now, you're in luck. Dumb luck. I'll do it, but only because I recently gave up giving a shit about so many things. I could even do a parachute jump.'

'I hope you won't have to. That's awesome. Come on, let me show you how it all works.'

'You don't think we'll die?'

'Nah. I'll do my best to keep you safe.'

★ ★ ★

'Now,' said Mario when Lara was zipped up in a heavy leather jacket with leather gloves, a hat, goggles and headphones looking like a motorcycle mama. 'If anything happens to your pilot, for example, I lose consciousness, just hit this red button. It releases the ballistic parachute and should see you landing softly ... somewhere. Hopefully not mid-ocean.'

'Good to know,' she said.

The sky lightened. Three or four bright stars still twinkled in the pale east.

'You all right?'

'I am,' she said. 'I used to be so scared of flying.'

'Not any more, though?' He asked, checking the wing.

'No.'

The ultralight hummed like a giant hornet on the runway. Lara sat at the back, legs dangling on either side of Mario's seat. In front of him he had a small instrument panel, like something she'd seen on a motorbike, Lara thought. Nothing else except the bright fresh morning.

She watched the tarmac speed by underfoot and checked the speedometer as they raced along the runway. At about a hundred and fifty kilometres an hour, Mario pulled the bar in front of him and they lifted upward into the air, as if on an invisible incline. Every wind gust or air pocket sent Lara's stomach lurching into the past or the future, while she tried to keep the world's supply of oxygen out of her mouth. Mario held onto the bar in front of him very tightly and steered into the blue above.

'Five hundred feet. You okay?'

'Fine,' she tried to say, through air bubbles in her cheeks.

'Try keeping your mouth closed,' Mario said.

She wanted to say easier said than done, but couldn't get beyond the blasting air and chipmunk cheeks to do it. She grunted. Below them, the waves broke slowly along the shore, and the sun burst suddenly from behind the horizon, flooding the sea with golden flecks, and blinding her for a moment. The radio crackled through. Air traffic control warned Mario of an approaching helicopter. Lara didn't see it until it was right overhead, and she could see the pilot's moustache.

'This is why I am not a pilot,' she said, managing the airflow into her mouth at last. 'I didn't see him.'

'It's my buddy Sam with the coastguard,' Mario said. 'You can wave if you want.'

She would have, only her hands were glued to the seat in front.

'Seven hundred feet. Look, whales.'

They flew out over the sea. The lighthouse gleamed

white on the headland. 'I'm going in closer. Hold on,' Mario said, and put the ultralight into a rapid nose-dive in which Lara fully suspected her internal organs were plotting to come flying out of her mouth.

She did, for a crazy moment, contemplate reaching forward and hitting the red button, but thought better of it. Instead, she grabbed onto strong shoulders and didn't let them go until the plane evened out.

The whales were right below them. Now this, Lara thought, is what a bird feels like. Lara and Mario skimmed along just above the waves and Lara would have happily given up being a human if she could be assured that life would be like this, day after day, until she grew too old and tired to fly and just fell into the sea. Suddenly, below them, a whale breached. It moved in slow motion. Before she could truly appreciate the magic of the moment, another one appeared and they almost felt the seaspray on their feet.

The sun warmed the beaches and the early morning cloud dissolved. Lara stopped swallowing so much air and stopped holding on too tightly. As some wise woman once said, once you passed a certain age, you only had so many shits to give, and this was obviously the time not to give one, even if this was the last day the planet existed. The world spread out, a tapestry of green bush and golden sands, and the rippling sea continuously crept towards that shoreline, moving under them. Lara felt her old London married-to-Brock self blow out the back in the wake of turbulence created by the flight. Her horizons, once so small and close and grey, extended out to where she imagined she could see the earth's curve.

'Check this out,' Mario said, going even closer to the water. At first all she saw were a few early morning swimmers taking a dip on a long stretch of beach. Then, just below, she saw what he saw — angular dorsal fins, recognisable from terrifying movies. There had to be about ten of them, she counted. Sharks. Not five hundred metres from the swimmers.

'Can't we warn them?' she yelled into her microphone. He used his mobile phone and got hold of coastguard Sam.

'Sharks parallel to South Golden Beach.' Then to Lara: 'Don't worry. This happens all the time and not too many people get eaten.'

'But some do get eaten?'

'On rare occasions.'

She watched the ignorant swimmers splashing out towards the breaking waves, while they checked out the dorsal fins of moving great whites. Do those swimmers have any idea how precarious and precious their lives are, she wondered? It was so obvious from this height that the sweeping big ocean was their territory. Did those flapping pink humans have any idea how close they were to being breakfast?

She turned to look west as they ascended, away from the ocean and over the rolling green hills and valleys of New South Wales. They followed an eagle, then a river, flew over a waterfall and then turned south along the coastline, following the highway.

'If we need to make an emergency landing, that utility road on the side of the motorway is perfect.'

'Do you need to make an emergency landing?' she asked, trying not to eat the microphone.

'Not today,' he said.

'You did once?'

'Sure.'

'Tell me that story another time.'

He laughed.

By the time they came in to land, the sun shone high in a cloudless sky. Lara didn't want to stop thinking like a bird.

* * *

Lara unbuckled her seatbelt, lifted the headphones off her head and climbed out of the plane. She stood unsteadily on the tarmac.

Mario walked around and opened his arms wide. She hugged him tight. 'Thanks,' she said. 'I had a great time. You get paid.'

'Great. On both accounts.' He laughed.

'I did almost see the headlines, "British Tourist Dies in Light Plane Crash", but I got over imagining that. It's quite cold up there.'

As heat from the ground radiated upwards, she broke into a sweat and took off the leather jacket.

'There's a nice little breakfast place in Brunswick Heads, which is only a five-minute drive from here,' he said.

'Sounds great,' she said. 'I'm starving.'

After tying down the plane's wing and making it safe and secure, they strolled towards the Saab. Lara's door wouldn't open. Mario bashed it with his hip to jiggle it loose and they laughed. 'You're so high-tech and mechanically able,' she said.

'It's my special talent,' he said.

They spluttered away from the Tyagarah airstrip onto the motorway towards Brunswick Heads. The wind tangled Lara's hair through the open window. Her face felt burned, alive. She hadn't cried for days and had hardly thought of Brock much in the past twenty-four hours. That had to be progress.

The restaurant overlooked the quietly flowing river, where birds and fishermen waited on the rocks for a flash of silver in the depths.

They'd just ordered when Mario's phone rang. 'Sorry, must take this.' He turned away from her. 'Hello gorgeous,' he said. 'You get back okay?' Silence. 'No. Should be finished by then. Okay, see you 'round two? Brilliant.' He put the phone down. 'Jodie,' he said. 'Girlfriend.'

'She, uh, must know about your job?'

'Of course. She's great. I'm seeing two women at the moment.'

'Oh, do tell,' she said. Her Dandy Latte, her new favourite, arrived and she slowly scooped the foam off the top. She tried to imagine what it might feel like knowing that the love of your life was off serenading other women and loving them in different ways. She didn't know how anyone could be that detached. She wished she had the guts or the disposition to try Room Two. Wasn't it the Buddhists who said practise non-attachment, she thought? Maybe these Room Two types were seriously evolved, and she was stuck in an old-fashioned world view. She felt miserable all of a sudden.

'So, Mario. Go on. Tell me about your girlfriends.' Her voice sounded nauseatingly cheery even to her own ears. She wanted to know whether this Room Two life of polyamory was entirely without drawbacks for those who lived it. She could not imagine it to be that easy.

'Sure.' He looked at her, eyes twinkling, tanned young face full of the joy of living and flying and having it all. Lara felt like an old witch who'd just

74

swallowed a lemon.

'I have, you could say, an expansive way of being.'

'Love to hear about it,' she said, trying to keep the caustic soda out of her voice.

'Well, I'm not into exclusive relationships. And I'm open about being open to many people.' His double espresso arrived. 'Been seeing Jodie for about five months. And seeing a German girl, Erika too, who does have a boyfriend. Both are experimenting with the idea of open relationships in different ways.'

'What fun,' she said, not meaning it.

'Yeah, yeah. It is, really.'

'Uh-huh,' Lara said. 'And I bet no one ever gets jealous or hurt and it's just shiny happy people holding hands day in, day out.'

'Well, I wouldn't say that,' he said. 'But I'd reckon it's a lot more honest and fun than the majority of so-called monogamous relationships.'

'I don't want to believe it.'

'Look, my lifestyle is a reaction to my life, if you need to know. My Italian father was an arsehole. He emotionally and physically abused my mother ... and she gave birth to seven children. Then he left us all. She had nothing without him. She eventually got cancer, died at age fifty, and had, in my memory, no joy in her life ever. At fourteen, I went to Italy, to boarding school, spent my teens there, and had my suspicions confirmed that marriage was a bullshit story for just about everyone. I swore that I would never, ever trap any woman in a relationship. I want all women to be free. Heck, I want to be free. The women I've known through my healing work are of a general consensus that men are mostly jerks because they're dishonest.'

'Now there's a thought,' she said. 'Well, sounds like

75

you've got the world all figured out. I dunno. I suspect it's not all rainbows and free love in Room Two, but what would I know?'

'No, you're right. I mean, even in Room Two, people sometimes get hurt or upset. I guess I look at the natural world and take my cues from animals who pursue pleasure, animals who are gay, lesbian, who masturbate, who use 'sex' to communicate — like bonobo apes, you know. Nature is pretty diverse. Who knows where we get this idea of monogamy? We share so much with the animal kingdom. Monogamy is not a natural law for all living things. It's a false expectation imposed by narrow-minded humans with ulterior puritanical and power-hungry motives.'

'Not entirely,' Lara said. 'I mean, there are in fact, penguins and other species who stay faithful to one partner for life, without vows or God or complex puritanical fears. And anyway, people have the choice to imagine how others feel, to be ethical and fair and kind, whereas animals don't really know much about that. Also there's love.'

'You're right.' He leaned back and drained his cup. 'I agree with some of that. But, maybe our species has to evolve a bit. For example, if I feel as though I'm getting attached to someone in my personal life, for one reason or another, I start to want to control them; what they do, what they feel. That's not love. It's awful. So I get outta there, for both our sakes. I don't want enmeshment or ownership, so I have to disengage. And sure it hurts, but then we're each free again.'

Their breakfasts finally arrived and Lara worked hard so as not to inhale her eggs on toast in one breath.

'You ever loved someone more than life itself?'

He contemplated bacon, sausage, fried tomato. 'Don't know.'

'Okay.'

'Maybe once,' he said. 'But never again.'

'When?'

'Years ago. Her name was Sophie.'

'Sophie?'

'Yeah. I reckon that's the closest to any kind of overwhelming love I've ever felt. I was back in Tassie after years in Italy. My mother was dead. I felt raw and open. And Sophie walked into that space.'

'Now you're talking my language,' Lara said.

'The thing was, I didn't have room for anyone else when we were together. She consumed me. I started to feel jealous of her interactions with other guys. I was terrified of trapping her in my desire. I hated that. So one morning I left.'

'Really?'

'Yep. Left Tasmania,' he took a giant bite of egg and sausage. 'Explained it in a letter.'

'That sounds cruel.'

'I had to do it.'

'You must've broken her heart,' Lara said.

'Nah. I don't think so,' he said, shaking his head as he chewed.

'How do you know, though?'

'She had other male ... friends. I didn't like the feelings that I felt. Had to resist being like my dad in any way. I was saving her from me. I'm sure she was relieved — eventually.'

They watched a fisherman reel in a big, flapping fish that knocked his cap right off his head as he brought it up from the river.

'How do you never get attached to a client – ever?'

'I have my protocol. I give them everything when I'm with them, and let them go when we're done.'

Well, she thought. Good for you. But he'd shown a chink in his chainmail. Sophie. He had known love and jealousy. He was human after all.

The big fish flip-flopped from side to side on the jetty.

'Son of a gun that's a giant,' Mario said. 'I hope he turfs him back.'

'Me too. When I was young,' she said, 'I was a fisherman's menace.' She told him about her numerous fish thefts and how she relocated captured specimens to seas and rivers.

The man did not throw his catch back into the river. 'Bastard,' she said. 'I'm tempted to do a relocation.'

She tucked into her egg, toast and tomato and didn't look up. When she did, Mario was staring at her. She smiled and put her knife and fork down.

'Look, I'm still considering … you,' she said. 'I just don't know how to get over my fears.'

'What are you afraid of?'

'Dunno. I'm worried about feeling ashamed, awkward, maybe getting hurt.'

'It wouldn't be like that,' he said. 'Think of it like a spa treatment, only a lot more fun.'

Would any newly abandoned forty-four-year-old woman sanely turn her back on that kind of an offer? Lara honestly could not imagine at this stage in the game, finding an opportunity to break with the past as good looking and sexy and delicious as this one.

'Here,' she said, getting a few crisp fifty dollar bills out of her purse. 'This is for this morning. And an advance to book you in for the, uh, spa treatment.'

'Thanks,' he said, and put the money in his pocket. 'What's next?'

'A date and time,' she said. 'And a venue. A remote beach comes to mind.'

'Done,' he said.

'Really?'

'Yes. I have a plan.'

'Good.'

'Okay if I drop you home after breakfast? I'll text you details.'

'Sure. You have a date with your girlfriend?'

'Yes.'

Lara drained her drink. 'I'm going for a run this afternoon. Let's get going. Before that bloody fisherman catches another one.'

11

Lara's phone buzzed. She hadn't checked messages for a while. She counted one hundred and thirty-seven unread texts and emails and after a moment of mild panic, realised that most of them were easily answered simply by hitting delete. Including one from Brock flagged urgent. And a message on her phone from Joanne: *Hi Lara darling. Mr Erotica – have you found him?*

She replied: re: *Mr Erotica. Stay tuned.*

At two o' clock, Lara, despite herself, imagined Mario arriving at girlfriend number one, Jodie's. She would be slim and young and brown, wearing a hippy wrap-around skirt, and tank top without a bra. Her perfect nipples would press against the fabric, her narrow hipbones protrude from the top of the skirt, and her waist-length hair would no doubt be cascading carelessly over her shoulders. Ten minutes passed. Would they be making love already? They were still young. Would they have sex three, four times in a row?

Was this insanity? Her husband had just left her for a pseudo-lesbian, and there she was fighting tiny green shoots of envy and unworthiness because of a sexy young Room Two connoisseur? Did she need her head read?

No, she thought. The new Lara did not need psychoanalysis. She was having an understandable reaction to recent events. The part of her that was properly insane was the old self — devastated because a narcissistic, boring, middle-aged bloke with shifty eyes had left her after more than two decades. That self had needed help. This self was suffering from Post Infidelity Stress Disorder. PISD, and according to her sleepless googling, could take years to recover from.

There were millions of former Room One inhabitants, she'd discovered. Recently or not-too-recently-betrayed, middle-aged women, they walked around heartbroken, wondering why they felt so traumatised, why they were so messed up, why self-annihilation seemed off and on like a viable way out of the pain. They developed all kinds of anxieties, relived events over and over, and cultivated their generally overactive threat-detection systems. Some of them escaped. Others ended up like Ruby, drinking too much and too often.

Lara had not allowed these thoughts until now. The universe, she mused to herself, had not worked in women's favour for centuries. Except in Southern Africa where a remote matriarch, the Rain Queen, Modjadi, hand-picked the men she wanted to have sex with, the men she wanted to father her children. She also had a few wives to help around the house. *That*, Lara thought, was in fact a sustainable formula given the current trend of overpopulation. Not that she had any rain queen fantasies.

She was absolutely sure of one thing, though: men had had their cake and eaten it too long.

Lara was ready to go somewhere she'd never gone before. Done with her waterfall of thoughts, she smothered her face in sunscreen, grabbed her sunglasses and hurried to her car. She drove into Byron and found a place to park right next to Main Beach. Clouds built in the distance.

Lara started to run and noticed that her legs didn't

seem as flappy as they had even a few days ago and she didn't feel quite as doughy or breathless.

Fine rain pockmarked the sand and the sun burst through the clouds in sporadic intervals. Her bare feet pounded the shoreline and she breathed in. This air came to her courtesy of thousands of miles of ocean, blasting across the Pacific. Oxygen therapy. Ozone therapy. For free.

She reached the rocks at the end, finally, and ran all the way up the steps. She stared out at the huge Pacific feeling like she could have kept running forever.

Since Lara had more energy afterwards than before her run, she wondered whether it was possible to stop time and start aging backwards. Start running at age forty-four and after two hours, arrive at age forty-two, and do that each day until you reached your perfect age at which point you could get lazy for a bit, age a bit again, and then run yourself backwards through time.

Energised, she went to pick up some supplies at Woolworths and the pharmacy. She arrived home after five. Ruby's back door stood open. Faint strains of jazz drifted over the lawn. She had a quick shower, pulled on shorts and a t-shirt and took the steps two at a time. She crossed the lawn barefoot disturbing a flock of rainbow lorikeets eating seeds from Ruby's birdfeeder. Ruby rushed to the door to wave.

'Come in,' she called. 'I've missed you, darl.'

Lara crossed the verandah into her house.

'You look radiant,' Ruby said. 'What are you doing?'

'Running my bum off,' Lara said. 'Hey, your place is so homey. 'I love all the artefacts and furniture Ruby. Where's it all from?'

'Bali, babe. My best place. Had some ripping sex there once. Here, have a seat. Tell me what you've been up to. I want to hear all your adventures.'

Lara plonked herself down on the couch. Ruby's breath told her ... whisky.

Lara ran her toes along the rug in front of the leather couch, gazed at the flat-screen TV worthy of a small cinema and marveled as a fluffy white cat the size of a dog sauntered in and looked at her with disdain; the hardwood dining room table with a vase of flowers at the centre spoke of home. The giant cat came towards her, hissed and then rubbed itself against her leg.

'Don't take Mimi seriously,' Ruby said. 'She's slightly bonkers. Want a Jack Daniels?'

'How about a gin and tonic?'

Ruby handed her a glass clinking with ice and sat down next to her.

'Thanks, Ruby.'

'What you been up to?'

Lara explained.

'You're joking!' Ruby wriggled into a comfortable position. As she reached out to put her drink on the coffee table, she spilled it. They both laughed. 'That's it? You flew?'

Lara couldn't help laughing. 'Flying's quite a wild way to spend the morning, don't you think?'

'Like, no hot sex, no making out, none o' that?'

'None,' Lara said. 'I had a great time.' She didn't speak of the plan, though.

'Honey,' Ruby said. 'You need to loosen up a little. Let your hair down.'

Lara sipped her drink. 'Relative to who I was last month, you have no idea how loose I am right now.' She told Ruby about Room One and Room Two and her proposal for ending both male domination of society and the environmental crisis with a unique rain queen approach.

'Darl, I'm on your side. Have always been. In fact, the first year of life after marriage, I made it my duty, no my mission, to sleep with as many men as possible. Mind you, I wasn't too worried about things then, like AIDS and so on. I learned the beauty of loving men one after the other, like chapters in a book, some of them very exciting, some of them just pages to flick through quickly without paying too much attention, some of them worthy of being slowly perused while you wished it would never end. Good times, darl. But not such easy pickings now at my age. Anyway, the thought of a few husbands at once? Nauseating,' she said. 'Three in a row would be preferred.' She reached out, took the whisky and skulled it. Her eyes rolled heavenward. 'Nearly as good as a good fuck. Nearly, I said.'

'Ruby! You're a one-track girl, that's for sure. Well, while we're on the subject, here's a personal question — you don't have to answer it ...'

'Oh, I love personal questions. Go on.'

'This is me being naive, okay, but ... when you hired one of these tantric workers ...' Lara dropped her voice to a whisper. 'Did you feel bad afterwards? Compromised, or, like you'd lost something?'

Ruby burst into raucous laughter. 'Darl, you're precious! Yes, I lost my fucking mind. Lose something? My virginity maybe. Oh, wait, that was long gone. Nah.' She laughed, enjoying herself. Then she turned to look at Lara with bloodshot, loving eyes. 'Lara, darl. Be a fucking hedonist. Hell, that guy the gypsy fortune teller told you about may be hiding just

84

up the street and you may as well enjoy life 'til he comes along.'

'That, my dear Ruby, will never happen. I am planning to Carpe the Diem, I just don't wanna Carpe the wrong part of the Diem.'

Ruby puffed out her big cheeks and blew. 'This is your time to heal, to get over an old life. My aging hippie advice? Grab life, and some dude, by the balls — and run with it.'

'Sound advice, I'm sure.'

Ruby laughed and downed the rest of her drink. She poured herself another. Lara had some more of hers.

'I shouldn't drink,' Lara said. 'When I was a teen, we'd go out to these clubs, and my friend Natasha would tell everyone not to give me any gin, because it was all over in five minutes. Apparently, I'm glad, then sad then mad and then snoring, in rapid succession.' She rested her head against the couch. 'I'm so tired,' she said.

'You skipped all the glad, sad and mad. You can't go to sleep now.'

Not long after, Ruby's own loud snores bounced off the walls. Lara slid out from her friend's leaning head, placed a blanket over her and tucked her in. Two empty glasses shimmered in the moonlight. Crickets pulsed in the bushes and bats squawked in the trees over the house as she crept out, using her phone-light as a guide. Late-night brown snakes had a habit of hiding in the grass Ruby had said and she felt properly alert and completely alive as she ventured back to her high house. She answered Mario's text about the next morning. Yes.

12

They drove south out of Byron. Twenty minutes out, they turned off the main road and drove on a narrow strip of rough bitumen into a dense tropical jungle. Tanglewood trees grew tall. Lara felt like she was inside a Tarzan movie. Or on the set of Jurassic Park. Dinosaurs could come to eat her any minute now.

'Parasites,' Mario said, pointing at the trees. 'Stranglers. Look. See how they grow around other trees? They surround them, use them to climb towards the sun. The inner tree, the original tree, dies, and the parasite reaches its ultimate dizzy height.'

'Oh, I know a few people like that,' she said.

'Who will remain nameless,' he said.

'Exactly.'

Trees that had elbows and knees and fingers appeared like strange trolls as they rounded another bend in the road. Lara's eyes, used to ivy-covered cottages and thick blackberry bushes in late summer, struggled to make sense of the things she saw in the undergrowth in this rainforest. It seemed like a drug-induced hallucination, only she'd never had one. Suddenly, Mario stopped. 'Up there,' he said, pointing through the front window.'Do you see him?'

'I can't see the woods for the trees.' Lara said.

'Follow my finger,' he said. 'That dark thing over there in the fork of those two branches is the fluffy bum of a sleeping koala.'

They got out and stood at the foot of a tall eucalyptus tree. Shading their eyes against the dappled sunlight, they walked around the base. As they trampled rainforest leaves into mush, they kept their eyes on the branches where the koala slept. She saw him then, with his face pressed against the side of the tree and his paw covering his nose.

'Gosh, that's cute,' she said. 'Makes me want to live here.'

'You are looking kinda happy,' he said.

'I'm thinking I could stay forever in a place where fluffy-bummed koalas hang out in local trees.'

The sun slipped behind a cloud and in the distance, they heard the rumble of thunder. 'Let's get going,' he said. 'I'll try and find you a snake before the day's out.'

'Very kind, but please don't go to too much trouble.'

They got back into the car and continued to drive down the jungle road. Heavy drops of rain began to splash down on the windshield.

Mario turned onto a narrow dirt track. The car rattled and bumped over ditches and potholes. At the end of the track he pulled into a clearing big enough for a single car. No way on earth would anyone who didn't know the area be able to find this spot, she thought. Rain hammered on the car roof and ran rivers down the windscreen. She was adrift in a new world in which anything was possible.

'So, now what?' she asked.

'Well, if we take off our clothes, we can walk in our bathers, and that way when we get back, there'll be something dry to change into.'

'But, Mario, I'm just not accustomed to hiking in public with all my wobbly bits hanging out, okay? I like to not expose every ounce of myself.'

He laughed. 'No one here gives a shit about wobbly

bits Lara. Look around. There's not a single damn soul to see us hiking. We could even walk naked. Anyway, you're a hot chick, okay? So, enjoy being you, amidst the other naturally beautiful things here.' He indicated the trees, the sky and the muddy ground.

'Do you also call seventy-five-year-old grandmothers hot when you're being your complimentary, tantric self?'

He grinned at her through dark ringlets. 'No. I don't if they aren't. I find what is beautiful and draw attention to that. I called you hot, because I meant it.'

Lara decided to stop arguing. 'Fine. Okay. Let's do it.'

'I've got a first aid kit and my backpack. I brought us a coupla snacks too. Also, it's snakey around here, but they'll be hiding in this weather.'

'I'm not too worried about snakes.'

'Great.'

'Unless they bite me. Or unless they're anaconda sized. Other things scare me more.'

Mario took off his shorts and shirt. His swimmers stretched and revealed more than they concealed. Lara stared.

'What are you most afraid of?' he asked.

'Right now? That if you walk behind me you will have a closeup view of my sagging arse dimpled with top-notch, middle-aged cellulite that will ripple with every step. It might damage you and I will be responsible. Do you have any idea what unconcealed cellulite rebounding off itself all over the tops of two wobbly thighs can do to a person's mental health?'

Mario shook his head, a wide smile spreading across his face. He took the backpack out of the car, threw his clothes on the back seat, slammed the door and dropped his pack on the ground. He came around to where she stood and put his hands on her shoulders. 'May I just?'

'What?' Her outside smile did not mirror the inside smile that hung upside down in her stomach.

'Get you half naked.'

'Oh my God.' Her voice shook and she giggled. 'Well, why not?'

'That's what today's for.'

'Sounds easy,' she said. 'I'm yours.'

He lifted her shirt, slipping it over her head. He opened the car door, and threw it on the front seat. 'Nice bikini,' he said.

He slipped his fingers under the elastic of her shorts. A second later they pooled at her ankles.

If, last month, someone had shown her a picture of herself standing in a rainforest in her bikini in the pouring rain, being touched by a bronzed sea god with wild dark locks, she would have dismissed it as photo-shopped fiction.

'Let's walk,' he said.

'Okay, go.'

Lara wondered about his sex life, his girlfriends, about separating sex from love, or more specifically, professional-healing-sexual-love from girlfriend-sexual-love and girlfriend-number-two-sexual-love. Confounding, she thought, to say the least. But she wondered just how many shits she had to give about all that just now anyway?

Room Two, she thought, here I come. An intimate tango with tantric Mario who had recently tangoed with a series of girls and women. How's that for pure unadulterated gutsiness?

'Keep your shoes on,' he said. 'It's a bit tricky

underfoot.'

Mario followed what Lara would have called a non-existent footpath, though he maintained they were on it. Quite a talent. They walked single file through undergrowth and patches of mud that sucked at their feet like hungry monsters. Lara felt sweaty even as the rain continued. Tall trees towered over them. Then, beyond the rain and wind, she heard the crashing of surf against rocks. The descent grew steeper. She thought of the original people of the land, traversing these hills.

They came to the edge of a cliff and descended down a steep embankment, small rocks tumbling down from under their feet. Her legs shook like the top of setting jelly as she tried to navigate the mud and stones and rocks. Mario took her hand.

'It's a bit slippery,' he said. 'Hold on.'

Lara wobbled and slid in mud and shrieked. Mario came to the rescue.

'Shit,' she said, looking down over a sheer drop of at least a hundred metres

'I gotcha.'

Her body trembled. Could he feel that? 'Last time I climbed something I was probably eleven,' she said.

'You're still the same kid,' he said. 'Being old is a state of mind.'

'That's crap,' she said. 'Try telling that to an eighty-five-year-old trying to run after a taxi.'

'Okay, I get your point,' he said as he caught her again. She tripped and stumbled her way down the non-pathway. She could hear the sea in the mist and rain but could not see beyond the thick forest.

After another ten or fifteen minutes she started to understand something. Muscles, which Lara had long since ignored, woke up. This was something she could do, despite a lifetime of city living, with shoes and socks and heavy clothing most of the time between nature and her. She felt her fingers, arms and legs, cramping, clinging, monkey-like to the protrusions of rocks that became their stairway.

Mario's fingers and the palm of his hand became her point of contact with safety.

'You're like a goat,' she said, 'leading a jellyfish. I would be tumbling down here arse over elbow, left to my own devices.'

He laughed. 'I've never seen a jellyfish with either an arse or an elbow.'

The jungle opened out in front of them, framing a stretch of sea and distant blue sky, and a hard-packed white sand beach surrounded by cliffs.

Lara followed Mario down the last rocky bit of pathway, losing inhibitions with each step she took. They reached the bottom. Only those who know the place and are reasonably fit could ever get here, she thought. Mario was right; she could've hiked naked. Lara was too busy trying to stay upright to give a hoot now about how her arse looked.

Boulders surrounded them. On either side, high green cliffs towered into the mist. A pounding, grinding, in-coming tide roared. Waves as large as houses crashed far out to sea. The downpour turned to drizzle. Out over the sea, the sun streamed through the clouds, turning the water beneath it to white gold.

Beneath her feet, the sand felt as hard as concrete.

'This way,' Mario shouted, running, pulling her across the sand. They wove their way between giant rocks. At the other end of the beach, they reached a cliff-face that had an opening in it.

'We have to hurry a bit,' he said, letting go of her hand, jogging faster. 'Tide's coming in.'

Lara followed, blinking away rain and sweat. She did not see the sight until they stood right in front of it at the other side of the beach.

A cleft in the rock opened up in front of them, the size of a cathedral door. Mario took off his shoes and motioned Lara to do the same. 'We're going in there?' she asked.

'Yup.'

'Into that giant vagina?'

'Exactly.'

'Tide's coming in, it looks like.'

'We'll be more-or-less trapped inside for some hours. It's safe though. Ready?'

'What's 'more-or-less?''

'We'd have to swim through this bit which will be a channel. Only if we wanted to get out.'

'Oh.'

'The point is, no one can get in without us being given a lot of warning. They'd have to struggle and splash and we'd hear them long before they'd see us.'

'Shit. Okay.'

He slipped an arm around her waist and hoisted her through the swiftly forming channel. The sea, warm, energetic, swirled around her thighs and the tide tugged hard as it pulled back out. She held onto him until they emerged from the channel onto packed sand that led upward into the cavernous vagina. The ocean roared outside. The cave narrowed to a point at the back and smelled like seaweed. Inside, powdery sand indicated that no water had made it this high up for ages.

Lara surveyed their surroundings. Water trickled

down the rocks overhead and every few seconds, dropped onto the ground.

'What d'you think?' Mario asked, indicating the high overhanging rock, the sea outside, and the moat-like channel beyond the mouth of the cave, keeping the world away. He dropped his backpack onto the sand and stretched his arms above his head.

'Sexy,' she said, gesturing at the dripping, algae-covered walls and the rivulets of water running through tiny crevices along the cave wall.

'Glad you like it,' he said. 'Because you're stuck in here with me for a few hours.' He unzipped the backpack. 'How does that feel?'

'I could ask the same thing. How do you feel about spending this lovely afternoon in a slit in the middle of God knows where, with a forty-something-year-old housewife?'

'Damn,' he said. 'It feels exciting.'

Lara felt herself flush. The air tasted salty. Like heaven.

As a teenager, Lara had devoured paperback romance novels at the rate of one every couple of days for an entire year, lasting from one Christmas to the next. After a staggering one hundred and four books, each one containing three or four explicit love scenes, she'd already had imaginary sex with more than a hundred Harlequin or Mills & Boon alpha male heroes. Lara's romantic paradigm was programmed. By the time she turned fourteen, she'd graduated to more intriguing works of literature. They didn't all have happy endings, proving she was capable of growth, though steamy romance had an enduring secret place on the top shelves of her book collection. Despite her romantic ideals and longing, Lara had never, in all her years of marriage, had a Mills & Boon/ Harlequin moment. Brock didn't have a romantic bone in his body. He had been a fumble-under-the-covers-till-you-find-it-kinda-guy. His pyjama bottoms had stayed wrapped around his ankles for two decades. From day one. Ninety-nine per cent of the time. Lara had known in the cold light of betrayed retrospect, that sex with Brock was like a cold potato supper with no bloody salt. Maybe it had been just with her. Perhaps with his other lovers he channeled a secret porn-star self. Now, she thought, if Brock had to compete with Mario in a five-minute beauty contest even four years back when the ponytailed twenty-two-year-old had captured Brock's imagination, and he hers, Mario could have walked in and stolen that girl in half a minute, hands — or pants — down. And that, she thought, was the truth. So, behold, at last, her own unique Room Two: an appropriately shaped cave – in which she was about to get to compare, contrast and evaluate many things male.

First, her dark-haired alpha hero burning with sensuality pulled out some soft cotton cloths from his pack and spread them on the sand. Then he took an amber bottle of oil and sprinkled some on the cloths so that a sensual aroma mingled with the saline air. His dark, Italian locks curled against his angled jawline and the colour in his cheeks rose when he looked up at Lara as she stood blocking the light.

He smelled delicious — like coconut oil, sweat and aftershave. The faint smell of seaweed, the sound of the waves lapping at the mouth of the cave and the sight of rain beyond the cave were all intoxicating. Lara sat down on the cloth. Mario reached out and slid his hands up her arms. Then, as if he knew what romantic heroes in cheap paperbacks always did, he pulled her towards him and she leaned onto him. Heat radiated from his hands against her back. He undid her bikini top and it fell into the sand. Her breasts pressed against his chest and her heart picked up its pace. He tangled fingers in her hair.

Their hips pressed together — only thin nylon separated their nakedness, and they sank down onto the cloth. She reached down into her bikini bottom and retrieved a condom she'd hidden there earlier.

'Great minds think alike,' he said. He put his hand into his backpack and unzipped a pocket, throwing things out of it. A whole array of condoms tumbled onto the cloth. 'But not yet.'

They laughed. Then he leaned over her and pressed her down onto the cloth until she lay on her back. He took her left foot in his hand and stroked it free of sand. Then he did the same with her right. When they were clean, he poured oil into his hands, and captured both her feet. Slowly, deliciously, he massaged each toe, her heels, arches, ankles, calves. She felt as though she'd fallen into a deep, warm bath. The massage went on for ages and she was both delirious and relaxed at the same time. Eventually his hands moved up her thighs, his thumbs pressing on the insides.

'Is this where we left off last time?' he said.

'That's what you tell me.'

'You comfortable?'

'No.'

'Why not?'

'You're a Room Two professional. I'm out of my zone.'

'Hey,' he said. 'This is your zone. You call the shots.'

A short while later, both of them naked, Lara felt

properly crazy with desire. Mario's sensual exploration of her body outlined every dip and curve – every part of her that had felt it didn't exist, now caught fire. Flames travelled the length of her nerves everywhere and she tingled. Imagine, she thought, never having this experience … this moment in which nothing mattered but the promise of ecstasy. Her head fell back and she gave in to being ravished.

With his thumbs, his lips, his fingers Mario aroused every secret fold and crevice until she thought her body would short circuit with pleasure. Beneath the cloth, the sand felt cool against her back.

She wrapped her legs around his waist.

Mario pressed into her imprinting her body on the sand. She let his rhythm shake her. Waves broke and receded, in the cave, outside the cave. Their bodies became one with the sounds and motions of sea and wind.

Lara and Mario made love three times in three hours. He showed her the tricks of his trade and she rode tidal waves of ecstasy, tumbling over and over until she almost forgot who she was.

Sometime later, she asked him to show her what men like, and he let her in on some secrets – massages and ways used for centuries by masters of the tantric arts, he said, that could ratchet pleasure up by ten notches at least.

Afterwards, they fell asleep. He woke her by trailing his finger over her now-sandy body.

'That's my world record,' she said, opening her eyes. She lay on his arm.

'Really? Well, honoured to have been here, ma'am while you reached your world record,' he said.

'I would have paid you anything for this.'

'I would have given it to you for nothing. I had a nice time too.'

They lay there, listening to the ocean do what it had been doing for millions of years.

'What was her name again?' Lara asked.

'Who?'

'The girl you left in Tasmania.'

'Sophie.'

'Sophie. Right. That's a sweet name.'

'I never think of her anymore.'

'Of course you don't.'

Silence.

'I did what was best, you know, leaving. I didn't want to lose myself, get entangled, that kind of thing.'

'Of course,' she said. 'I don't know, though. Maybe you aren't completely the emotional Room Two Superman you think you are.'

'Why do you say that?'

'Maybe after years of giving countless women the best sex any of them could dream of, you'll think, I could have been there, loving this girl, maybe having children with her, sharing everything, being there for each other, growing old together. You know, good old Room One stuff.'

'I can't see it,' he said.

'I know. You live in Room Two. I couldn't stay in here, even if I tried. So it's hard for me to imagine people who do.'

'Why?'

'I can be in it with you, Mario, but that's because I'm paying you and you're nice and because this is your profession. I mean, do you think, that being with one person over time, having children, going through stuff, et cetera, that maybe it's got something to offer, besides broken bodies, broken hearts and stretch marks?'

'From everything I've seen, no.'

'Why?'

'Too much suffering.'

'But you can't guarantee you won't suffer in life.'

'I know. But I can do a hell of a lot to avoid it.'

'But how?' she said. 'I mean, look at me. I tried my best.'

He looked at her. 'Life's unfair, is all I can say.'

'See this?' She pointed at the silver stretch marks below her navel. 'This is the visible trail of destruction left after making and giving birth to two actual human beings. The other scars are in places that won't see daylight ever. They're the stuff that happens when you put yourself aside as you pander to the growing-up needs of the two aforementioned creatures. There's a mound of rubble under your heart that lasts, I believe, forever.'

'So childbirth, you say, is not much fun?'

'Society's biggest conspiracy.'

'Why?'

'They don't tell you that women have one hole missing, and it's bloody enormous – ten centimetres by ten centimetres. If God had been a woman – and this is how we know for sure she isn't, the proper design for a female human would have been a kangaroo, where the baby grows in your pouch. You can even check on it as it grows. Your nipples are in the pouch, or nipple, so no hassles with stupid issues around breastfeeding. You can even do it in public. When it's time for the world, the kid just leans over and starts eating grass, or broccoli, as the case may be. No pain at all.'

'And so God, if there is one, is …'

'A colossal fucking jerk with a twisted sense of humour. None of it is funny for women.'

'It's that bad?'

'Try chewing off one of your own limbs with your teeth.'

'Oh … that's terrible.'

'Exactly. And I'm not making this up. They did a pain study in Canada and found that for most women the pain of childbirth is the equivalent of what people experience when they chop off a finger, or a hand. Wanna know how it was? Have a ten-centimetre red-hot iron slowly inserted into your arse for approximately seven to twenty-four hours, while some imbecile sits next to you and asks you to breathe.'

'That's revolting. Why would anyone do that?'

'For every first child? Ignorance. Oh, and the conspiratorial silence of others. After that? Hormones and insanity. After my first, I swore to the universe that I would never go through that again. But the thing was, I thought Brock's love was part of the equation. Bloody idiotic me. I did it again. Which is why I'm here broken, body wrecked and betrayed, lying in a cave with a sex god telling him, stupidly, to consider Room One. Ignore me, Mario, and all my advice.'

'What men do to women is terrible.'

'I'm with you on that,' Lara said. 'But you guys can do something about it. I mean for one, roll out the red carpet for all those mothers out there. Help them, appreciate them and tell your friends to do the same. Most importantly, don't hurt them.' Lara paused. She took a deep breath and sighed. 'I'm sorry, Mario. You didn't ask for a sermon, but you got one for free. You hit a nerve.'

For a moment there was only the sound of the sea. 'I

appreciate it,' he said.

'Really?'

'Yep.'

They were both still relaxed. She looked at the roof of the cave and noted how lichen grew in coloured patches on the rock. Deep gashes led far into the earth.

Mario broke the silence. 'Hey, you know, that takes me back to our animal stories,' he said. 'I have one you'll like.'

'Sure.'

'It's about the emu. She just lays the eggs, and that's it. Then she's out of there. The male does the rest of the work. He sits on the eggs, keeps them warm and does all the child rearing. He's a one hundred per cent stay-at-home dad and she can do whatever the hell she likes. He's always there for her, forever.'

'I do like that. I should've been an emu. Or an African wild dog.'

'Yeah?'

'My favourite. They live in packs made up of a bunch of males and only one or two females. The top dogs, a male and female, mate for life. They're the only ones in the pack to mate and have offspring, and then the rest of the dogs look after the pups. The best thing about them is they actually take care of their old dogs.'

'Sounds like a good world.'

'It's better than ours,' Lara said. 'Ours is the dog-eat-dog version. The actual dog world is a class act.'

'It's true. Lots of animal models out there are superior to ours.'

'Most of them, actually, because none of those critters are into lying and cheating. They do their thing — just do it. If others come along to threaten a union, they bite them, or rip out their throats.'

'You need some serious self-love,' he said.

'Easy for you to say, Mario. If I were you, I would adore myself, really, I would. You're delicious, and you know it. But if you were a fifty-plus woman with chin hair that had to be plucked once a week, skin like leather and a body like a bus, you'd have a heck of a time loving yourself.'

'Hey, that's why I do what I do.' He rolled onto his elbow. 'But that image isn't you. She's your fear.'

'Maybe not for now. But she could be me in a few years' time. And she's real. She lives and breathes in many women.'

'Why don't you focus on living your own sexy life with all your heart?'

'I'm trying,' she said.'And you have given me the chance to have a go at that Cartesian trick men are so good at.'

'Oh yeah?'

'I'll never master it, but I think I've achieved it this afternoon. I managed to separate mind from body, head from heart, sex from love.'

'Aha! Congratulations. And was it fun?'

She laughed. 'Mind-fucking-blowing.'

They lay there a while longer. The tide reversed and the water drained away from the cave. Mario had packed sandwiches, drinks, and fruit. For an hour or so they sat in the cave. Lara imagined they were like the first humans at the beginning of the human world. They laughed and told jokes and dusted sand off each other's bums.

★ ★ ★

Late afternoon. Lara and Mario walked naked into the sea. She ducked under wild waves and body surfed to the shore. She let the foam dissolve any vestiges of her old self and felt it disperse in the blue of the Pacific.

In the sea, she found her essence.

Lara lost track of time. When Mario came up behind her and caught her on a big swell of blue-green water, she learned that the sea offered unique opportunities for lovemaking.

The late afternoon sun shone down on them as they climbed back up the cliff. Lara held onto the rocks and felt the earth as if for the first time and understood that she was one of its creatures. Ahead, Mario moved with primal strength up the cliff. She followed close behind, tapping into her own animal self, enjoying being scratched by bushes or bumped by rocks. She welcomed her new level of fitness.

She'd done it and she felt elated. She'd wiped out a chunk of her old narrative, deleted the version of her life in which she played the jilted, saggy, unlovable wife sitting on her own, trying to piece what was left of her life, together. In this new story, Lara played a single forty-four-year-old who'd just had mad sex at and in the sea with a genuine superbly endowed sex god. Yeah.

10.50 pm.

Lara: Dear Joanne,

Sorry for my long silence. Re: Mr Erotica – I did actually feel the earth move. On the sand and in the sea. May be seeing him again. How are you?

10.53 pm.

Joanne: L!!! What the, L?!! So happy for you. Where were you? Is that possible? A beach on this planet in a country full of people where you can get up to that stuff?

What's his name?

10.54 pm. Lara: Mario.

10.55 pm.

Joanne: Mario. Gorgeous name. I thought I would let you know – I saw Brock in Sainsbury's (on his own). He asked if I'd heard from you. I said you were having an incredible time, and that by the sounds of things, you'd met someone. I know that was naughty, but you should have seen his face. It slid all the way down and hit the floor.

10.59 pm.

Lara: Ugh, the thought of him ruins my day.

11.00 pm.

Joanne: Sorry. Just thought it might help. Forget him. Tell me about Mr E.

11.01 pm.

Lara: Young. 30s or so. Appendage size: XXXL!! Whooo hoo! Whoever said size didn't matter never did an internal comparative analysis! Plus, best tongue for rent or free on the planet. Not a permanent state of affairs, but tons more enjoyable and cheaper than psychotherapy.

11.05 pm. Joanne: Oh, I'm coming … there! Give me his number! 😆

11.06 pm.

Lara: No! 😆

13

The next morning when Ruby came around at ten for a cup of tea, Lara couldn't contain her exultant mood.

'You look like the cat that got the cream,' Ruby said. 'What happened?'

Lara gave her a few juicy details. She held back on some things, feeling ever so slightly possessive. Nonetheless Ruby devoured each word, one by one. Her cheeks flushed the colour of her flaming hair when Lara volunteered Mario was proportioned spectacularly.

'You know,' Ruby said breathlessly, 'you're lucky he didn't pass out. All that blood in his dick, there'd be none left in his head.'

'Rubes! Really! Anyway, wonder of wonders, he was both conscious, and erect.'

'Ha ha! Darl, he sounds like the pick-o'-the bunch.'

Ruby helped Lara make the tea. 'Let's go somewhere today,' she said. 'I'm agitated. I feel the need for some sensual sights. You wanna come to a nude beach?'

Once, as a teenager on a Majorca holiday with her family, Lara had wandered by accident fully clothed through a nude cove. She'd been too prudish and shocked to look at anything, and had jogged away. Until Ruby's offer, that was the total of her nude-beaching experience.

Ruby and Lara climbed, stumbled, laughed and fell through thick undergrowth and tangled jungle vines on a narrow pathway to get to a spot that Ruby called Freedom Bay.

'Naked beaches are effing hard to get to,' she said. 'Can't make it too easy for the masses. Also, from the shade over there you can look up at the path and see who's coming down.'

The bay lay surrounded by thickly forested cliffs on either side. Thunderous surf crashed into the rocks to the left and right out to sea. Between the cliffs lay a secluded bay. Gentle waves lapped at a golden shoreline.

'Where is everyone? Are there sharks or something?'

'No.' Ruby laughed. 'The nudies are all under the trees there. See those pinkish blobs? Sun's too hot for their tender parts.'

At one end of the beach, trees cast black shadows on the sand, and under those trees, pink shapes moved about.

Lara thought of her own tender parts and how confronting it would be to take off her clothes right there and dive naked into the sea, watched by a contingent of shade-dappled people-blobs. But, what the hell, she thought.

'What are you doing?' Ruby asked.

Lara dropped her bikini bottoms in the sand, took off her top, and bounded headlong into the water. A wave caught her and knocked her over, and she fell in, swallowed by froth and salty surf.

'Wait for me,' Ruby yelled. When Lara looked back over her shoulder, Ruby's enormous pale breasts were swinging wildly as she rushed into the waves.

'Isn't this gorgeous? The water's like heaven,' Ruby squealed. 'Oh my, you're gutsy darl.' A wave dunked Ruby. She went under and came up spluttering.

They stood, backs to their audience, staring at the oncoming breakers.

'Ruby, if I had not come to Australia, I'd be certifiably crazy by now. I'd probably be stalking the streets of London with a kitchen knife, tailing the lesbian lover of my once husband. Now, I'm just me.' Lara flung her no-longer-young arms into the air. A thousand droplets sprayed out around her, catching the sun in starbursts of light.

They emerged, dripping, smiling, middle-aged mermaids remembering who they were. 'I know that every moment under this gorgeous sun is potentially carcinogenic, but since my boobs have never actually seen the sun with their own eyes until this moment … a few minutes won't hurt us, will it?' Lara said.

'Nope,' Ruby said. 'Here's your towel.'

Lara felt the seeping warmth of the sun on her entire body as she stood there, drying herself. They walked a little way down the beach where a flat, black rock jutted out into the waves. They climbed onto it, set out their towels, and lay down to soak up the sun. Lara did not honestly give a shit about wrinkles, when the whole sea and sky were around her naked self, embracing her for who she was. She didn't need Brock. She didn't need Mario, or any man.

Lara lost track of time. She lay on her back, her hand across her face, marveling at the dappled light playing a kaleidoscope of images across her eyelids. At a certain point, a shadow darkened the picture. She moved her arm, looked up and then sat up and pulled her knees in against her chest. A man stood right over her. A naked man. Ruby sat up too. The guy was tall. He had skinny legs and a balding head with a few strands of scraggly shoulder-length hair,

106

which hung down over his shoulders in ringlets. Lara concentrated on looking at his face. Then she glanced over at Ruby who had focused her sharp eyes on the man's crotch and gave him a slow, cool, once-over. It was possibly approving, but Lara found it hard to tell.

'I beg your pardon,' he said politely. 'But me and my mates saw you ladies having a good time and wanted to, um, invite you to join our little party.'

'How kind,' Ruby said, a satisfied smile on her face. 'Politically, though, I just don't think it would work.'

'Why's that?' he said. 'What's your affiliation?'

'It goes like this,' Ruby said. 'If you guys are left-wing, then consider us right. If you're right, we're left. If you're gay, we're straight. If you're straight, we're gay. How's that?'

'Sounds like us,' he said. 'A perfect fit.'

Lara had trouble not looking at what dangled pinkly, disconcertingly close to her face, and which sported a shiny ring near its end, as casually as other folks might sport wedding rings.

'Maybe not,' Ruby said.

'Well, I like to think of us as all-embracing,' he said. 'Politically speaking, that is,' he added. 'Girls, didn't mean to disturb. Anyway, you have a nice day anyway.'

When Lara looked again she noted the sunburnt bald patch on the back of his head and his slightly saggy buttocks sliding up and down as he walked away, each cheek dusted lightly with fine, golden sand.

'That was a bit funny,' Ruby said.

'What was that all about?' Lara asked. Ruby began to laugh. Her whole body shook.

'Was that a come-on?' Lara asked.

'Who knows,' Ruby said, laughing more, wiping her eyes.

107

'What's so bloody funny?'

'Did you see his schlong?'

'No ...'

'Honey, it was right in your face.'

'I was trying *very* hard not to look at it ...'

'Ha ha ha,' Ruby laughed. 'That's what's so funny. You must have puritan blood in you. That was the guy from the bar the day we had too much beer.'

'You recognised him without his clothes on?'

'Course I did. I mean, his schlong, it wasn't exactly eye candy in porno terms. More like a piece of work from the comedy store. But hon, it looked to be in good, working order, and I can only imagine what it could do when it gets happy. Anyway, it's good to get a look, isn't it? That's what we came here for, didn't we?'

'Did we?'

'Well, didn't we?'

'You mean *we're* the perverts?'

'Oh, don't be so crude,' Ruby chortled. 'I wouldn't put it that way!'

'You are a pervert, Ruby.' Lara was laughing too.

'Alright, alright. I am too,' Ruby said, turning her ample body over to get her dimpled bum into the sun. 'This is what I wanted. I came here to get an eyeful. Preferably a face full.'

'You got that all right.'

'I'd say you got the face full.'

They lay there. Lara felt torpid with heat and laughter. The sun kissed all their white bits through the ever-decreasing ozone layer. In her imagination Lara would forever see the face of Mr Long-Schlong. She knew that if she did run into him on the street fully clothed, she would, unfortunately, recognise him.

Five hours later, no amount of aloe vera gel could assuage the stinging. Lara tried to lie carefully between her lavender sheets, but the fiery touch of an almost equatorial sun had found her, and she had underestimated its power.

★ ★ ★

So much for her all-over tan. After two days, the burn began to peel.

Mario called and left a message. She decided to wait before returning his call. She hoped that the burnt skin would peel off and reveal a gorgeous, smooth flat tan beneath in due course. She also wanted to have some time to gather her new self together, without running straight back into those sensual arms, or setting up a weekly direct debit into his bank account.

★ ★ ★

Lara had not checked emails for some days, and when she did, she found no less than nine messages from Brock. She deleted them all and blocked the sender.

She spent the next few days on her own, out of touch, hardly at home. She ran, walked, climbed and ate ice-cream all around the Byron Shire. She found a Five Rhythms dance event one evening and went there, to gyrate and pound and wiggle with a hundred and fifty other sweaty bodies. They moved through five different rhythms, from slow and sensual to hip-thrusting, pounding, let-your-inhibitions-fly-free energy all the way back down to loving the earth. A man in a skin-tight silver bodysuit with a sizable crotch bulge shadowed her across the room, gyrat-

109

ing behind her, then in front of her, trying to catch her eye, despite her blatant non-verbal message of *dancing alone tonight*. She lost him to a youngster with dreadlocks she could smell across the room and who looked like she matched him beat for beat.

If she'd wanted to make out with a stranger, this was the place. If she wanted to dance her head off, ditto, and she did. If she wanted to stay in her own bubble of self-discovery, she figured it was imperative to stay away from the dude in the moon suit.

The next day, in Byron, she checked the community notice boards. Her rental car, was getting to be expensive. She found an old Toyota Yaris for sale for a bargain price and within six hours had returned her old faithful to the local Thrifty Car Rental agency, and was the proud owner of a shiny, red Yaris of her own. She felt like she'd just been born. She had no idea why she should dream of any kind of permanence while on a holiday visa in a foreign country. Nonetheless, she owned something here now.

Delirious with new-car ownership, she went into town for an LSD. She was sitting sipping her drink, crowd-watching, when two tall delectable men walked by. And one of them was Mario.

'Well, hi,' he said. 'You've been hiding.'

'Hi guys. Have a seat.'

'Okay, sure, for a minute. Hey, so this is Jean-Luc, by the way. Jean-Luc, this is Lara, a good friend.'

Not a customer? The blonde man stretched out his hand. 'Lara,' he said, sounding French. 'Pleased to meet you.'

Jean-Luc, tanned and chic and a little older than Mario, told Lara he was doing a photo shoot for a French magazine he worked for. Mario was his model for the day. As he spoke, she noticed how Jean-Luc looked at Mario, as though besotted, visually devouring him second by second.

They sat down on either side of her and ordered coffees and raspberry chocolate cakes to share.

'Hey, Lara,' Mario said, mouth full. 'I have an idea, but only if you like it. Come with us. What do you think about some impromptu modelling? Jean-Luc is exceptional and you'll be great. Don't you think, Jean-Luc?'

The Frenchman blushed under his tan. 'Of course,' he said. 'It would … how you say, add a little spice.'

I'm too old, Lara's old self screamed. *And ugly. I'm not a model. I sag. I have wrinkles and acne and cellulite.*

'It sounds like fun,' she said. 'Why not?'

* * *

Lara might have guessed that she'd be posing half-naked with a mostly-naked Mario for the best part of two hours. She lay with Mario on a rocky outcrop at a deserted point of the beach wearing only her bikini bottoms. Then she lay by herself under an overhang with her arms only barely covering her breasts. Later she stood with Jean-Luc admiring Mario's physique as he posed Adonis-like in the afternoon light.

'He is so beautiful,' Jean-Luc whispered to her as he clicked away.

'He is,' Lara agreed. 'Don't fall in love with him.'

'Too late,' Jean-Luc said.

'How long have you two known each other?'

'Since teens. In Italy. I came here to be with him, to heal. My heart has been broken over there after three years of relationship. Even when you don't love

111

someone with your whole heart, to be rejected is terrible. Lara, I tell you something. I have been depressed since I was four years old.'

'That sounds awful Jean-Luc.'

'Yes. It gets so bad sometimes. This time, I was going to kill myself. I called Mario to say goodbye. Mario say, come here, do your work from here, stay with me for a while. He is so kind. I think I have loved him since a long time. When I was eighteen, and he was only fifteen years old.'

'That sucks,' she said. 'Does he know? How you feel, I mean?'

'Yes. We are close. But he can't love me back the same, for many reasons.'

'I guess I know some of those.'

'And, he loves *les femmes* too much. Hey, Mario, lover boy, what about some shots *sans* everything, hey? Just for me?'

'I'll drop my pants for you, Jean-Luc, but you're the only guy in the world I'd do that for.'

Jean-Luc hid behind his camera. Lara took in the view, appreciating the art, the awkwardness and the natural sexuality of the moment.

Then Jean-Luc turned to her and said, 'I want that you two form a sculpture. Rodin's Kiss. I'll do it black and white. We can do that?'

Jean-Luc coached his subjects into nudity and into position. Onlookers were at a distance but the models weren't completely alone. Lara and Mario sat on a rock, Lara's arm around Mario's neck and his hand on her hip. Her naked breasts were fully exposed. When in her life would she have ever have imagined doing this?

'The story,' said Jean-Luc, 'is from the thirteenth

112

century. Francesca da Rimini is the woman. That's you, Lara. You have fallen in love with the younger brother of your husband. His name is Paolo. When the husband finds you, he will kill you. So Mario, your lips and her lips don't quite meet. Your love is doomed. Beautiful. Now Mario. Pull her towards you. Lara, hold him close.' Mario's lips hovered so near Lara's, she could feel his breath. She enjoyed being compelled to embody the beauty of forbidden love in the shadow of grief.

Later, when they went out to eat together, Jean-Luc showed her the day's photos.

She saw shadows and light and shapes of bodies, and an erotic conversation captured forever in black and white.

'I'm very happy with these pictures,' Jean-Luc said. 'Something magic happened here.'

'It helps that you have beautiful models,' Mario said laughing.

'Jean-Luc, I think you have real talent,' Lara said. 'What you've captured isn't even in the bodies, or the poses. It's outside of us. It's really something.'

'If I want to use these, may I get you to sign a permission form? I will pay you if I get paid.'

'You can just use them if you like,' she said. 'I don't want any money, honestly. Email me some copies and send me prints if and when you have them. Anyway, no one will ever believe that's me.'

'Of course,' Jean-Luc said. 'And do you also want some naked Mario shots?' He laughed.

'Oh yes. Absolutely,' she said. 'For my pin-up collection.'

Mario leaned over and kissed her ear. 'You haven't returned my call yet,' he whispered. 'I might show up at your door, if you don't.'

When Lara left, Jean-Luc kissed her on both cheeks. 'Look after yourself,' she said.

'You too,' he said.

'Thanks, Jean-Luc, for an amazing day. You don't know what you've given me.'

They hugged in resonant empathy.

She walked back to her car on air.

14

Ruby came to the door at nine and knocked. Lara invited her in for breakfast. She was making scrambled eggs and toast.

'Nah, but thanks, Darl. Gonna try and lose some weight. I'm sick of looking like a fridge with a head.'

'Oh come on, Ruby. You do not look like that at all.'

'No, really. You don't have to be kind. I told myself, you know, that my body knows what it's like to be thin and why the fuck should I walk around looking like this, right?'

'Well ...'

'I want some of what you've been getting.'

'Egg?'

'No. Young, hard cock.'

Lara almost choked on her piece of toast. She swallowed half her tongue and her laugh. 'Check out the ads in the paper,' she said, echoing Ruby's earlier advice.

'You're on,' she said. 'Where you been?'

'Running, walking, modelling for a gay French photographer. And I bought a car.'

'Fuck me! That's your car? You own it?'

'All mine. Gave back the rental. I now have something, one thing of my own, you could say.'

'Oh darl, that's wonderful. And how's the glorious Mario?'

Lara loved Ruby. Her landlady felt like an old friend. But every time she talked about Mario now, Lara wished she'd shut up.

'He's fine,' she said. And then her phone rang and she saw it was Joanne. Thank God. 'Gotta take this, Rubes. It's my good friend from the UK.'

Ruby mumbled that was fine and disappeared out of the door and down the stairs.

'Lara?'

'Joanne?'

'Oh my God, I can't believe it. I actually got you. I was beginning to think you'd given me the wrong number.'

'It's so good to hear you. Is everything okay?'

'Oh, just perfect,' she said. 'Except for missing you. Are you avoiding calls or something?'

'No, not really. The reception's really bad here. And completely random. Sometimes calls come through, other times not. They say it's an Australian thing. What's up?'

'How is it? Gosh, I want to know everything about Mr Erotica and how that's going!'

Lara revealed her secrets and told Joanne about her hilarious new, though brief modelling career.

And then Joanne said she had to ask Lara's permission about something.

'Go ahead.'

'I'm going to the opening of a friend's art show at a gallery tonight. I know Brock will be there because he knows Greg, the artist. If Brock asks me about you, can I tell him?'

'Tell him what?'

'That you're having a fantastic time, that you're in a relationship and your life is glorious right now?'

Perhaps Lara went quiet for too long.

'You there, Lar? If that's too trite and uncomfortable, I won't say a thing. I just feel like I want to be

116

your emissary. I will say anything, or nothing to him, on your behalf.'

'I was thinking …'

'What?'

'I suppose, I don't give a shit, Jo. You do whatever.'

'Okay.'

'Anyway, I had a brilliant day today being a betraying thirteenth century beauty, Francesca, featured in Dante's Inferno and the inspiration for Rodin's Kiss. I'm living my own life and I don't give, as they say here, a flying fuck about Brock right now.'

Joanne said, 'that, Lar, sounds a-mazing. I couldn't be happier to hear it. I miss you but honestly that's not reason enough to return to our miserable, grey UK. How are your kids?'

'They're great. Rose is enjoying her work at the gallery and Simon's band is making a new album. I think they're both relieved I'm not going mouldy in some damp bedsit in Wimbledon.'

'I'll be in touch with them soon,' Joanne said. 'I promise.'

* * *

Everyone in the world should have a Joanne, Lara thought, as she lay staring up at the dark ceiling and listening to crickets. They'd been friends since they were thirteen. Joanne had always been top of the class. Now she made an excellent living as an actuary. While the teenage Lara read romances, Joanne read detective novels. Later, when Lara went to clubs and stayed out till the small hours, Joanne stayed home and did advanced mathematics or swam miles in the indoor public pool. They had nothing in common, except familiarity. A friendship beyond time. Joanne had no desire to marry or have children. When Lara met Brock, married him, had children and lost all her single friends, Joanne stayed on as the only individual who not only still came around for dinner, but actually *brought* the dinner, and threw her buddy a lifeline of adult conversation regardless of the two toddlers and their tantrums. Joanne reminded her that it wasn't the onset of the apocalypse when Rose hit puberty and decided to pierce her left nostril and her belly button, and have a tattoo on her right buttock that said kiss my ass. She mentioned that when Lara'd had four holes pierced in one ear, her parents had also seen the end of the world coming. And now, regardless of distance, Joanne remained a dependable fixture in Lara's life. So if Joanne wanted to tell Brock to go and eat his toweringly phallic office block, or anything else, on her behalf, she could go right ahead.

Marriage, Lara decided with more clarity, was a black hole. Decade after decade women risked vanishing into it. Motherhood was even more dangerous. She thought of her body. After her marriage, it became nothing more than a vehicle with a utilitarian function. Sexual organs were (badly designed) entrances and exits for off-spring. Breasts were fast-food for same aforementioned offspring. Women's bodies risked being nothing more than a shared residence. From the role of wife, to mother, to Brock's affair, Lara thought of her married life as an utter cliché. She wished she could warn every new bride with starry eyes that she was about to encounter an event horizon and perhaps be sucked into a dance all the way to oblivion. She didn't think she was jaded and sour; she thought she'd seen the light.

On waking, late the next morning, Lara's head hurt and her forehead burned. Rain poured from a solid indigo sky and a fire raged in her throat.

The grey universe and fever signaled that her fantasy of nude beach combing was going to have to take a back seat. She groaned and pulled the covers over her head.

She felt too weak to even get up and get a glass of water. She imagined she might just lie there and dehydrate and eventually die and no one would find her until she'd begun to decompose. In the humidity this would be rapid. She hoped Ruby wouldn't stay away too long. As she felt herself descending into self-pity, there was a knock on her door.

'Come in,' Lara croaked.

The door opened and Mario stood there, all six-foot-something of him. 'You okay?' he said. He strolled across the room and sat down on the bed. Lara turned her head away. 'You don't look too good,' he said.

His hand felt icy on her forehead. 'Too cold,' she said hoarsely. 'Don't come near or you'll get sick.'

'Have you had anything to drink? Your lips are parched.' He filled a glass of water, brought it over, sat on the edge of the bed again, lifted Lara's head and held the water to her lips.

'Thank you.'

'I came because you didn't call me back.'

'Sorry.'

'I was worried about you.'

'Why?' she coughed. 'Don't you have, uh, paying clients and girlfriends to take care of?' she asked, taking another sip of water.

'I wanted to know how you were,' he said. He put his hand on her cheek. 'That's furnace temperature.'

119

'Don't say scary things to me. I'll be okay soon. How's Jean-Luc?'

'He's doing okay. A bit all over the place.'

'I feel his pain,' she said.

'Yeah, I guess you two have some parallel themes going on.'

'What's he going to do with his broken heart?'

'Not sure.' Mario shrugged. 'Maybe I can help him ... '

She grabbed his wrist. 'No bloody way,' she croaked, with more force than she knew she had. 'If you're considering sleeping with him, don't, Mario!'

'Why not?'

She let go of his wrist and fell back. 'It's not the answer to every heartache.'

'What do you mean?'

'Your penis, Mario, though stunning, is not everyone's salvation, okay?'

'But I could heal him.'

'Oh my God, Mario, listen a minute. Don't be a jerk, okay? I might be sick as a bloody dog and out of my head, but that poor man is already in love with you. If you seduce him, he's going to lose his mind. Then you'll move on, or possibly just go to work. You'll mangle his already broken heart. Seriously. Just be a good friend.'

'How do you know all that? He doesn't love me. He lusts. Some other dude did the heartbreaking.'

'You're wrong. We talked. He's loved you since he first knew you when you were teens. If you go all tantric on him or mess around with him, you'll destroy him. He's even less Room Two material than I am. You have to trust me on this one. Stay away from him. In that way.'

Through her delirium, Lara thought Mario might be considering her words. 'I see,' he said.

Footsteps clunked up the stairs.

'Darl? Lara? You okay?'

Seconds later, Ruby entered the room.

'My, my, hello there,' she said.

Lara, though feverish, caught the seduction in Ruby's voice and her on-heat vibes ricocheted through the room. 'I'm Ruby.'

'Mario,' he said, introducing himself and holding out a hand. 'You're the landlady?'

'I am indeed. Oh, darl,' Ruby said, grabbing Lara's aching feet under the sheet. 'Honey, I know exactly what to get for you. It's an old wives' remedy and it works every time. Vinegar socks. They'll bring your fever right down. I'm so glad I came up here. I hadn't seen any movement from the cottage and I got worried.' She stood at Lara's feet, a silhouette of voluptuousness dressed in a green kaftan with peacock feather designs all over it, see-through against the back light, radiating sensuality.

'Honestly, I'm not dying. You guys can, you know, get on with your lives. I'll be okay.'

'Good to hear,' said Mario. 'But, hey Ruby, those vinegar socks sound like a great idea. This is a pretty high fever. I'll stay here until you get back.'

Ruby hurried out and down the steps. Mario stayed by Lara's bedside. 'I came over here thinking I'd find you hot – but not this hot,' he said.

'Sorry to disappoint. Anyway, I don't want to get addicted.'

'To what?'

'To you. It would be easy. I'm practising restraint.'

'Aha, I see. I didn't ever consider such a problem.'

121

'Yeah, well, consider it now.' She put her arm over her eyes. Footsteps clunked up the stairs.

'Here's Ruby with hot vinegar socks.' His nose crinkled. 'Now that smells absolutely vile. She's a sweetie, your landlady.'

Indeed, Lara thought. 'You guys can go, now. Thanks for dropping by. I'm glad I don't have to worry about dying of a fever by myself, and rotting here for days, leaving you with an inconvenient mess to clean up. Thanks Ruby.'

Mario stood up. 'That vinegar smell is unforgettable,' he said to Ruby. 'I'll drop in again soon. If she gets any sicker, get her to the doc, or give me a call.'

'Oh, hon, of course I will.'

They exchanged phone numbers and Mario left. Ruby fussed over Lara, pulling the disgusting socks over her feet and wrapping them tight in a towel. She gave Lara Ibuprofen and promised her a big pot of chicken soup in the late afternoon.

'Text me if you need me, darl,' she said. 'And ooh, that man. I get it, I get it! Yummy yummy.'

After she left, Lara added nausea to her list of complaints. The acrid smell of apple cider vinegar now permeated the cottage. She slept, and when she woke, she cried.

She had no home. No one loved her. The cave and Mario and the photo shoot all seemed like something she'd imagined. They were fake anyway, bits of rainbow against a stormy sky, a brief and chance illumination, nothing long term. She missed being comfortable in her own place with all her own stuff. All of that was gone. Taken. Lost. Sold. She was left with nothing left but a shivering body and a befuddled mind.

15

A week of soup and honey and lemon juice and vinegar socks did not have the desired effect. Ruby had been in and out of Lara's acidic-smelling abode tending to her for days.

'I reckon it's time to see the doctor, darl,' she said, as Lara blew her nose hard into a tissue. 'You look like a drunken bloody sailor and I'm worried about you.'

'Thanks. I don't want to burden you with having to find somewhere to bury my body. So, do you have a doctor to recommend?'

'Not really,' Ruby said. 'I'll bring you a list of docs and you can call around the medical centres and see who's free today.'

Lara estimated Ruby had probably run a total of five full miles on her account during the last week of being a nurse. Lara owed her. Mario had phoned twice and she'd told him optimistically that she was getting better and would be in touch as soon as she made it out of Mucousville.

Ruby returned with the numbers. She seemed in a hurry.

'I'll see you later. I have to make a phone call. I may drop in and see you tonight.'

'No need,' Lara said. 'I'll probably find a doc, get drugs and come straight back into bed.'

'If you need me, don't hesitate, okay darl?'

'Thanks, Ruby. You've been an angel.'

'No dramas. Good luck at the doc.'

Lara called three of the five doctors on the list. One of them, a Dr Andrew Roberts answered the phone himself. He said he could see her immediately. This meant she had to get into her car and drive twenty minutes into the middle of somewhere else. The directions to his office were amusing, and not just because of her fuzzy state of mind. They lead her up a narrow mountain road into the folded green hills. Lara was certain she'd taken a wrong turn, but Dr Roberts had assured her that when she got to the end of the road, the dirt track that lead to the left was the driveway. Her car rattled and bumped over the rough road and came to a stop outside a white-washed high-set home with a single car in the drive and a view over the distant ocean. She switched off the car and slowly got out, looking around. Below, a stream ran through the property, and forest crowded the hills on either side of the stream.

This had to be wrong. No sign of a clinic anywhere.

'Hello.' A figure appeared at a glass door.

Lara climbed out of the car. 'Hi,' she said hoarsely. 'I think I'm lost. I'm looking for Dr Andrew Roberts. D'you by any chance know where I'd find him?'

The woman's slick dark hair was pulled back in a tight bun. 'This is his office,' she said. 'You are here.' She smiled, pointing to a small wooden sign on the door. *Doc Roberts* said the sign. *Family Physician.* 'Come in, come in,' the woman said. 'Is not very easy to find. I'm Valencia, housekeeper.' She held out her hand with a warm smile.

'Nice to meet you, Valencia.'

'You have bad cold,' she said. 'Doc Roberts will be

124

available soon.'

'Thank you.' Lara forced a return smile and was led into a waiting room attached to the large house. Light poured in through a skylight. The room was bright and cheerful, if a little sparse. Pale-blue oil paintings of sea and sand and shells graced the walls, and a wooden counter with a bell stood between Lara and the doctor's room.

'He see you in a minute,' Valencia said, and went to rap on his door. Then she dusted the counter and shuffled papers into a stack. Lara tried to control her hacking cough. She sounded like a dog barking. Looking up she noticed a piece of paper pinned to the reception desk: *part-time office assistant required. 3 mornings per week.*

How did patients ever find this doctor, she wondered? How on earth did he make a living out here?

The door opened. A tall man with grey hair and blue eyes stood in the doorway in khaki trousers and a purple shirt.

'Lara? Please come in.'

'Thanks,' she said and got up. Her head spun and she sat down again.

'Valencia, would you get a glass of orange juice please?'

'Yes, of course.'

'I'm fine,' Lara said, taking the cold glass from Valencia with shaky fingers. 'I mean, thank you.'

'Well, Lara, what can I do for you today?' the doctor asked once she was seated in his room in a comfy red chair. His voice sounded calm and reassuring. Lara wished she could just lie down in his office on the floor and go to sleep.

'My throat's been on fire,' she croaked. 'For about a

125

week. I feel like I've coughed up both lungs and I still have a temperature.'

A smile tugged at the corner of his mouth. 'Poor you,' he said. 'Let's have a look.' He put on glasses and touched her chin with warm hands. Lara stared at his clean-cut jaw, sharp eyes and slightly protruding bottom lip while she gagged on an ice-cream stick he held against her tongue. A shiver ran through her that had nothing to do with her fever. Either this was delirium or Doc Roberts was the most good-looking man she'd ever seen. She wondered whether she might be turning into a predator. She'd never reacted to a man like this before. It had to be the fever.

'You on holiday?' he asked, removing the stick from her throat.

'I'm on an extended trip.'

'I see. From the UK, I presume?'

'London. Yes.'

He listened to her breathing, his hands brushing her feverish skin, while he focused on detecting what was going on far below the surface. She noticed his fingers, and the sinews on his hands.

'Well, Lara, it sounds like bronchitis. If you were at home and able to relax, I'd say go ahead and lie in bed for another week, and nurse yourself until you get better. But since you're on holiday and not in the comfort of your own home, I'll prescribe antibiotics and let's see how you go.'

Handsome. And sensible. Not a drug pusher but giving her drugs nonetheless. 'Thanks,' she said. 'I'll probably take them.'

'Good,' he said. 'Anything else I can help you with?'

Run your hands over my skin again. Do that thing with the stethoscope. Take me?

126

Oh goodness, she thought. Was she becoming a Room Two woman? Had Mario flipped a switch?

'No, that's really all. Thanks very much for everything. I've just had enough of feeling rotten.'

'I hear you,' he said. She watched him writing out the script in an unreadable scrawl. A gold wedding band on his left hand caught the light. Damn it, she thought. Of course.

'Please get in touch with me if you don't see any improvement over the next five days.'

'Thank you,' she said, and stood up. 'I will.'

He opened the door. 'Hope you feel better soon,' he said. 'Goodbye Lara.'

What an attractive man. And much older than thirty.

Valencia was at the door as she left. 'You feeling better now?'

'Thanks, yes. It was the first time I've been out of bed for a while.'

'You eat properly and take proper care,' she said. As she turned to go Valencia called out. 'Miss?'

'Yes?' Lara thought maybe she'd left something behind.

'I'm housekeeper here. But I thought I ask if you know of someone who is a secretary? Dr Andrew, he going away for one month. He leave big mess of papers. I not able to do this job. Spanish is my language and my English is not so good. So I am asking if you maybe know someone?'

'I'm so sorry, Valencia. I'm new here. I don't know very many people.'

'S'all right,' she said.

'I'll keep my ears open, though,' she said, climbing into her car.

Lara drove straight to the pharmacy, got the antibiotics and bought a large bunch of flowers and a box of handmade Belgian chocolates for Ruby, in loving thanks for her devotion over the past week. Then she drove home, feeling light-headed.

Lara parked. There under the trees, she spied Mario's Saab.

Mario and Ruby; these people had been so good to her she could hardly believe it. She thought she might have bought flowers for Mario too, but, that could have looked odd.

Lara trudged upstairs and found her place empty. She presumed he'd come to see her, and finding her not at home, had gone over to Ruby's. They were, she thought, probably having tea together, eating muffins. She made some honey and lemon juice and took her first dose of pills. Then she stood at the large window overlooking the garden and peered down at Ruby's house. She contemplated rushing right over there with the flowers and chocolates, but tiredness overcame her. Instead she lay down on her bed and soon fell asleep.

When she woke the sun was low in the sky. Afternoon heat pulsed through the cottage. Sweat ran rivers down her temples, but already she could feel the fire in her throat had been dampened by Doc Roberts' victorious antibacterial prescription. What a hero, she thought, and got up. She made herself another cup of lemon and honey, drank it slowly, and then washed her face, picked up the flowers and chocolates and trudged over to the main house.

Walking across the lawn, Lara felt a sense of disquiet, but dismissed it. As if she shouldn't be walking here, now. No sound emerged from the house. The

128

back door stood open, so she tiptoed inside. No Ruby, no Mario. She looked around the kitchen, located a vase and filled it with water, arranging the flowers and placing them on the coffee table. Maybe they'd gone for a walk, she thought. She heard the floor creak upstairs. Low tones emanated from Ruby's bedroom.

Lara suddenly felt like an intruder. Her heart rate accelerated. For reasons unfathomable, she tiptoed across the room to the stairs, which she took two at a time, stealthy as a rat at midnight. The faint sound of Spanish guitar music floated down from the bedroom. On the stairwell, she stopped.

'Look hon, I know I'm probably the oldest and least attractive of all your clients,' Ruby was saying. 'But, FYI, I was a hot little number until my twenties.'

Mario's low intimate tones followed. 'Ruby, you should love yourself. Every inch of yourself.'

'Big boy, holy fucking moly, all I want is every inch of YOU!'

'Fuck,' Lara muttered and smothered her mouth with her hand.

'You bet,' Mario said. His laugh rumbled out under the door.

Shit, shit, shit, she thought, her heart exploding from her chest. She tiptoed back down the stairs, without breathing. Speeding up, she bounded like a kangaroo across the lawn back to her cottage, her heart trying to pound its way right out of her chest. The room swam. The world swirled in shards around her ears. It had to be the infection making her dizzy and delusional. She was monstrously green with jealousy. She knew it was misplaced; Mario, the tantric sex worker, was at work, wasn't he? And Ruby was the one who'd suggested the bloody classifieds in the first place. She had the right to call his number too.

Lara suddenly detested her beloved landlady who had showered her with kindness and concern. Whether Ruby deserved a good time with a tantric sex worker or not did not register in Lara's logic. She began to pack. Lara balled her clothes into her suitcase, tipped her toiletries into a plastic bag and dumped everything from the fridge into a cardboard box. She left Ruby the week's rent in cash. As the sun turned the sky to evening magenta, Lara hauled her suitcase down the stairs and dragged it over to her car. Two trips back to the cottage and her entire life lay in her Yaris. She drove away from the cottage without looking back and without a clue as to where she would spend the night.

16

Lara had no idea which direction to take as she drove down Main Street, but she knew she had to put some physical distance between herself and the place where things had happened. Twilight wrapped blue arms around the hills. Lara knew her actions did not meet the requirements of intelligent planning, running away like this, but she could not see an alternative. She wanted to get away, and fast. Further south, lay the beach town of Lennox Heads. It took twenty minutes to get there and as the sky grew dark she saw a sign pointing to a caravan park. She turned in.

The glass door to the reception area was already shut, but a woman inside who was busy counting out her day's takings, saw Lara's gesturings outside, and came to open up again.

'I'm sorry,' Lara said pathetically. 'Do you have any cabins available for tonight?'

'We're closed,' she said.

Lara must have looked desperate, she thought, because the woman sighed.

'Twenty-three-A is available. I can check you in before I go.'

'Thank you so much. Twenty-three-A sounds perfect,' Lara said. She succumbed to a coughing fit.

'You okay?'

'I'm fine. Not infectious.' She hoped.

The woman wasn't going to take any chances. She took Lara's credit card with a thumb and forefinger, and after swiping it, lathered her hands in antibacte-

131

rial foam from a bottle on her desk.

She gave Lara a set of keys, a map and some sheets and blankets sealed in plastic.

'You're on the end, closest to the sea,' she said. 'Enjoy.'

As Lara left the office, the woman sprayed the air with disinfectant.

Lara could hear the crashing sea as she parked her car under the shelter next to the cabin.

Ruby and Mario; no doubt, he was giving her the time of her life while Lara pushed her face into her pillow and half-suffocated in tearful misery. Every time she turned over in bed, the cabin rocked. The roar of the sea played through her dreams, a reminder of Mr Erotica and the cave at the end of the world. She dreamt that all her teeth fell out, and she scrambled across the floor trying to find them. When she did, she tried to put them back into her mouth.

Her own snores woke her. Lara, unsettled and ill, spent the remainder of the night not knowing which end to put over the toilet bowl. Maybe, she thought, she had finally arrived at the point of breakdown she'd been fearing. She'd likely been under the equivalent of a general emotional anaesthetic these last few weeks and Mario had been the drug. What stupidity, she thought. What the hell had she been doing? She'd thought the kind and sexy things Mario had said to her were uniquely aimed at her, but of course, it was his job to make women feel special. She hadn't learnt to distinguish reality from fairy stories yet. Every seductive phrase of Mario's was part of his business, used a thousand times over. She'd done it again – had become another cliché, the one where you fall for the sex-worker and think that somewhere in all that is an actual meaningful relationship. Oh God, she had been a sucker. And Ruby? Lara felt terrible. She would have given the poor woman lifelong sex with some young sea god as a present if it had been in her power – until the moment she'd heard her in bed with Mario. Now, instead she wanted to punch her.

Screeching black cockatoos flying overhead announced the morning. Nothing awaited Lara. No plans, no people, no work. No one needed her, or wanted her. After lying on her bunk all morning, she realised that every decision she'd made since meeting Brock at twenty-two, and before coming to Australia, had depended on other people, on him, the kids, a long line of obligations and other people's wishes and needs. She'd never woken up and thought, 'today is my day, this is my life, what should I do?' She'd never lived as an adult, in the world, on her own, and that, she thought, was tragic.

Which was why it had been so easy for her to come to Australia. She had so little to tie her to her own life, she had dropped out of it leaving barely a ripple behind. So this was her landing point. This was the real Lara. Sick and alone in a metal cabin on a New South Wales beach.

The small cafe at the caravan park provided Lara with a late breakfast in the form of orange juice and a microwaved croissant. She took the next dose of pills. Already she could feel her battle being fought for her. God bless antibiotics, she thought. Her throat no longer hurt. She felt weak, but after breakfast, she strolled out onto the beach. The sun came out. She walked along the shoreline for hours, noticing the light, and the way each wave broke, different every single time. In the distance, on the horizon, a morning thunderstorm brewed. Behind her, grassy dunes caught the breeze.

Lara's fever had gone, and the internal inferno with it. If she couldn't trust other people, she could, she realised, at least trust herself to preserve herself. She'd had the guts and gumption to walk away from Brock and her old life in London. And she'd stopped eavesdropping on Mario and Ruby before hearing any more and had raced away. She did, after all, have a survival instinct. At this point in time, that was nice to know. As she walked along the beach, she noticed how her shorts hung on her. She looked down at her legs. The last time they'd been this slim she had been fifteen. Running and walking, sex, tears and fevers had moulded her into a new shape. Her hair had grown longer and she'd stopped trying to tame it. Her face felt like it had had too much sun and her nose was raw with blowing it but she didn't care. Looking down, she was thankful for this body. It was, with a little help, managing to get better. All that wasted energy and regret, she thought. How about something new? She imagined looking back on her forty-four-year-old self when she was twice this age. There would be so much to appreciate about being here at this age at this place and time. So, she asked herself, why not do it now?

'Fine,' she said to the wind. 'I'm starting now, okay? I like myself. Like my hairy legs that can walk and run. I like this body that's returning to health. Yes, even these arms, they're alright. My legs are pretty strong and good for climbing up rocks and cliff faces, oh, and while I'm at it, I like my wobbly bits too, do you hear me, world? This body has survived the ripping and third-degree tears of childbirth, twice, and has recovered to be able to function pretty well. If I ever get the chance I'm going to roll out the red carpet to middle-aged, betrayed women everywhere. I'm okay, you hear world?'

Lara had found, on the lonely beach, a new kind of love and appreciation. She'd once read a book called *A Beginner's Guide to Constructing the Universe*. The book showed how maths and geometry were both at the root of everything beautiful and profound on earth and in outer space.

She wanted to find the sequel, something like *A Beginners Guide to Constructing a New Life*. She reckoned that it would be full of emotional and practical geometry, some defining lines and structures she could use to plan her next steps. She needed a context. And maybe she just needed to get a bloody job.

As she stood on the beach, the nothingness that stretched out in front of her was a perfect beginning.

17

For two more days Lara walked her foamy beach, and spent hours of solitude in her cabin. She subsisted on orange juice and croissants. There was no mobile phone reception, so no one could reach her. On the third day she decided to go into Lennox Heads to buy some fresh food and make a call.

When her phone found itself within reach of a tower, it buzzed. Sweat poured down her back. She pulled into a car park and wrestled the phone from her pocket. Nine new messages.

Message one: *Hi Lara, this is Mario. Just checking in to see how you are. Talk to you later.*

Message two: *Hi again. It's Mario. Came round to see you and found you'd moved out. Let me know where you are.*

Message three. *Hi Lara, it's Mario again. Calling on Ruby's behalf. She's um, pretty cut up about you moving out. Could you give her a call when you have the chance? 62039901.*

Message four: (static) *Hi. This is Ruby. Did I do something to upset you? Call me.*

Message five: *Hi Lara, it's Brock ...*
DELETE

Message six: (sing-song voice) *He-ey, this is Mario again. I'm not stalking you. Just want to know if you're okay. Don't be a stranger. Bye.*

Message seven: *(static, engaged tone).*

Message eight: *(static, engaged tone).*

Message nine: *Hey Lara, I need to speak to you. It's*

Mario. Call me when you get this.

Okay, she said to the universe. It would be infantile to ignore some of this. She could respond with a single text message. It would be better to do it before she thought too long about it.

Hi Mario, got all your messages, thanks. I'm fine. I'm enjoying some space for a while. Tell Ruby the same. Best, L.

Next she called the office of Dr Andrew Roberts. Valencia answered the phone.

'Hello, this is Valencia.'

'Hi, This is Lara. Remember I came there the other day and you so kindly gave me orange juice?'

'Yes, I remember. You still sick?'

'No, I'm much better thanks. I'm actually calling about the job. You know, the office assistant Dr Roberts needs.'

'Oh, you find someone?'

'Well, I thought I'd like to apply.'

'Okay. Yes,' she said. 'This is good. But the problem ees, Dr Roberts he gone away. Back next month. I tell you what. You give me your number and I call him and tell him.'

'All right. Thanks.' Lara gave Valencia her number.

'I give him this today. He can call you what time?'

'Any time before the end of the day's fine. Thanks.' She knew that this meant committing herself to stay in town all day.

★ ★ ★

Lara spent the morning at a cafe enjoying a hearty meal of avocado, egg, tomato and toast, sipping a flat white. She jumped when her phone rang.

137

'Hello, this is Andrew Roberts returning your call.' Radio DJ voice.

'Dr Roberts, hi. This is Lara. I was in your office the other day with bronchitis. I don't know if you remember me.'

'Yes, Lara. You're feeling better I hope?'

'Very much so. Thanks for the drugs.'

'You're welcome. It's what I'm here for.'

'I was actually calling about your ad for a part-time office assistant.'

'Are you a part-time office assistant?'

'Not exactly.'

'Sounds perfect then.'

'Well, ironies aside, Dr Roberts, I'd like to apply for the position.'

'What relevant experience would you have?'

'I was a teacher for fifteen years. Some of that time I was the administrator of a small Catholic school.'

'Look, Lara. I'm away working in Western Australia for the next few weeks. I do need someone to answer the phone, take bookings for when I return, and to sort out a rather large backlog of mail and do some filing. That's the job description for the moment. Think you could do it?'

A dark and seldom-revealed secret was that Lara had never had a job interview. Her teaching position had developed organically from the school her children attended. First as an assistant, and then, while completing her degree in education, she stood in for a teacher who was ill, and over time became a full-time employee. She really didn't want to blow this belated step towards independence by admitting she felt like an amateur.

'I'm sure I could help you with that, Dr Roberts.'

'Andrew.'

'Andrew. And, um ...'

'Yes?'

'I would offer to do this at first on a volunteer basis.'

'Why's that?'

'A mixture of altruism and not having a work visa.'

He laughed, a sound that felt like honey pouring into the cracks in her soul. 'Ah. A small issue not to be overlooked. Well, Lara, hmm, let me think about that for a minute. Look, here's the thing. I need the help, and there you are, so on that basis, if I can make a contribution to your room and board and food for three days a week of volunteer help, we could have a deal.'

'I'll take it.'

'Done, then. Would you stop in at my residence sometime today and speak to Valencia? I'm going to send details through to her. If it's agreeable to you, you could come in say, Mondays, Wednesdays, and Fridays, from nine in the morning until about two or three? Starting as soon as possible.'

'I could start next week.'

'That sounds good.'

'Perfect.' Lara couldn't understand why her heart suddenly lifted.

'Thanks. I'll see you when I get back. Any questions, get my email from Valencia. Phone contact isn't advisable as I'm very busy for the next few weeks.'

Lara put her phone away with shaking hands. She'd done it. She had her own car, and now room and board and food. At the rather ripe old age of forty-four, Lara had become a self-sufficient human being. Even if Brock left her nothing, she would be surviving now, not, as she'd feared, scrabbling across the floor to col-

139

lect her lost teeth. And that was the Beginner's first step to re-building her own life.

Half an hour later, in the Byron Hinterland, she drove up the winding road, towards the property at the end with the river running through it.

Valencia ran out of the house, a wide smile on her face. 'I am happy today. This is good, very good,' she said. 'Welcome! I knew it was right thing to ask you. There is too much paperwork – is all a big, big mess, and no one understand me properly on the phone. And they speak too quick so I not understand them. You starting next week?'

'Yes,' Lara said, still standing by the car.

'Come in, come in. I get you something to drink.'

The email that Valencia printed out had come through from Andrew Roberts' phone. It was brief:

Thanks for taking this on. Make yourself comfortable around the office. Answer the phone, take appointments starting Monday the 7th (Valencia will show you the booking system). Sort mail.

'Is that all?'

Valencia gave Lara a guilty look.

'There is big problem,' she said. 'I show you.'

Lara followed her into a storeroom at the side of the office. Valencia opened the door and pointed at two massive cardboard boxes, waist high, each one filled to overflowing with unopened mail. Above that she saw yet more mail, on the shelves.

'Dr Andrew, he not open his letters for *long* time.'

'Oh. Wow, Valencia. This mess could have major personal and financial ramifications, right?'

'Sorry?'

'You're right about the big problem here,' Lara said. 'This must cause a lot of stress for the doctor?'

Valencia grabbed her arm. 'Miss Lara, I worry so much. I worry that maybe he will lose … everything. You see? I am happy you are here. I try to help you. Okay?'

'Okay,' Lara said. 'We can do this.'

'Sorry,' Valencia said. 'Let me get you juice.'

'Not to worry.'

They went back out into the reception area. Lara had to wonder at the mental health of someone who didn't open his mail. And where in all this was his wife?

'Here,' Valencia handed her a glass of orange juice. 'Come, sit.'

Lara sat down in the waiting area. Clearly, For Valencia, orange juice was the solution to all problems. 'I'll tackle this all next week.'

'Oh, thanks God,' Valencia said and hugged herself. 'This is good, good. Thank you, thank you. I can't do this anymore.' She sounded close to tears.

Lara wondered whether Doc Roberts might be in some state of mental decline. The sparse office, the surroundings, the boxes of unopened mail – it didn't quite make the 'normal' mark. But his demeanour had been so gentle, so capable, though a guy who left boxes of letters overflowing with no doubt, several years of unopened mail had to have a problem.

'Valencia, look, I'll be here on Monday. I have to sort out things where I'm staying.'

'Doc Roberts he say to me, you can stay in the cottage. If you like to. Is self-contained. By the hill. Mrs Roberts, she used to live there. I will make it clean and tidy for you by Monday.'

'Doc Roberts' wife?'

'No, no. Mother. Now she too old. She gone to old

people's home. One bedroom okay?'

'Of course. Can I have a look?'

★ ★ ★

The walk up the hill behind the main house gave no hint of another living space. And then Lara saw it, a beautiful wooden studio-cabin.

The veranda caught the sun. Emerald-winged, red and blue and purple-breasted rainbow lorikeets watched hanging upside down on a nearby wattle bush.

The door was unlocked. Valencia pushed it open. Dust rose from floor. Beneath a grey coating, shiny hardwood floorboards peered through. A bed frame stood in the centre of the room. Behind that, there was a closet. They walked across the floor making footprints in the dust. To the left of the bedroom stood a small kitchenette, complete with cobweb-covered appliances. It was like a Sleeping Beauty cabin after a hundred years. The bathroom had handrails along the wall, and a large jacuzzi tub.

'Perfect,' Lara said, like a prospective renter. 'I'll take it.'

Valencia's face beamed.

'I clean everything for you and make it very nice for Monday,' she said. 'Last time he rent this was nine, ten months ago. Then he decide, no more renters, nothing.'

'So, he rented this when his mother moved out?'

'Yes. For one year. One problem is, no bed, no mattress.'

'Don't worry,' Lara said. 'I'll organise that. I'll try and get one delivered by Monday. Thanks so much for your help.'

* * *

On her way back to the caravan park in Lennox, Lara decided to check her phone before she went out of reach again. No new messages. Then it rang.

'Hi my dearest!'

'Joanne! Wait, I need to pull over. Give me a second.'

She found a lay-by surrounded by trees, and skidded to a halt on the sand.

'I have to relay news to you, Lar.'

'Good news, I hope.'

'Well, it depends on what cheers you up. I think it's good anyway.'

'Do tell.'

'I saw Brock at the party.'

Lara's heart went heavy, like a grey river stone that would always sink.

'Right.'

'He seemed fine. Looked a bit strained, but I went to talk to him and he seemed terribly glad to see me. He asked me all about you.'

'Hmm.'

'I told him you were in Australia, having a wonderful time. I said you'd met someone and were having a magnificent affair.'

'I see.'

'He looked slightly pale, then smiled and said that was great, he was very happy for you.'

'Mm hm.'

'So, I explained to him that it looked like you'd really moved on, found yourself, and a new exciting love. I told him you sounded happier than you'd sounded in years. He tried to keep the smile on his face, and then asked me in the most earnest way whether I knew when you'd be back. I told him I believed, not yet. Did I do right, Lar? I honestly thought I saw actual pain in the man's usually incredibly confident face, but maybe I'm just reading into things.'

'Yeah, I think you are. He's a class act. Should be in Hollywood. Had me fooled for long enough.'

'I know it. But I sensed something.'

'If he was capable of experiencing anything beyond entirely selfish emotions, I'd grow wings, but after twenty years, I have serious doubts.'

'Okay, maybe you're right, but I did my thing, and he now knows you aren't somewhere, lonely, unloved and pining.'

'I suppose that's probably a good thing. But I wouldn't believe his "sincere" look. He's been practising that in the mirror every morning and has clocked up his ten thousand hours. He's an expert. I don't know how else he could have made dishonesty look like sincerity for so long.'

* * *

As the images Joanne relayed to Lara played over in her head, she felt better. It was important to her that Brock would never know that she had contemplated driving off a cliff. The thought of him sitting in the cold light of early spring, imagining Lara to be having a rollicking good time with a young lover was inspiringly funny. She smiled, finished the call and drove on.

2.00 pm

Hi Lara, this is Jean-Luc. Attached are the pictures I took. I hope you like them. I will email higher resolu-

tion versions and also, if you choose some, I will print and frame and have them sent to an address if you can give me one. I would like to see you again if you are free. I go back to France in ten days. It was very nice to meet you. X J-L.
  2.05 pm
  Hi J-L
  Thanks so much. Am free if you want to come to Lennox Heads maybe on Saturday morning? Coffee on me. Come alone. Don't tell friends, or Mario. L

Lara scrolled through the pictures. Wow. She didn't look too bad in that light with that filter. And the contours and shadows and shapes were gorgeous and the masculine-feminine energy was, well, potent. Bloody Mario. He looked sultry and handsome. Pity she was so bad at being a Room Two Person, she thought.

18

The cafe overlooked the sea. Jean-Luc was hard to miss. His height and broad shoulders and his shiny blonde hair caught the sunlight. When Lara waved, he hurried towards her and wrapped her in his arms. He kissed her full on the lips.

'Thank you for seeing me,' he said, and sat. Several customers stared.

'No, thank you for coming down,' Lara said. 'It's good to see you.'

'Are you okay? I heard you were sick.'

'I'm better now, thanks.'

'Mario was worried.'

'Really?'

'Just tell me, okay? Did Mario break your heart?'

'Nope.'

'But ...'

'No, Jean-Luc, really, he didn't. My heart had already been thoroughly broken by my ex. Mario just went into some of the cracks and widened them. I had to get away.'

'He has been very sad about you.'

'Really?'

'He felt bad. He doesn't like to fail.'

'He didn't fail. He did his job. I failed.'

'Yes, but his job is to make women feel wonderful.'

'He's probably too young to understand, but life's a bit more complicated than he thinks. Maybe he's not the answer to every woman's, or man's prayers. You'd know, right?'

'Yes,' he said.

'So, is that why you're here? To find out what Mario did wrong so you can go back and tell him?'

'No. No, I have something to ask. And I wanted to see you before I left.'

'Okay. Sure. Meanwhile, how are you? You doing okay?' She motioned the waiter to come over.

He nodded. 'Yes. Feeling good again. Australia is so beautiful. Being in the sun is good for me. I have met some nice people. I have a six-month contract with a magazine here for next year.'

'That's fantastic,' Lara said. 'Which one?'

'It's called *Wild*.'

'The women's magazine?'

'Of course,' he smiled. 'And why I wanted to see you. Lara, they would like to use the picture of you and Mario *The Kiss*, for their cover at the end of the year. They will pay me and my French magazine will pay for the other pictures. And I will pay you. But are you okay with that? Because I will only say yes if you feel comfortable.'

The waiter came over. They ordered coffees. Lara recommended a fat piece of chocolate pavlova, which she described as an Australian diabetes-enhancing special made with meringue and whipped cream and berries and sometimes chocolate, so sweet it made your cheeks meet on the inside. Jean-Luc thought that working on achieving blood sugar imbalances wasn't a bad idea.

'I'm fine with you using the picture,' she said.

'Thank you so much,' he said. He leaned across and kissed her on each cheek. 'You've made my day. Really. Your picture has given me an unexpected new avenue in my career.'

147

'You're welcome. And Jean-Luc, just for the record. If anything, I was mad with Mario, not heartbroken. You can tell him that it's my issue, not his if you like.'

'Yes. I will.'

'And you're good? I was hoping he wouldn't cause you any more pain. And he obviously hasn't, right?'

The coffees and pavlova arrived.

'No.' he said. 'Mario said to me: "Jean-Luc, if we did anything sexual, I would break your heart. I love you my friend. I cannot hurt you."'

'Mario said that?'

'Yes.'

Lara reached out with her coffee spoon and took a giant scoop of Jean-Luc's pavlova and stuck it in her mouth. 'Wow,' she said.

'I'm sure he would like to see you, to talk with you sometime. He told me all what happened.'

'What, that I heard him with Ruby, my landlady?'

'Something like that, yes. That's what he was afraid had happened.'

'Yeah, well, it was horrible. But in the end, he was at work. I'm a bloody idiot, but I guess I already knew that.'

'I think, Lara, he is learning some things about life.'

She ate more pavlova.

'You can blame Mario for being arrogant, and your ex-husband for being a lying bastard. I can blame my ex, Pierre, for being the arsehole, but that's not going to fix anything, no?'

'You're right,' she said. 'And eating all this crap is only going to make me feel better for five minutes. Don't you just sometimes want to, I don't know, make these jerks feel the pain they cause?'

'Yes,' he said. 'But this is not for us to do. Let's go

for a walk on the beach.'

'Perfect.'

★ ★ ★

That night, lying in bed, Lara reflected on the high-lights of her day; eating pavlova and sharing break-up stories on the beach with Jean-Luc, whose tragedy equalled hers. He'd returned home early from a business trip and wanted to surprise his lover Pierre, but instead was surprised himself when he found Pierre having sex in his shower with someone else. Jean-Luc had taken a whole bottle of sleeping tablets and woken up in hospital after getting his stomach pumped. At that point he'd been furious to still be alive While walking with Lara on the beach he said how grateful he was to actually still be alive.

It was also refreshing for Lara to hear Jean-Luc say in his classy French accent, "Brock is a stupid fucking bastard."

Lara slept for twelve hours. She woke as the new day burst over the horizon and got out of bed feeling well again. She decided to go for a jog.

As she ran, the pounding on sand soothed her. At some point into an hour of running, the distress of the Mario-Ruby scenario evaporated.

19

Lara stood on the veranda of her new abode with Valencia.

'It looks like a different place,' she said. 'Honestly, I feel like I'm moving into a resort, Valencia. Thank you.'

'I'm happy you like it,' she said. 'I like to make this place nice again. I find the curtains, wash them, put them up. The tablecloth too and the flowers from the garden. You sure that mattress company is coming now?'

'Yep. They just called.'

The air resounded with screeching lorikeets. In the distance, she could hear the sound of water over rocks. Behind the house, was a forested hill. In anyone's book, this was absolute paradise. And all Lara had to do to live here was answer the phone and sort the mail. What a stroke of good fortune, she thought.

Eventually the truck arrived. Two men slid the new mattress onto its waiting base. Valencia gave instructions to the mattress guys in a no-nonsense voice. 'I want that everything is perfect for you, Lara.'

The studio gleamed and smelled like pine. After they left, Valencia picked up a pile of folded sheets and a quilt.

'I give you sheets, bedding from the house. I can help you make the bed?'

'Look.' Lara held up a large packet from Big W. She'd bought herself a sea-coloured Bed-in-a-Bag. She figured that her own buying-of-bed-things-ritual

150

was an important step in the Beginner's Guide to a new life.

'Okay,' Valencia said. 'I can wash them first? You don't like to sleep in shop smell.'

'Good point. Thank you. Though I don't really mind.'

Valencia was adamant. She helped Lara make the bed with the sheets she'd brought. Lara looked closely at her face. It was hard to tell how old she was with her olive skin, dark eyes and hair, and solid, energetic body.

'Looks lovely,' Lara said.

'Is good,' she said.

'I think it's time to get to the office now,' Lara said. 'It's nine.'

'Yes, good. If you need anything else, ask me. I think Doc Roberts is very happy to have you here.'

'Let's hope so,' Lara said.

She closed the door of her new home behind her and they walked down the pathway towards the main residence.

Nine fifteen am. They began with the mail, Valencia helping Lara to heave the massive cardboard box of letters out into the middle of the waiting room. Lara took one look at the overflowing waterfall of unopened mail floor and shook her head.

'Looks like we'll need to sort them into piles first. There's personal correspondence, business, bills and other stuff. I'll open the ones I'm unsure of first.'

'He need everything to be organised. Is a big mess.' Valencia said.

Valencia went to do laundry and uninterrupted, Lara began to sift through the chaos of a stranger's life.

151

A good portion of the letters showed date stamps that were two years old. She put those in a pile and decided to open a few. What was the doctor's story, she wondered? And was the mail from hospitals in Sydney work-related? She opened one. It referred to a blood transfusion. Had he been ill?

She opened a letter that looked like a bill, It contained a plain card with a picture of white lilies. *Thinking of you, Chris, Diane and Debbie.*

There were three letters from a hospice organisation. Lara put those into the 'business' pile without opening them.

She opened a few letters from a law firm in Sydney. Those went onto the business pile.

She grew curious. Had the doctor been diagnosed with a disease? Was he in denial? She sorted a letter from a cancer research centre, and another.

Another letter, in business-like type, was addressed to Dr Andrew Roberts. No clue which pile it should go into, so she opened it. *Andrew, please call us if you need support, emotional or spiritual. Rev. Steven Muir and Cathy Muir.*

Valencia would know what had happened here and Lara could just ask her, once she got to know her better.

Intrigued, Lara continued. She sorted real correspondence from junk mail and read letters when necessary. There were no mortgage or bank statements or payments. Had he paid his house off? Those details were most likely online, she thought.

Lunch time came and went. When her stomach groaned, Lara looked at what had been done and the small dent she'd made in the heap, and decided to call it a day.

In the afternoon, Lara drove to Mullumbimby, and shopped for a week's worth of healthy food and a few new items of clothing. She spent a hundred dollars an hour for three hours. It had to be done. When she got home, Valencia's Hyndai was gone. Lara was alone on forty acres of bush land. That was a real first. She sat on her new deck picking at a large plate of salmon salad and surveying the vista of trees and green in front of her. Movement above her on the rafters of the veranda caught her eye. An arm-thick snake cruised on top of an inch-wide beam right above her head. It wobbled from side to side. Lara froze in disbelief. She didn't scream. She had prided herself at not being afraid of snakes, but that was before she'd sat underneath a quavering, slithering one of this size.

To her relief, Valencia's car pulled up. As the door opened, Lara called out at the top of her voice.

'Valencia?'

'Lara? You okay?'

'Snake!' She yelled. 'Above my head. A really big one!'

Valencia stomped up the path. Released from her trance, Lara scrambled to a standing position, dropped her salad plate and leapt off the wooden decking.

'Oh, glad you're here.' She stumbled towards Valencia.

'You okay? You hurt?'

Lara shook her head. 'No. I'm fine. But look. Up there.' She pointed over her shoulder.

'Oh, that snake? He no problem.' Valencia said with a big grin.

'What do you mean?'

153

'Is carpet python. He live here. A good snake.'

'A what?'

'A carpet python. A good snake,' she said, slowing herself down. 'He eat brown snakes and keep mice away.'

Lara watched the snake's three-metre length vanish into a gap beneath the roof of her new accommodation and looked at Valencia. 'It just went into my roof!'

'He live there,' Valencia said and laughed. 'Don't worry, Lara. You will be used to this. Many house in this rural area have one maybe two carpet snakes in the roof.' She picked up Lara's plate. 'What a pity — you drop your lunch.'

'So, I have to live with this snake? I mean, Valencia, I have nothing against him, but I prefer snakes outside, and not over my bed in the ceiling, or hanging over my salad.'

'He not come in your bed.'

'Well, that's a relief,' Lara said with some irony. It was clear Valencia wasn't going to call a Snake Man to relocate the roof resident.

'Tell me about brown snakes.'

'Very, very venomous,' Valencia said. 'Don't walk outside in dark. Always look where you go.'

Damn, Lara thought. Her non-fear of snakes had blossomed into edginess. But when in her quiet British life had she had the opportunity to encounter anything like this? Her experience of snakes had come from visits to reptile parks in foreign countries. She threw a look at the gap between rafters and roof. Okay, python, we're housemates, she thought. No alternative — they had to share the roof. In light of the brown-snake information, she thought, this would have to become an acceptable companionship.

'There's more salad inside.' Lara said to Valencia. 'Let me dish you up a lunch plate.'

★ ★ ★

The following day, Valencia left for three days to visit her eldest son in Brisbane. On the day she was due back, Lara still sat between piles of mail reading and sorting with the same anticipation she might have felt watching a gripping mini-series. She'd moved the piles of letters into the reception area so she could be there in case the phone rang. Dramatic loose threads dangled in her mind. Details around a crucial event were missing from the correspondence. Until now, she'd only opened letters that couldn't be judged by their envelopes, not wanting to intrude. The next letter looked personal. Driven by curiosity, she opened it.

Our dear Andrew,

Gabrielle will always be in our hearts as the most beautiful of all flowers. She is now at piece with your little Luke. Heaven is a brighter place with both of them together in it. Jean, Michelle and family

Lara opened another, a card with stars and the moon against a dark sky.

My dear friend,

So sorry for your loss. Mike

She felt her throat constrict. She had uncovered the link to a another's terrible family tragedy. Outside, the stillness of the day stretched out, layered with heat and the scent of eucalyptus.

An hour later, Valencia returned. Lara heard her footsteps and looked up as Valencia appeared at the open door.

155

'Hello Mrs Lara. You okay?'

'Hi Valencia. Yes, I'm okay. How was your trip to see your son?'

'Was good. What happen? You crying?'

'Me? Oh, I was. I just ... read something. Was Gabrielle the doctor's wife?'

Valencia nodded. She put down her bag, and put her hands to her face. Her eyes were tearful. 'Only forty-three. She die so young,' she said.

'That's terrible,' Lara said.

'Everything been bad here. Bad and sad for very long time.'

'She died two years ago?'

'Two years ago, yes,' Valencia said.

'Some kind of cancer?'

'Yes. A bad cancer. In the bones. Everywhere. Terrible.'

'I see,' Lara said. A doctor who couldn't save his own wife from cancer. Devastating.

'Such a good family. They help me so much. I come here from Spain. Divorce and come to live in Sydney with my sister, but she very poor. I come here to get out of the city when my boy was ten. Mr Andrew and Mrs Gabrielle, they help me. I work for them and help them and we like family. They look after my boy and I'm like a grandmother. And they love each other so much. They have a baby boy, Luke, and we all so happy. But then Luke, he die.'

'Their little boy?'

She nodded. 'Two years old.' Tears spilled down her cheeks.

'How?' Lara whispered.'

Valencia shook her head. 'Miss Gabrielle, her heart is broken. Two years later, she die.'

Lara got up from the chair, put her arms around Valencia.

She said. 'You see? There is big sadness and mess here. Maybe you won't stay. Because here is very heavy. And I want to help Doc Roberts, Andrew. He such a good man, but he just work, work, work, never do anything else.'

'Don't worry. I won't leave because of the sadness,' Lara said. 'At least some things make sense now. Like all the unopened mail.'

'Yes,' Valencia said. 'And thank you. You know, he always do kind things for people, and then such bad things happen. This life is not fair,' she said.

'No. It's not.'

Valencia made tea. Lara kept working, feeling the weight of the tragedy. She moved swiftly through the mail now, knowing where to place things. She hunted for unpaid bills (she found only three) and put Valencia's mind at rest that there were no outstanding mortgage payments to be found. It looked like he probably had his finances mostly under control. She understood why he perhaps didn't want to touch his mail and read all the condolences and notes from friends, which would just make his loss real and fresh all over again. So, not a mentally ill and shady character, this doctor, but a grieving husband and father. Lara took a break, walked over to her veranda and sat down, leaning back in the old canvass-covered chair. She admired the purple bougainvillea and the yellow passionfruit flowers that climbed up tall old trees near her cottage.

A loud scuttling in the underbrush startled her. At first she thought she was looking at a deer. She'd read in a nature-walker's guide to the east coast of

157

Australia, the difference between wallabies and kangaroos. If it has a horse-face, she remembered, it's a kangaroo. If it has a rabbit or deer-face, it's a wallaby. Her wallaby bounced up to the veranda and paused at the bottom step, watching Lara, twitching its nose. It was unafraid, paws dangling, ears turning this way and that.

'Hello there,' Lara whispered. Moments later, the wallaby bounded away into the bush. Lara felt alive. She wondered how much of every moment she'd taken for granted up until this point. What in the world had she been doing, wasting time not appreciating things, getting angry at the wrong bloody things? She realised she needed to be properly done with fretting over Mario and Ruby. She had done the right thing getting away. Yes, she loved Ruby and her foul mouth, and she missed the feeling of those days of thrilling anticipation with Mario within reach. And yes, it had been awful hearing them in bed. It had also been okay, she thought, to take some time to herself to figure things out and get over everything, including herself.

20

For the first time in a long time, when the weekend arrived, it felt like a weekend. Lara went out onto the deck, in new pyjamas, at dawn, holding a mug of tea. The wallaby sat out in front, eating grass. Other wallabies joined one-by-one. At first they kept a safe distance from her, but after a few minutes, they too ventured out into full view. It didn't take Lara long to establish personalities. The biggest of the tribe was bold and adventurous. The joey at his side seemed shy. Any sign of movement from Lara and the young wallaby bounded away into the bush. The third stayed close to the big guy and copied everything he did. If he stopped to sniff the air, ditto. If he decided enough grass from a particular patch, ditto. She probably had all their relationships wrong. What did she know about the secret life of wallabies? It was all projection. Maybe that was her tragic flaw, she thought. How much of what she loved in Brock had been projection? What had she actually loved about this man, to go through childbirth twice, to have spent thousands of hours in his service, going unnoticed by him, trying every day to re-find the man she'd thought she was in love with?

When they were young, Brock was a handsome athlete studying architecture in London. He had lots of admirers. His father had instilled in him a firm mantra; marry your own kind. By this, he meant, if you value domestic bliss and a dishwasher-safe existence, don't commit to a blonde, buxom beauty. Lara

159

was, Brock said, the best candidate in the eyes of his parents. She'd thought that was a good thing. At first she'd been overwhelmed by the attention of such a perfect specimen of masculinity. She'd spent her early youth shy and self-effacing, reading romance novels, and then found her heart in sport. Volleyball and clubbing with friends occupied her life in her final high school years. She'd found short-lived fame as the best volleyball spiker on her team and went on to play at university.

She met Brock at a university volleyball match when he was watching her and cheering her from the sidelines. He'd watched her spike a few balls and publicly praised her elegance and fury. After they started seeing each other, she went to play in Ireland over a long weekend, and Brock sent her off with a poem he'd written. A love-poem. To her. Perhaps at that moment, the Ultimate Romantic Hero, as created by Lara, aided and abetted by hundreds of Harlequin Mills & Boon heroes, delivered itself as Brock. But he'd never played his part, either in words or deeds, beyond that one poem. He was crass about sex and intimacy at the best of times, and joked (mostly at Lara's expense) about it, though he knew that she'd wanted to keep their intimacy sacred and romantic.

Brock wanted his father's approval, and Brock's father thought Lara would be The Perfect Wife. So Brock proposed. That was the not-very-exciting narrative of the romance, through her present eyes. Through the years, every time Lara saw Brock when he'd come home from work, or from a trip, she could now admit, she'd had a nano-second battle with disappointment. He was always distant, unimpressive, vacant and talked about himself non-stop. Both of

160

them had him at the centre of their universes. Lara had to keep conjuring images of a Romantic Hero who wrote her a beautiful poem and appreciated his perfect wife. It was her way of supplanting the colossal egotist he grew into after they'd married.

Her disappointment had pervaded everything, she realised now. It came when he looked at her, or rather past or through her. It was there when she saw his body slouching into middle-age in front of the television, paunch extended, oblivious to the person next to him who would have loved a candle-lit dinner and maybe a new love poem after ten, fifteen, twenty years. Lara had tried valiantly to remake him despite the smallest offerings of affection he gave her. Given the tiniest bit of encouragement she resurrected a construction of him time and again, and made herself fall in love with him. That had been the tragedy. Looking back, she couldn't believe it. In fact, the tragedy wasn't losing Brock, it was the possibility that if it hadn't ended, she'd have spent another twenty years wasting her life, in love with a bloody ghost of her own creation.

★   ★   ★

Moody, thunderous clouds, and an early storm threatened the bright morning. Valencia had told her that twice in the last eight years the property had been flooded in, cut off from civilisation. No one had been able to get in or out for a week. The small river at the bottom of the property could rise by two metres, she'd said, which explained the sign on the road: *Road Subject to Flooding.*

Lara showered, got dressed and walked, mindful of brown snakes, towards the main house. Valencia lived in a two-bedroomed apartment next to the reception and doctor's office, on the ground floor of the large house. Lara knocked on her door.

'Hello Mrs Lara!'

'I just got a text from you. You wanted me to come over?'

'Yes, yes. Come in. I just get message from Dr Andrew. I tell him we do big job in the office, and I want show you the message.'

'Oh. Right.'

Lara followed her through a beautiful living area with wall-hangings and pictures that had echoes of Spain. A big poster of Gaudi's Sagrada Familia Cathedral graced the wall above Valencia's dining table.

'I love Gaudi,' she said, admiringly.

'Oh, we both love Gaudi,' Valencia said. 'But is good here. Australia is good. No bad husband, and only nice people. I have my life.'

'Yeah. Funny thing, isn't it? I have my life, too. No bad husband.'

'Where is your husband?'

'The guy who used to be my husband is in England.'

'Divorce?'

'Separated. Divorce ahead. Yes.'

'Another woman?'

'Ah yes. Many. Yours?'

'Lots of women. And beating me.'

'What a fuckwit.'

'Pardon?'

'Sorry. Not a nice person.'

'Yes. One of those.'

Lara laughed. She'd joined the club of millions of women worldwide. Admission was free after you'd been through the ritual of betrayal and she'd inadvertently joined the allegiance. She found comfort in the knowledge.

The email from Dr Roberts came up on Valencia's computer.

Thanks for yours, V. Just tell Lara to sort the mail. Prefer if she didn't open or read. Just sort into piles as best she can so I can tackle when I get back. Glad to hear things are going well. Thanks for holding the fort. Take care, A.

'Bloody hell,' Lara said. She hated being told today what she needed to have known almost a week back. Too late for that, Dr A, she thought.

'Why bloody hell?'

'Well, I've opened the mail. I've read things I shouldn't have. I know his whole story. He could have given me those simple instructions before I started.'

'Not to worry.'

'Hmm.'

'Lara, he very kind man. You din't know. So is okay.'

'He'll probably fire me.'

'No, no.' She waved her hands, wiping the air clean. Nonetheless, Lara felt tense.

'Tell me.' Valencia said. 'You have kids?'

'All grown up.'

'You too young to have grown kids.'

'I'm forty-four.'

Valencia laughed. 'You look younger. How old you think I am?'

'I have no idea. Fifty-one?'

Valencia burst out laughing. 'Sixty.'

'Sixty?'

'I stay young inside,' she said. 'Being married make me old.'

'You look wonderful. You have beautiful skin. You're

163

very lucky.'

'Thanks, thanks. Men, you know, they make you old. No more for me. Only nice friends. Ladies.'

'I get it,' Lara said.

'Yes,' Valencia said. 'For me that's good. But you are still young. You can find a good man.'

'I don't want any man, good or bad,' Lara said. 'I'm learning to be just fine without one.'

Valencia said, 'I worry about Dr Andrew. He not going to lose the house?'

'No. There wasn't even a single mortgage statement. He must have that under control.'

'Thanks God!' she said. 'I also worry that he needs to have a good woman. He's so young still and handsome. I like him to find someone.'

'I'm sure he will one day,' Lara said.

★ ★ ★

In just two weeks Lara became one with her setting and grew into a bush woman – well, that concept was relative. When the python appeared one afternoon going down the gutter on the side of the veranda, she stood at a respectful distance and said hi. When a hand-sized Huntsman spider scuttled out from behind the toilet and sat on the wall watching her, she said, 'look, please do whatever you need to do, but stay the bloody hell out of my bed.'

Butcher birds sang in thirds and fifths and made tunes that composers would envy. The mob of wallabies now treated her with fearless regard. She may as well have been a bush or a tree. She could sit on the steps and they ate grass close enough that had she reached out her hand, she could have stroked their

164

soft red fur. She could sit under the Poinciana tree with pieces of watermelon in her hand, and two rainbow lorikeets took turns in perching on her wrist to eat. One evening, she shared the veranda with a prehistoric-looking water-dragon who begged for food as if he had once been fed by humans and was expecting dinner.

In the same two weeks, she made it through the box of letters and a whole shelf of Dr Andrew Roberts' unopened mail.

Valencia explained his situation. He worked away for weeks at a time for the flying doctor service in remote outback areas in Western Australia. He had a part-time practice when he was back home, to keep busy. Otherwise, his colleague in town, Dr Peter West, saw his patients. Lara had made up-coming appointments for him which would fill his calendar after his return in another two weeks.

'He like to keep working,' Valencia said. 'Most times, flying doctors, they come home and relax. He not know the meaning of relax. Only work.'

The phone rang just as Lara was about to finish for the day.

'Hi, this is Debbie from Caramere Aged Care. Is Dr Roberts there?'

'No, he's away for another fortnight,' Lara said. 'Can I help?'

'Oh, pity. No, that's all right. I'm the now full-time diversional therapist and I thought I'd forgot to mark the calendar. He usually comes in when he's here, so next week he would have been over to play the piano for the residents. His mum gets a walk out in the gardens with him. But never mind. I'll explain that he's away.'

'I'm Lara, Dr Roberts' new office assistant.' Then, on impulse she said, 'I can't help you with the piano bit, but I'd be happy to come over and chat to residents and take anyone who would like to go for a walk out into the gardens.'

'Well that would be wonderful, Lara. Do you mean that?'

'Yes, of course. What time and when?'

She took down details and directions, and was tempted to ask for a definition. What was a diversional therapist? It sounded like the person hired to divert your attention from the fact that you would be kicking the bucket sometime soon.

So, she thought, the doctor played the piano. She tried to imagine him bent over a keyboard, lost in a musical trance. She banished the image from her mind.

To modify the overriding theme of white-on-white, she cleaned the office and placed a vase of flowers, an explosion of colour from the garden, on the front desk.

21

Friday evening in Byron: the usual hippies, the tie-dyed clothes, the stoned youngsters, a dog wearing sunglasses, and an old lady walking with a kitten in a handbag. Lara had a smoothie and walked to the beach. She no longer gave a second thought to the quirky residents and passers-by.

A girl and her boyfriend strolled along the sand. He wore shorts, she wore nothing. She walked by, enjoying the view, holding his hand, her hairless and completely naked body drawing a few stares, her breasts pale and bouncing in the evening breeze. Lara looked at her. Had she ever been that young, that carelessly graceful?

She had just turned to go back into town and think about what she might eat, when a figure caught her eye. Or perhaps an energy field caught her attention. Whichever, she turned around. A man in a pair of dark trousers and a tan shirt cut a conspicuous figure as he walked towards her. He wore mirror sunglasses and dragged his luggage behind him. Loud wheels rolled over the gaps in the paving. 'Lara! What a coincidence.'

Lara's heart turned to concrete.

'Hello Lara.' He took off his glasses.

Was this a ghost, a trick of a stressed brain? No, Brock looked real enough with his pasty face and his drooping eyelids. All Lara's millions of previous nano-seconds of disappointment stretched into an eternity of Seeing Things as they Really Were.

Any strength she had felt in the preceding moments drained from her limbs.

'What the hell are you doing here?' she asked so loudly that the lady walking past stopped in her tracks and gave Brock a filthy look. 'Are you insane? How did you get here into my hemisphere? How did you find me?'

'I flew here for a purpose and coincidence, or divine providence, whichever one you'd like to call it made our paths cross this instant. I'm staying at the Blue Sails Resort down the road, and had planned on locating you sooner or later. Why weren't you answering my emails or texts?'

'You walked out of my fucking life, remember?'

'Don't be foul-mouthed. It doesn't suit you.'

'Oh please. I'm not nearly as foul as your behaviour.'

'Come on Lara. I've just made a forty-hour journey across the world to come and find you and talk to you.'

'So generous. You're forgetting one thing. I didn't invite you.'

'I tried to ask you. You ignored me.'

'I think you should be able to read that as not interested. Stay the fuck away.'

'I don't appreciate it when you swear. It's vile and disgusting, Lara.'

'True, but again, not nearly as vile and disgusting as you. Not as gross as someone who goes around secretly fucking other women and then feigns faithful sincerity when he comes home to his wife. Not as vile as that.'

Brock went pale. 'Look, you're still upset. Let's get out of this public place.'

'What do you want? A romantic dinner venue?'

'I want to talk to you,' he said, his lips thin and mean.

The longer Lara stared at this man, the more fiery she felt.

'Fine. Since you're here, Brock, I do actually have some important things to say to you. Let's go there.' She pointed to a cafe on the other side of the road. She knew it had a seating area at the back away from the street. She stormed across the main road, heedless of oncoming cars and a screech of tyres, while he tripped along, dragging his luggage, trying to keep up with her.

They sat down opposite one another at a table in a far corner of a courtyard. She was reminded of their final dinner in a former life when he had told her he had fallen in love with Jacqui. Now they were upside down in the universe and at the bottom of the world, and yet Lara had never felt more right-side-up.

'I'm surprised at you,' he said, leaning back in his chair. Sweat had stained his shirt all down the front and she wondered for a perverse moment who'd done his ironing.

'Really? I'll take that as a compliment.'

'You're just angry. It's understandable.'

'No, Brock, I'm not just angry. I'm changed.'

'Can we have a decent conversation?'

'Decency implies honesty and truthfulness. In my almost twenty-one-long-year experience, you haven't shown me you have those.'

'I was honest with you.'

'Are you serious? I only figured out recently that you were in the pants of Allyssa of the blonde ponytail four years ago, when we went on holiday to her

169

parent's place on the Isle of Wight. I woke up and wondered where you were at 4.00 am, and you rushed in from the garden, looking guilty as hell and smelling like someone else, telling me some bullshit story about not being able to sleep, and walking along the beach, thinking. And two years ago, all those late nights with doe-eyed Maria BigTits. I remember at that Christmas party, you and her in a bizarre little besotted bubble, you putting your coat around her chilly shoulders and whispering in her ear like you guys were on a fucking *honeymoon*. I stood at the bar like a stupid fuckhead, not hearing a word the barman said to me because I could not believe what I was seeing. You, Brock, are a piece of fucking work. Telling me *honestly* about the lesbian and your reason for leaving me, after the fact, does not constitute honesty. I thought that I was in a marriage with someone who loved me. You made a mockery of my life.'

Lara's voice and temperature rose at the same time.

'For God's sake, Lara, please!'

'What? Please stop? Why? You don't like this narrative? Oh, sorry, but it's the honest truth. Then again, you wouldn't know honesty if it hit you on the head with a cunt-shaped baseball bat.'

'Stop being so disgusting and overdramatic. It wasn't like that. I told you it had nothing to do with you. I fell for someone else. And I wanted to be honest about that. And she's been decent enough to stand back and allow me this time to come here and try and work things out with you.'

'Oh, that's rich. You think that makes you noble? Makes her decent? Fuck off! By the way, a reminder. Even though you think the world revolves around you, guess what? It doesn't.'

'You didn't exactly waste any time throwing your-self at the nearest available man. Joanne told me about your mid-life crisis escapade.'

'Escapade?' She dropped her voice. 'No, Brock. My stud was a goddamn game-changer. And he wasn't the nearest available man. I had to avoid many near-est available men. My beach god was well-endowed, young and flawless, who did things to me beyond a lifetime of your narrow imaginings. He showed me, Brock, what a man could be. As a result, I'll never be at risk of going back to a mediocre life like the one I lived with you'

Brock had turned a strange shade of grey-green. For the first time in her life, Lara had made Brock miser-able. Did he have penis-envy, she wondered? Was that what finally got to him? A waitress approached, but Lara looked at her so fiercely, she retreated.

'What do you want, Brock? Why are you imposing on me?'

'Well, thanks for the break in your selfish tirade. I came to tell you that things have changed.'

Lara remained silent.

'I'm re-evaluating my life. Jax understands that I need some time. I miss having you at home. I'm not sure I want to spend all my days with someone who is still attached to the idea of being a part-time lesbian.'

'That's something you should have checked out before you did the trade-in. Listen, Brock. I don't give a shit what you do with your life or your lesbian slash polyamorous slash bisexual lover. I deserve bet-ter. If you think I would ever consider being back with you while you try to figure out whether that person is worth it or not, you are out of your fucking tree.'

'If you'd stop with the appalling language for one

minute, I could finish telling you what I want to say. I miss you being there when I get home from work, folding the laundry. I miss the smell of your cooking, your comfortable body in my bed at night. It was exciting to try something new, you know that now as well as I do. But I've thought about what I want for the future and I miss what we had. Look, I'm going all out here. Come back, please, Lara. You can't have just stopped loving me after all this time.'

'What world do you live in, Brock? Folding laundry? Comfortable body? That's a winning appraisal. Listen to me properly, Brock, if it's the only time you ever do. I'm not going back with you, or to you. Once, I loved you, or an idea of you. But not anymore. I don't even like you. You were a bad habit. I've broken it. You never deserved me. I've come to understand that you walking out on me was the biggest favour you could have done for me.'

'You're just saying that.'

'No, I'm not. I mean it.'

'You'll regret it.'

'I couldn't. I already regret so many wasted years with you. Being without you is relative bliss.'

'You won't want to grow old alone.'

'I would rather grow old alone or with a three metre long python than with you. You might have considered those sentiments before embarking on your decade-long fuck-around.'

'I made a mistake,' he said. 'Millions of men make that mistake and their wives take them back.'

'I'm one in seven billion,' Lara said. 'And also no longer your wife and also, not taking you back.'

'You're heartless,' Brock said. He wiped sweat from his pink forehead, his eyes distant like they used to be,

172

not seeing her, not seeing anything beyond himself.

'No, I'm not. I was full of heart and you had your chance. Now you're out of my heart for good.'

He leaned back, sullen and perspiring. 'You'll be sorry one day when you look back,' he said. 'I came here all this way to lay my life on the line and ask for you to compromise and make a go of things. And this is what I get.'

'Yes, Brock. This is what you get. We both get something. I get my new self. And the more I see of her, the more I like her. No compromises. Anyway, I need to get out of here,' Lara said.

'Aren't you even going to order something?' he asked.

She pushed her chair out and stood up. 'No thanks,' she said. 'I don't need anything.'

Lara walked away from him without looking back.

22

At first Lara couldn't remember where she'd parked her car. She walked down the street, her mind as blank as a new whiteboard. She had to stop and relive the moments before she'd seen Brock to remember where she was and find her Yaris.

Waking early on Saturday morning, Lara decided that she needed movement, distance and space. She went for a drive.

Over the weekend, Lara put nine hundred kilometres on her car, travelling across New South Wales to places where the stars at night seemed close enough to hold, where the Milky Way splayed out across the heavens so thickly the stars looked like a misty cloud. She climbed a mountain alone and found flakes of pure gold in a stream nearby. When she slipped and fell into the mud, she emerged with three blood-sucking leeches stuck to her ankles through her socks. Her heart didn't skip a beat. She pulled them out of her skin and out of her socks, leaving bloody trails all over her legs. The encounter was no longer terrifying to someone who had no more shits to give. She re-found her centre and stopped feeling like she was standing on the edge of an abyss, primed to fall into it at any moment.

As she drove through miles of foreign territory, she realised Australia held her in its wild embrace. She leaned into it and knew that she'd never felt such a sense of belonging as she did here in a red Yaris, with an empty road stretching out in front of her.

When Lara arrived back at the practice late on Sunday night and finally crept into her bed, her body ached with tiredness. Her legs stung where the leeches had tried to suck the life out of her. She knew she would only be able to properly relax once she knew for certain that Brock had taken his sorry arse away for good. She needed to come up with a plan to ensure that.

★ ★ ★

On Monday morning the phone in the office rang.

'Hi Lara, it's Andrew.'

'Oh, hello. How nice to hear from you.'

Was her voice tremulous because she knew more than she was supposed to know about him? Or because his vocal presence had a mysterious magnetic impact on her circuitry?

'You and Valencia have been holding the fort, I hope?'

'Yes, we have.'

'Good, thank you very much. And your accommodation? How's that working for you?'

'It's perfect.'

'I wouldn't go that far.'

'I would. It's great.'

'Good, good. Look, would you mind taking care of a small matter? I'm in a rush right now, so could you call the Carremere Retirement Home and apologise to the diversional therapist, Debbie? She likes a bit of a longer chat if I call her. I was supposed to be there today and I didn't let her know in advance I'd still be away. Here's the number.'

'Consider it done,' Lara said, because it was.

175

'Cheers. See you soon, Lara,' he said, and hung up. She held the phone in a sweaty hand.

At eleven, Lara told Valencia about her date with the residents in Carremere and about going to visit to spend some time with old Mrs Roberts.

'Is good you go. They all get so lonely. Mrs Roberts, she now maybe ninety. She have a very sharp tongue,' Valencia said.

'Well, in my opinion, if you reach that age, you're allowed to have a bit of attitude.'

★ ★ ★

Lara arrived at a beautiful bushland setting. She drove up the long drive through dense foliage peppered with red and yellow flowers. Surely there could be worse things than growing old in a lovely place like this, she thought.

At reception a tired-looking woman with black hair and a smart blue and white dress greeted her. Lara got a whiff of something putrid in the air.

'Oh, you must be Lara. It's good of you to come,' she said. 'I'm Debbie.'

'The doctor sends his apologies,' Lara said. 'He's sorry he didn't let you know on time.'

'No worries. He's very busy, I know. But they just love visits and something different. They're playing games in the common room now and I did tell Mrs Roberts you were coming.'

'Is she okay with that?' Lara asked.

Debbie grinned. 'Well, since you asked. When I told her you were coming she said, "Who the hell is that?" Be warned, she doesn't mince her words.'

Lara laughed. 'That sounds promising.' She had an

extended moment of self-doubt. Here she was coming to visit her new employer's mother, when she didn't know her, or him really, and without him having any knowledge of it.

In the common room, ancient people sat around white tables playing scrabble, eating biscuits and drinking tea, or simply staring out into space.

'Nice piano,' Lara said.

'Do you play?'

'No.'

'It's a Steinway, donated by a resident who passed away. The doctor is quite a talent. You heard him?'

'No, can't say I have.'

The smell made her wrinkle her nose.

'Ah, here's Mrs Roberts. Dot. DOT! This is Lara. If you'd like to, she's here to take you for a stroll outside. Maybe you'd like a bit of fresh air?'

'What?'

In a wheelchair, sat a tiny woman with short white hair and dark eyes.

'THIS IS LARA,' Debbie said

'Chrissakes, I'm deaf not stupid! Back off, will you?' she said to Debbie. She turned her head. 'So you're Lara, are you?' she said. 'What can I do for you?'

'How are you today, Mrs Roberts?'

'Oh, Lord Jesus. Call me Dot and don't patronise me. I'm fine today, can't you tell?'

Well, Lara thought, they were off to a flying start.

'Apologies,' she said. 'Would you like to go outside?'

'Yes. Get me out of this urine-soaked prison.'

Lara grasped the handles of the wheelchair. Debbie threw her a look that was both thankful and apologetic and the two set off out into the expansive gardens.

'Lara, don't take me left at that fork over there. I

hate going past the pond. It's a goddamn mosqui-to-infested swamp.'

'Oh, of course,' Lara said. 'We can have a forest walk.'

'No, *we* can't. I'm not exactly on legs, am I?'

'No, you're not. So, I'll have the forest walk and you can enjoy the view.'

'What view? It's wild and overgrown. No one's tak-ing care of it. Forest walk, my tits. It's fit for crocodiles and belly-crawlers, not human beings' Dot muttered, shaking her head. 'Take me to the top of Everest. Now that's a view.'

'I agree. We can arrange that for some time in the future,' Lara said. She couldn't tell if Dot was amused or appalled.

'Look,' she said, as Lara wheeled her along a path that wound through eucalyptus trees and brushbox. 'You don't have to make polite conversation, Lara. I hate small talk. If you don't have anything intelligent to say, just walk me through this insipid vegetation. At least it doesn't stink to heaven.'

'I agree about the small talk,' Lara said. 'So I'll be real. That smell is terrible. This place looks really nice, but what was that revolting aroma I smelled when I walked in?'

Dot turned her head. Lara moved so they could look at each other.

'That, my dear, is the smell of piss. Lots of it. Every-one wets themselves here. It's old folks home smell. Get used to it.'

'Isn't there a way to get rid of it?'

'Aside from getting rid of the pissers themselves, no idea. You'd think there'd be a product for it, wouldn't you? So, distract me. Tell me about yourself and I don't mean superficial nonsense. You have a British accent, and you're volunteering your time. What's your story? And yes, keep pushing me. We can go through the forest to the end of the lawn over there and sit in the sun.'

'Hmm. Okay. I've just been tailed to Australia by my ex-husband who has been having several affairs over the past decade culminating in a final one with a woman who claimed for exotic reasons that she was lesbian. He left me, and then decided he wanted me back, telling me millions of men do this and their wives take them back all the time. I said no. That's my life up to the end of last week.'

'What a clod,' Dot said. 'You should have relieved him of his goolies.'

'It crossed my mind. I decided not to stoop that low.'

'Ha!' From the back, Lara sensed Dot was smiling. 'Yes, well,' Dot said. 'If you would have, you would have been well within your rights.'

'Thanks for that. So, how are you today, really?'

'Lousy. How would you feel? My legs don't work and I have to get help to take a crap and to pee. It's very undignified. My eyes are bothering me, and I can't hear a thing out of this ear. Apart from that, I'm fine. My mind is sharp and that's a perpetual suffering. You get the picture?'

'I do,' Lara said, walking her through large palm fronds and ferns. 'It sounds totally awful, Dot.'

'Youth is wasted on the young, they say, and it's true. You should live for the moment and enjoy the benefits. I can't advise that strongly enough. Have you had sex with anyone since he left you?'

Lara choked as she inhaled her own spit and then

179

cleared her throat. 'Uh, yes,' she said. 'Yes.'

'Good, good. That's the first thing to do. Break the bonds. Who was it?'

They had emerged from the forest and she pushed Dot across the lawn to a bench in the partial shade of a Jacaranda tree. Lara positioned the wheelchair so that sunlight shone onto Dot's lap and legs. Then she sat on the bench opposite her new friend and entwined her hands together.

'He was a tantric sex worker. I paid for sex. You know, like …'

'No, but it sounds interesting. Tell me more.'

'Like a male version of a prostitute as in, you pay for sexual favours, but also not like a prostitute in that the goal is sexual and emotional healing, not just having sex.'

'Oh. That's a good story.'

'It was a good story.' Lara smiled. Dot's eyes creased into amused wrinkles.

'Now that makes me less grumpy. I have no idea what a tantric sex worker does. Tell me the details.'

Lara told Dot everything. She talked about the massage, the sex in the cave and about Jean-Luc, and the photo shoot. She showed Dot the pics Jean-Luc had given her, scrolling through them on her small phone screen. When she'd finished, Dot's face was bright red.

'You too much in the sun?' Lara asked.

'No dear. I'm blushing for the first time in a few decades.' Dot chuckled. 'And it feels good.'

Lara laughed. 'I have his number if you want it.'

'Jesus Christ,' Dot said, turning a deeper shade of red. 'If I'da known this ten years ago, I might have given it a go. You're good for me,' she said. 'Don't go

180

away now and be a stranger.'

'I'd never dream of it,' Lara said. 'So what did you do, you know, when you were younger?'

'My life? Oh, it was one big surprise. No one thought I'd make it to adulthood. I wasn't supposed to live past my teens. You try growing up with everyone looking at you as if you're about to kick the bucket. Heart problems after rheumatic fever, they said. But whaddaya know? I kept defying the odds to spite them. I got up every morning and I'm going to keep doing it until I don't feel like it anymore.'

'Wow,' Lara said. 'What was your profession?'

'I would hope you might have been able to tell. I was a newspaper columnist. Political and social satire before anyone really knew what that was. Long ago. I'm so goddamn old I was an adult when I saw the Sydney opera house go up from scratch. I had my son late in life, after I'd had a successful career. I defied the odds on that account too. But, enough of all that. Remembering makes me tired. Any minute now, I'll be talking rubbish.' She waved her hand in the air, as if clearing it. 'You can take me back. It's time for a nap. But listen. Come again and tell me your stories. I'd like to hear more.'

Lara wheeled Dot inside. They paused at a table where a scrabble group had just begun a new game.

'Would you like to join them, Dot?' A carer sitting with the group turned to Dot as she went past.

'I'd sooner be a stuffed kangaroo,' Dot snapped. 'Lara can take me to my room.' They moved onwards. 'Look, over there, that's the lieutenant. His mind's pretty sharp, but a nasty stroke left him drooling. It's a pity. It's taken away his dignity, hasn't it Harold? Oh, and he's deaf too, so you can't be blamed for imagining he's a fool. But he's not.'

Harold didn't react as they trundled past.

At room forty-nine, which had a bed, a chair, a TV and a window that looked out over the lawn, they stopped.

'Come in,' Dot said. 'Help me get into my recliner, will you? I'll instruct.'

Lara followed instructions and ensured Dot was safely helped from the wheelchair into her chair.

'That'll do,' Dot said. 'Thank you for your help. Not as elegant as ballet on ice, but not bad. When will you be back?'

Lara did not hesitate. 'Next week if that works for you?'

'I'll check my calendar,' she said. 'I'm very busy and important.'

'Of course,' Lara said and smiled.

'Ah, I've just remembered. Nothing of note happening next week. Come whenever you're able.'

'Be back in seven days,' Lara said.

23

Saturday. Two days before the doctor's return.

Lara had imprinted the name of the resort where Brock was staying into a deep part of her brain. She wondered whether he was still there. She mused on the idea of revenge. She thought cinematically how her life might be made into a movie right now: the character, Lara Winters, walks calmly into a kitchen shop and purchases a simple knife, Charlotte Corday-style. Cut to a shot of her surprising her ex in the bath. Or: Lara Winters arrives at the resort, convinces him to come outside for a chat and then runs him through with her weapon.

No, Lara thought. She didn't want to see Brock come to any physical harm. She wanted him to come to emotional clarity, to maturity and even remorse, rapidly. She also wanted reassurance that he was the hell out of her new life. She could feel he was still around. The thought ruined the security of her hard-won Brock-free zone. Paradise had been infiltrated by a serpent.

Determined, she drove out of Byron towards the resort. She'd noticed it on the way to the nude beach, and while driving with Mario on the way to his cave. Images of Mario, of being with him, flickered through her mind. At least, she thought, she had slept with someone after Brock. She had been the object of a young man's desire, and although his words may have been nothing more than work-place patter, clichéd and over-used, his body had been gorgeous, and hers, for several hours. She held onto that thought as she pulled up outside the Blue Sails Resort.

She went through to reception.

'Hi,' she said, no kitchen knife in hand. 'I'm here to see Brock Sinclair. Is he still here?'

'Indeed he is, my dear. Room thirty-eight.' The receptionist barely looked at her. 'Shall I buzz him?'

Australians are so casual, she thought, about privacy.

'No need,' Lara said. 'I'll find him.' She walked through to an outdoor walkway, feeling something outrageous growing inside her. She followed the signs, found the numbers from thirty to sixty, and walked briskly to her destination. Outside the door, her heart hammered against her ribs, pumping all the blood away from her head, and into her feet. Even her toes tingled. She knocked. The distance she'd travelled since arriving in Australia could be measured in light years. Light years.

There was a pause. She heard footsteps and the door opened. A tall, slender woman, with blonde hair in a bob, a nose-ring in her left nostril, and wearing a revealing white top and a black and orange mini-skirt stood there. She looked at Lara with surprise. Baggage stood in the entrance. The destination on the tag read BNE.

'May I help you?' the sexy woman said, her voice low and husky. For a lightning second, Lara thought that she'd knocked at the wrong door. Then she recognised the face. Minus the nose-ring and mini and barely concealed model-body, behold the pseudo-lesbian assistant she'd encountered once at the office long before she knew what was going on.

'Is Brock here?'

The woman cast a slow, quizzical look over her shoulder. 'Brock, darling. There's someone at the door to see you. I'm very jet-lagged, but she does seem familiar.'

Brock darling.

Lara's thoughts tumbled over each other, like rocks falling in a slow-motion sequence down a hill.

The man who, until recently had been her husband, appeared barefoot on the white tiled floor, his hair wet from a swim or a shower, his nose sunburnt to traffic-light red, his garish shorts and unbuttoned shirt flapping in the breeze from the open door, his beer belly protruding.

'Lara. This is a surprise.'

'Lara?' said the lesbian, draping herself alongside him.

'Ahem. I'm sorry.' He cleared his throat. 'I should have introduced you. Lara, this is Jacqui. Jax, this is Lara, my um ...'

'Soon-to-be-ex-wife,' Lara said. 'The reason, I presumed, Brock came to Australia.'

'Right,' he said.

Lara stared at Jacqui's full, sultry lips.

These were the snakes in her basket.

'Hi,' Lara said.

A long uncomfortable silence ensued. Brock looked squeamish. His eyes darted to the door as if he wanted to escape. 'What can I, um, do for you, Lara?'

He sounded cold, foreign. She took a deep breath and turned to the woman who towered over her.

'Well, firstly, what, in fuck's name, are you doing in Australia, Jacqui-the-lesbian?'

Brock's face turned deep red.

Jacqui took it all in her stride and didn't miss a

beat. 'I was made an offer I couldn't refuse.'

'Oh really?'

'Truly,' she said. 'A first-class ticket and a week in a resort, and this man finally devoted to me? I thought, why not, didn't I, darling?'

'Brock couldn't manage for five minutes on his own,' Lara said, kicking off her flip flops and walking past them, inviting herself in, and taking a long, cool look around the glamorous, spacious, five star living area. 'One minute he's flown all the way across the world to grovel at my feet, and within days, he's got his two-timing floozy on her eager way over.' She plopped herself into a white couch and put her feet up on a glass table on which stood two glasses of mid-morning champagne and a half-empty bottle. Sand fell from her toes onto the table. Her heels left smudges beneath them. Champagne! Now there was a nice idea.

Brock's face was an image of horror and embarrassment. Lara leaned forward, reached over and took one of the glasses. Swirling the bubbly around like a professional taster, she brought the glass to her lips and took a sip. 'Mmm. Excellent. Now, Jacqui. A word of advice. You'd be better off going back to your girlfriends. Brock will move on to more exciting pastures in due course, so you may be wasting your time. I'm guessing that the only attractive thing you found about him was the fact that he was married to me. It's always exciting, tasting forbidden fruit.'

The next sip she took was a large one and it burned all the way down into her stomach. 'But now, I'm not in the picture anymore, so ...' She took another long sip of champagne. 'The excitement's worn off and he's not that attractive anymore, is he? What is nice about him though, is that he has a fat bank account, which you're obviously already benefitting from.' Lara made a sweeping gesture to indicate the luxurious accommodation. 'But as I already own half of everything and he's not about to write you into his will, he'll be using you for as long as you'll let him.'

When Brock found his voice, it was cold and cruel. 'You're ruining my holiday. Get out of my apartment.'

'Ah,' Lara smiled. '*Your* holiday? I'm staying right here until the two of you pack your bags, and get the fuck out of *my* holiday.' She took another sip of champagne emptying the glass. She refilled it.

'You're drunk,' Brock said, coming over to her. He tried to take the glass from Lara's hand.

'Not as drunk as I could get,' she said, holding the glass away from him, while reaching for the other glass with her other hand. The only way he was going to get anything from her was by wrestling her for it. He wasn't going there.

Lara took the second glass of champagne and skulled it.

Brock said, 'you're crazy.'

Lara said, 'No, this is a sane person's response to insane behavior.'

'I have no idea who you are. I've never seen you like this.'

'Brilliant,' Lara said. 'The new me.'

'Maybe I'll let you two do some talking alone,' Jacqui offered, her lips drawn into a straight and uptight line.

'Oh, please don't go,' Lara said. 'I want you to hear every bloody word I say.'

The more unsettled Brock and Jacqui became, the

gutsier she became. The alcohol had made her bold. 'You deserve each other, you two, but you need to know a few things. Jacqui. God, it must feel awful to come out here knowing you're his second choice. But now you're here, you might as well know that Brock is a classic male chauvinist pig. Women for him are either kitchen and laundry personnel, or sex personnel. For a while there, he thought he had both. But alas, all good things come to an end. I resigned from kitchen, laundry and sex duty. It's sad but true, and you may not know this, but he said he really misses having a wife, and if you don't want to play the domestic kitchen-laundry-sex duty role, he is likely to find someone who will. And you, Brock of the middle-aged, flaccid-penis-without-Viagra, this is my place. My hemisphere. Byron Bay isn't yours, it's mine. So, fuck off out of it, both of you.' Lara dropped both empty champagne glasses on the tiled floor where they shattered into millions of slender shards.

Brock's face went from florid to pale.

Lara wiped her hands on her thighs, and walked past her ex and his lover, out of the door.

She got into her car, rolled down the window and put her head on the wheel. This was not the time to drive, she decided, overcome with exhaustion and elation after doing such battle with the past. Everything she wanted to say had been said. There was nothing left festering inside her, no residue, no lingering sense of injustice. She needed to just catch her breath. The champagne had also begun to have its effect. She closed her eyes.

★ ★ ★

188

Lara had no idea how much time had gone by, before she became aware of voices, and then a cold cloth on her forehead. Someone was shaking her arm, speaking too loudly into her ear. 'Lara? Lara, darl, wake up. It's nearly evening! I don't want to have to call the ambos but you're scaring me.'

'What?'

'You okay, darl? Thank God!'

Ruby's familiar face loomed large.

Lara sat up. 'Ruby? Where am I? Why are you here? Shit, my head hurts.'

'Here, sip this.'

Lara's head felt it was the size of a watermelon. She leaned back in her seat.

'Darl, it's five pm, and you're at the Blue Sails Resort. Reception found my number in your bag. They were afraid you were some homeless person moving into their car park. You do look a bit ragged. Ruby nodded. 'I wasn't sure you wanted to see me but they said they didn't know who to call. I thought, what the hell, you're gonna need someone, so I came over.'

Lara reached out and hugged Ruby's round shoulders. 'I've been awful,' she said. 'I'm sorry. Thank you.'

'Nah, darl,' Ruby said. 'It was pretty ordinary … ya know … what happened … I'm sorry. That was not nice at all. And after you came to bring me flowers and chocolate … what a cow I've been.'

'Forget it,' Lara said. 'Do you know why I'm here?'

'I think I might.'

Lara filled Ruby in.

'I'm pleased to tell you that I saw them leaving,' Ruby said.

'Really?'

'Yes, they were checking out as I arrived. Tall blonde,

middle-aged beer-belly with one-way goggles? Nice British accents?'

'Yes.'

'Your ex and his appendage have fled.'

'Really? Brock and his Succubus are gone?'

'Yep. Not a trace of 'em left behind. We can go and make sure if you like.'

Lara sat up. 'No. I think it's all good. And I'm feeling better already,' she said.

'You can go back home to wherever you're living or you can come back to my place. I can make you dinner and we can talk about it all. Either way, I think it's time to not overstay the welcome at the resort.'

Lara took a deep breath and looked at Ruby's lined and kindly face.

'Your place please. Can't imagine anything I'd like more, Ruby.'

24

Lara left her car in Byron and let Ruby drive her back to the house where she hadn't been for what felt like a lifetime. Ruby looked happy. She was uncharacteristically wearing pink shorts and a floral shirt. Her hair was unkempt but her face looked less ruddy, less ravaged.

'Excuse me for saying this,' Ruby said as she pulled into her drive, 'but fuck a fucking duck. I thought you'd vanished off the face of the earth. It's a miracle to see you again, in however decrepit a state. I am so happy!'

Ruby reached over and clasped Lara to her ample bosom in a suffocating hug. 'WELCOME back!'

'Thanks Ruby,' Lara said. Tears of gratitude welled.

'I don't have tissues in the car, so if you're going to leak body fluids, darl, let's go inside, where I have all the necessary supplies.'

Lara walked with Ruby across the lawn to the familiar house where the kitchen light shed its golden glow across the twilight backyard. Her previous abode, high in the trees, stood empty.

'Come in and sit down. Before you say anything, let me make some tea.'

Ruby's house seemed warmer, more comfortable, like home. They chatted about small things while Ruby made tea and pulled out crackers and cheese and Byron Bay cookies.

'Darl,' Ruby said, 'when you left I cried as if I'd lost the love of my life. I saw the flowers and the choco-

191

lates and I realised what had happened. I wanted to run after you. Hon, I would have traded in a thousand Marios for you.'

'Ruby, I'm over it. It's fine, really, I promise.'

Tea-cups in hand, the two women sat on the couch.

'Darl, though, I'm sorry. What a fuck-up.'

'You did nothing wrong, Ruby. Both you and Mario were entirely within your rights. It was me. I was carrying a lot of baggage and you guys gave me a perfect canvas. I transferred all my betrayal wounds and projected them onto you two. I mean, Rubes, he's a sex worker and you're my friend. What was my line of thought?'

'Dunno. I should've talked to you before I hired Mario. I would have done otherwise if I'da known what would happen. I can live without Mario, but I didn't want to lose you.'

Lara could hear the shower upstairs and pointed to the ceiling.

'What, or who's that?'

'That? Ah. Yes, that. I'll show you in a moment.'

'You got company, hon?' the male voice wasn't very deep, or very familiar, but when he poked his head over the stairway banisters and Lara looked up into his eyes, she knew him. His face was burned into her memory. Mr Long Schlong himself. She turned to Ruby and whispered, 'The nude beach dude?'

'Nigel darling, this is Lara, a dear old friend. You may have met before?'

'I don't think so, hon. Nice to meet ya, Lara. I'll be down in a sec.'

'You think he doesn't remember me? How did this happen?'

Ruby smiled. 'A short story.'

'I thought he was a predator,' Lara whispered. Ruby laughed.

'No, darl, just lonely.'

'How did you end up together?'

'Believe this or not. I actually went and got him off the nudie beach. Not a bad move.'

'You went into the shadows where all those guys were hanging out?'

'Well I lay around sunning my arse for a good while. Then I went on a treasure hunt.'

'Plucky!'

'Sure. But darl, you know me, I wasn't too forward. The gay guys weren't worried, and I asked Nigel if he'd step into the sunshine with me. When we got out from the shadows, I made him a proposition: meet me for a cuppa with clothes on. He agreed.'

Nigel came down the stairs. His long straggly hair had been cut short and combed back. His skinny body didn't look too bad in stonewashed jeans and a faded denim shirt.

'So, you're Lara?' he stretched out his hand and she took it, and shook it.

'Good to meet you,' she said. If he was pretending they'd never met, he was making an excellent job of it.

Nigel went to the kitchen. He pulled out pots and banged around, and then went out into the garden.

'He's one helluva cook,' Ruby said. 'Puts me to shame. Now. There's something we need to do.'

'What?'

Ruby got up and went into the kitchen. She returned with a familiar-looking box of chocolates.

'I saved these,' she said. 'I thought, even if I keep these suckers for twenty years, I'm only gonna eat them if I get to eat them with you. You think they'll be alright?'

'Oh Ruby, I don't give a shit if they're stale. I'll only go home once we've finished the box. They'll help my headache.'

'You sure?'

Ruby hurried over, tore the box open and placed it in front of Lara, taking one and popping it into her mouth. 'Heavenly,' she said. 'Here, have one. Or three.' Lara took one. She looked at the box, her gift. Sure, it carried a memory of pain, but as the sweetness melted on her tongue, her headache and any echo of past pain, receded.

'Bloody delicious,' she said to Ruby. 'I have good taste in chocolates.'

'You do, darl. They're almost as good as the sex I've been having with the beloved owner of the longest schlong I've ever had.' Her eyes twinkled. 'And he knows what to do with it, even if it's not the youngest one on the block. Experience can trump youth.'

'It's that good, is it?' Lara whispered.

'Darl, you should hear the angels sing.'

25

Doctor Andrew Roberts was due back in the late afternoon. The entire day, Valencia bustled about cleaning and organising. Lara had long since sorted all the mail. After her volcanic eruption at Brock, after tea and chocolates with Ruby, a chapter in her life was resolved.

Brock was gone. Her fickle-hearted ex and his attached leech would make a good pair, she thought. They were a much better fit than Brock and she ever were — narcissistic opportunistic egotists who matched each other perfectly. Why hadn't she seen that before? As a result of Lara's confrontation with Brock and Jacqui, Ruby had come back into her life. This, Lara thought, was an unexpected blessing. Mario was probably at work somewhere, doing what he did best, and good for him, she thought.

Lara felt reborn, remade. All she had to contend with now was a touch of anxiety about how she would feel and act when the doctor finally returned to his home and saw that she knew more about the details of his life than she was supposed to.

* * *

An indigo storm came rumbling in from the sea. The first drops of rain hit her as she walked to her cottage from the house. The air smelt like ozone. Lightning flickered overhead. Lara now figured that nothing could have hastened her process of coming to terms with Brock's betrayal. The timing had been right. The eruption had happened at the perfect moment. She felt free to be who she really was, and that included having a foul mouth and foul thoughts when necessary.

As she boiled the kettle for a cup of tea and listened to the pouring tropical rain drumming on the roof, she noted that every last smidgeon of green and yellow jealousy in her had evaporated. Taking courage and daring from the glasses of bubbles and saying everything that had been festering in her heart to Jacqui and Brock, had dissolved it.

Outside, pandanus leaves bowed and dripped. The storm passed and birds began to sing. Poor, Ruby, she thought. She'd had to wear Lara's displaced angst for too long. But that heavy stuff was gone too now. Lara imagined it all being, washed clean down the hillside in the rivers of iron-oxide-red mud that made tiny trails through the trees, on their way to the creek at the bottom of the doctor's property.

From her kitchenette Lara could see the end of the drive. A blue Toyota hybrid made its way up to the main house at exactly 4.00 pm. Lara approved of her employer's taste in cars and wondered whether she should go down and say hello right away or whether he might want some peace.

She felt nervous about seeing Andrew again. Probably just her guilt, she thought. Also, he was good looking and had inspired illicit thoughts while he examined her. Would he have the same effect on her sans fever and post-Mario?

Forty-five minutes later she ran a comb through her wild hair, and slipped on rubber flip-flops. She walked down the sodden pathway to the main house.

Her heart beat a bit too fast and her feet were muddy. When she reached the main house, she had to stop outside, breathe deeply, and rinse her feet under the outside tap. Because of the stormy sky, lights were already on inside. She went as noisily as possible up the stairs to the front door. Lara had not been up there before as it was above the practice. She rang the bell. She waited for five minutes, growing uncomfortable. She rang the bell one more time and waited. Still, there was no answer. Either the doc was busy, or, he didn't want to be disturbed. Lara didn't want to be disturbing.

She turned and ran down the stairs and just as she was about to start up the pathway, the door above the offices banged open and he stood there, framed by the light behind. He was wearing blue shorts and a white t-shirt and he was barefoot. She stood in her cutoff denim shorts and loose pink shirt, feeling awkward. They'd only encountered each other dressed formally as doctor and patient, and now that relationship had changed. She waved.

'Hi Andrew. Welcome home.'

'Hello, Lara. Sorry. I was in the shower. Are you on your way out, or would you like to come up here again?'

'Sure, I'll make the trip again,' she said, and turned back.

Andrew hadn't shaved, and though his eyes looked tired, he was bloody handsome, she thought.

'How's everything going?' he asked.

'Oh, it's lovely, thank you. How was your time on the west coast?'

'Busy-busy. I'm tired. Thanks for taking this all on. I couldn't have done it without you.'

Lara smiled. 'My pleasure.'

His eyes were kind, but guarded. Lara wanted to apologise right away for opening too much of his mail, for stumbling on his private life, but she was too anxious to say a word.

'I, um managed to get through all the mail and sort it for you to look through.'

'Good,' he said. 'Thank you for making the appointments for the rest of the month. It's looking a little busier than usual.'

'I'm trusting that's a good thing?'

'Yes. I suppose it is,' he said. 'Well, Lara, I'd love to stay and chat, but I haven't slept more than four hours in four days, so I'm heading off to relax. Thanks for stopping by. I'm very glad to have you here.'

'My pleasure,' she said.

'Right. If you're here at about ten, we can talk logistics.'

'Good idea,' she said. 'See you then.'

★   ★   ★

That evening, alone in her mountainside home, Lara felt wistful. It was clear as day to her now. She was a woman in the middle of her life, alone in the world, single, loved but no longer needed by her children, and free to do whatever she wanted to do. Somehow this didn't seem as exciting as it had sounded when she first said it to herself.

She had a distinct sense that the doctor needed his space. She had felt his capacity to be kind yet distant. Perhaps, she thought, she should stop letting her thoughts linger at all on his handsome jawline and capable hands.

She couldn't sleep that night. Koalas grunted in the trees. Rain fell periodically and wind whipped through the forests. She fell asleep to the sound of the dawn kookaburra chorus.

When she finally opened her eyes and looked at her watch, it was already nine-thirty. The doctor wanted to see her at ten. The sky had been washed clean by the rain and a single wallaby lay quietly in the shade of a gum tree.

She got out of bed, and stumbled to the shower. It was also her day to visit the old people, and take Dot on a walkabout during which she would no doubt fill Lara's ears with hard-hitting and acrid commentary on the state of the world and its woeful inhabitants. During her walk Lara would share anything that might make Dot grin or better yet, blush.

She put on a blue and white sundress and went to the trouble, rare these days, of adding a touch of mascara and eye-liner, aware that she was nervous about being in the presence of the doctor. Her hair hung in damp ringlets over her shoulders. It was obvious, she thought, looking in the mirror, that she hadn't been awake very long. The bags under her eyes reminded her that skin at forty-four did very different things after a bad night, than skin at twenty. She hadn't felt self-conscious in this way for a while, and she didn't relish the feeling.

At one minute past ten, Lara slipped on her sandals, and opened the door to reception. Andrew Roberts sat at the desk. His glasses were on and he was focused on his computer screen.

'Hello,' he said absentmindedly, glancing over the rim of his glasses. 'I'll be with you in a minute.'

He finished, took off his glasses, and leaned back in

the chair. The vase of beautiful flowers Lara had left on the counter was gone.

'I'll get another chair from my office.' He stood up. 'Why don't you take this seat,' he said.

She walked over and sat down. He rolled another chair in and sat opposite her, on the patient-side of the counter. She couldn't help but notice the way his silver watch-strap caught the light, the careful way his white shirt sleeve cuffs were folded back and the way his pressed pants creased at the knees as he bent forward.

'You managed to sort through all the mail,' he said. 'That was quite a bit of work.'

Her mouth went dry. 'Yes. I hope it's what you wanted.'

'Partly,' he said. 'I did email Valencia quite explicitly about sorting, and not opening any of it. That's obviously *my* job.'

'Yes.' Why on earth had she even done it? What kind of ludicrous momentum had possessed her to open a stranger's mail? She'd feared this moment, and couldn't put it off any longer. 'I heard from her after I'd opened a few letters which were not clearly marked. I learned too late that this was your preference.'

'Yes, I noticed,' he said, looking at her directly. She stared back at him. 'Did you not consider, perhaps, the issue of my privacy?'

He had clearly inherited a certain quality of acid straight-talking from his mother. Lara had only had one training session in managing it thus far. She straightened her spine.

'Andrew. I'm terribly sorry. I had no idea what I was doing when I arrived. I simply wanted to get everything organised and sorted out as efficiently as possible. When I opened the letters, I realised that ...' She shrugged, lost for words for a moment, but did not take her eyes off him. 'I realised that I had stumbled onto something I had no right, and in fact, no desire to know. Will you please accept my sincere apology?'

His jaw was tense, and his face was not unkind, but distant.

'I have to be able to trust anyone I employ,' he said. 'I do see, but this makes it awkward for me now. Can you can understand?'

'Of course,' she said. 'I'm sorry. I was unaware of ...'

'I accept your apology. Please take into consideration that anything you've read is confidential and that I've no wish to talk to you or anyone about any of it, now or ever.'

'Yes. Yes of course.'

Lara had seen cats poised on the brink of pouncing, every muscle taut, focused. Andrew Roberts, at that moment, resembled such a creature. He then leaned back in his chair, picked up a pen, slid a piece of paper out in front of them and began to click the back of the pen. 'I was thinking of the equivalent of two hundred a week, in terms of rent,' he said. 'If that sounds reasonable to you?'

'Oh, yes. That's reasonable. Is it enough?'

'Of course. It's not a place I intended to use to generate any income. I rented it out once and decided it wasn't a good decision.'

'Right. Well, I promise to take good care of the place while I'm here,' she said.

'That was going to be my next question. When you

201

came here sick, you said you were on holiday. Has anything changed in that regard? I'm not saying that I won't employ you, but the arrangement as we discussed may have to remain informal.'

His eyes were blue. The left one had brown flecks in it, making it appear to sparkle every time he blinked.

'Nothing's changed,' she said. 'But if you found someone more suitable with an actual proper work visa or better still, a local, I'll move on. I'm here to help. My visitor's visa will expire at the end of next month.'

'Well,' he said, and slid his fingers up and down the pen. 'I've been looking for someone and no suitable applicants have appeared. If you're available, and able, I'll be happy to deduct rent as well as pay you some cash as a form of donation for your volunteering. I'll confirm the cash component with you later.'

'That's fine,' she said. 'I'll be in the office first thing tomorrow morning. I think you have Ms McWilliam first, and then a Mrs Jenny White.' She stood. 'Well, I'd best be going, if that's okay. Have a lovely day, doc,' she said.

'Likewise,' he said. 'It's going to be busy tomorrow.'

'Of course. I'll see you then.'

Lara was shaking as she stood up. She hurried from his presence, which was making her feel like she was sliding downhill on a slope covered in black ice. Also, she did not want to be late for her appointment with the mother of the doctor, the original qualified tongue-lasher. Lara would have, under normal circumstances, told him outright that she was off to visit his aging parent, but she'd already invaded his personal space to his chagrin, and she feared that revealing this small fact now might annoy him more.

Sooner or later Lara would have to find a way to explain herself. But not right bloody now.

She had to remember to ask Valencia what she'd done with the vase of flowers.

★ ★ ★

'Oh, you look lovely,' Debbie said when Lara arrived at the front office at Carremere. 'I'm so glad to see you,' she said. 'Mrs Roberts has been foul tempered this past week, probably missing her son. He'll be here in the late afternoon, I hope, to play the piano. The lieutenant had to be taken into frail care, I'm afraid. He has an infection and had trouble breathing. I'm sure they'd both love a little extra attention.'

'I'll be sure to pay the lieutenant a visit after I see Dot,' she said.

Debbie, though she ran around like a thirty-year-old, looked haggard and tired today, and Lara could see grey along her side-parting where the dark brown hair dye had grown out.

'Thank you,' Debbie said. 'This way.'

They went into the community room. Lara wasn't sure whether anyone remembered her, but she made a point of saying hello to each of the residents.

Dot was sitting in her wheelchair with her back to Lara, staring out into space. Lara said her name loudly before she appeared in front of her.

'With all the trouble in the world, how do you manage to look so cheerful?'

'Hello, Dot. It's lovely to see you too.'

'Indeed. And Lara my dear, where on earth did you get those ridiculous clothes? Off a dead fairy?'

'Of course,' she said and smiled, taking both Dot's

hands. 'I won't ask you how you are, because I can see you're miserable. Would you like me to take you for a walk through an insipid green forest, by-passing the mosquito-infested swamp, on a pointless twenty-minute journey back to where we started?'

'Yes. I'm glad to hear you talking some sense,' Dot said. Her face was grey and sombre, her lips dry, her hair thin and wispy. 'Let's get going,' she said. 'What's the delay?'

Lara went behind Dot and pushed her wheelchair.

'They fine people for speeding on those pathways,' Dot warned.

'I know,' Lara said. 'You warned me last time. I promise to keep myself in check. There'll be no speeding.'

'His majesty's gone to Never-Never-Land.'

'Meaning?' Lara said, nudging the wheelchair onto the pathway.

'The lieutenant. He's gone to the place from which no man, or woman for that matter, returns. They call it Frail Care. It's the last exit to Brooklyn.'

'Debbie told me.'

'Hmph,' was all Dot said.

'Your son got back from his travels yesterday. He seemed tired. I should mention. He makes me nervous.'

'Hmph,' again.

'Also, this week, I chased my ex-husband and his apparently-lesbian lover out of the country,' Lara said.

'Tell me that story. Did you hound him with a machete? A shotgun?' Dot brightened.

'No. Two glasses of champagne. They thought I was utterly insane. They left in mortal terror of being followed everywhere by me.'

'You must have been magnificent,' she said. A satisfied snigger escaped her lips.

'I was,' Lara confessed.

'Excellent,' Dot said. 'But tell me. I don't understand. Why would he want a woman who wants other women? What's the attraction?' she asked.

'Because he's a cliché,' Lara said. 'Her fancying other women doesn't threaten his masculinity.'

'I hadn't thought of it that way,' Dot said.

They made their way further own the pathway.

'Anyway,' Lara said. 'I'm happily not part of the tribe that goes through the usually female agonies that are unnoticed and unappreciated. You know, the upper-lip-bleaching, leg-waxing, eyebrow-plucking, bikini-waxing tribe – the constant bloody battle with nature that starts when you're thirteen. I've narrowed that stuff down to only the aerodynamically enhancing essentials like the occasional leg wax.'

'And the essentials will be completely unnecessary when you're ninety. I'm pleased to tell you, that by that time you won't give a rat's ass whether you have a beard, a moustache, or both, because you're just trying to stop dribbling and wetting your pants … it's all priorities, isn't it?'

'Yes, I suppose.' Lara said, seeing things from Dot's perspective. 'So, Dot, where do we get the idea of "happily-ever-after?" And why do we swallow it so thoroughly?'

'We generate it because the human race is essentially weak and pathetic and altogether fearful of reality,' Dot said. 'Slow down, will you? I'm losing my false teeth!'

'Oops, sorry!'

'That's why I wrote. I was the self-appointed

bullshit-detector of my generation.'

'I'm sure lots of people were grateful for your words.'

'Oh, bollocks. They were nothing of the sort. I had so much hate mail I could have wallpapered my house with it. People don't like being told the truth. Or hadn't you noticed?'

'Dot, can I ask you something?'

'For God's sake Lara, you don't have to ask me if you can ask me something.'

'No, of course. I haven't told Andrew that I know you, and I'm afraid that if I tell him, he might think I've overstepped boundaries, muscled into territory that I have no right being in.'

'This is why he makes you nervous? Get over yourself,' Dot said gruffly. 'You're too sensitive. Anyway, it's none of his business whether you come here or not. I'll tell you straight if you ever make it onto my shit-list. Right now, it's long enough and you aren't on it.'

'Well that's good news,' Lara said.

'Don't take me inside yet,' she said. 'Let's walk another lap.'

'You mean, I walk another lap.'

'Now you're talking,' she said. 'Tell me more about the world outside this confounded twilight zone. You need to find a good someone and get on with things after your husband did the dirty on you.'

On the next lap, as she put it, Lara told her again about Mario, and at Dot's request added the gory details about what happened with Ruby and Mario, about what she heard and did after finding the two of them upstairs in Ruby's house.

'Well, my, my, you got the short end of his stick.'

'Dick?'

'What?'

'I got the short end of his dick?'

Then Lara heard an extraordinary sound. It wasn't a cough, and it didn't quite make it into the category of laughter, but Dot Roberts was capable of mirth. It warmed Lara's heart as Dot emitted a sound not unlike a cackling kookaburra.

'Time to go back now,' she said, wheezing and taking a few moments to recover. 'One crisis per day is quite enough.'

'Crisis?'

'Every event is a crisis at my age. Laughing included.'

When she brought Dot inside, she wanted to go straight to her room. 'All that fresh air did my head in,' she said. 'Time for a nap.'

At that moment Debbie appeared. 'She's taking me to my room,' Dot said and pointed ahead of her. 'That way.'

'No lunch?' Debbie asked her.

'The hell with eating,' Dot said. 'It'll be one less crap I have to take, won't it? One day I'll give it up altogether.'

'If you need a snack, just ask,' Debbie said.

Lara smiled at Debbie as she pushed Dot in the direction of her pointed finger.

'The trouble with that woman,' Dot grumbled. 'Is that for all her sweetness and light, she can't help talking to us like we're imbeciles, or children, or an unfortunate combination of both.'

'I know,' Lara said. 'But her intentions are kind and well-meaning.'

'Yes, yes. The road to hell is paved with her sort.'

Lara helped Dot into her room, out of her wheelchair and into her bed. This time the effort made

207

beads of sweat roll down her temples.

'Bet you never expected this bag o' bones to be such a dead weight,' Dot said.

'It's good exercise,' Lara said. 'Can I get you anything before I go?'

'No. Will you be here again next Tuesday?'

'Yes, of course.'

A framed black and white photograph of a mother and toddler stood on Dot's dresser next to her bed. The mother had smooth skin, a firm jaw and her hair was swept into an attractive bun. In her arms she held a laughing, pale-haired boy whose chubby hands clasped hers. Both of them were smiling at someone to the side of the camera.

'That's Andrew,' Dot said. 'And me. His uncle took it. We're looking at Andrew's father, who's being a silly bugger. When I die, my ghost is going to look like that. It was a time in my life when I was most happy.'

'He's adorable,' Lara said, looking into the laughing eyes of the little boy.

'Yes, now get going before I lose the desire to nap. And don't forget to visit the major.'

'The major?'

'Oh, you know who I mean. The lieutenant.'

'I'm on my way.' She bent over quickly, and kissed Dot on the cheek. Before Dot could reprimand her, she slipped out of her room.

★   ★   ★

Frail Care was like a hospital ward. The lieutenant lay half-sleeping on his bed, hooked up to a drip. She sat down on a chair next to him and took his hand. Icy cold. 'Good day, sir,' she said. 'I don't know if you remember me? I'm Lara.'

His eyes opened. He stared at the ceiling.

'I had a lovely day, that day I came here.' She patted his hand. 'I believe you fought in two world wars.'

There was an almost undetectable pressure on her hand.

'That makes you quite something, I'd say. And quite a hit with the ladies.'

She held his hand between both of hers to warm it. 'Dot seems to have her wicked eye on you. Her tongue's pretty sharp though. Anyway, I know she would have come here herself if she could have, but you know Dot and her priorities. She's taking a nap instead.'

Lara could see he was ill. She stayed, watching his face, listening to his laboured breathing. 'Anyway, it looks like you need a bit of peace and quiet, but I'll be back next week to say hello and see how you're doing.' She got up, leaned over and kissed his forehead, still holding his hand in hers. This time, the pressure on her hand was stronger, his fingers trembling with the effort. He was still here, and she knew it, and he knew she knew it. She held on for a moment longer, and when his fingers loosened their hold on hers, she tucked his blankets around him, and left the room.

Lara saw Debbie on her way out. 'He's not too good, is he,' she said.

Lara shook her head. Her throat felt tight. 'He's still here, though,' she said. 'He knows everything.'

'I know,' she said. 'Don't worry. He'll be looked after. This is the nature of this place.'

'I'll be back next week.'

'That's good of you,' Debbie said. 'We'll look forward to it.'

'Just don't tell Doctor Andrew Roberts, if you don't mind.'

'Tell him? About what?'

'He has no idea I've come here to visit his mother. I don't think he'd approve. I'm an employee. Not family. Dot is in agreement with me for now.'

'No worries,' Debbie said. 'As long as it's what Dot wants. No need for anyone to know.'

'Right,' she said. 'See you.'

When Lara climbed back into her car she felt as though she'd travelled to another dimension. She was back in life after being halfway to Neverland. Carremere was, as Dot put it, a twilight zone. Lara found herself thinking about the lieutenant. Don't let him suffer, she thought.

★   ★   ★

Valencia was standing outside in the garden, beating a small rug with the back of a carpet brush when Lara arrived home. Lara had shopped and arrived with four bags of groceries. When Valencia saw her hoisting them out of the car, she hurried towards her.

'I'll give you a hand,' she said.

'That's all right, I can manage, really.'

'No, no,' she insisted, taking two of them. 'Good for me. How you find Mrs Roberts?'

'She's all right,' Lara said. 'She had a good laugh today.'

'You very good Lara.'

'I'm not really. Also the doc doesn't know and I'd like for this to stay our secret if that's okay.' It was getting to be demanding, all this secret-keeping for no understandably good reason.

'Yes, okay,' Valencia said. They squelched through the mud up to the veranda. 'Is going to be a big storm today. Later.'

'I saw the clouds on my way home.'

Lara opened the front door and Valencia stepped inside. 'You make it so nice in here,' Valencia said. 'Chase away the ghosts.'

'Really?'

'All the bad feeling is gone. I like your flowers. You need a proper vase,' Valencia said. 'I get you one.'

'Thanks. Oh, and I wanted to ask you. Do you know what happened to the vase of flowers I put on the reception desk?'

'Gone,' she said, obliterating everything in front of her with her hands.

'Who took them?'

'Doctor Andrew, he ask me to take them away.'

'He doesn't like flowers?'

'No, no. I think he like flowers. The problem. They remind him. So I no put flowers anywhere. The funeral, you see. People send too many flowers.'

Lara stared at her in silence. 'I see. I didn't know.'

'Yes,' she shrugged. 'That's why I no tell you. I think, maybe he change. Maybe some colour is good. But no. I put them in my bedroom,' she said. 'They smell very sweet.'

'Right-oh,' Lara said. 'Well, I'll make sure not to indulge my desire for such things in future. I suppose he wants everything just the way it is,' she said.

Valencia nodded. 'Just the way it is,' she said.

'Thanks for your help, Valencia. You're a dear.'

'I go finish my jobs now, Lara. See you later.'

Lara stared after her. Valencia had one of the

warmest, kindest hearts of any human being she'd yet encountered. Lara couldn't understand what she'd done to deserve such generosity from her.

That night, Lara woke up with a fright. A loud crack of thunder above the house rang in her ears, followed by a brilliant flash of lightning. The heavens opened, and the next minute, she heard a roar unlike anything she'd ever heard before. The volume of rain sounded like it would take the entire studio cottage down the hill and into the river. Her body felt on edge. The deafening clatter of rain on the roof continued until dawn.

26

By morning the sheets of rain swept down over the mountainside. They were like white curtains, or ghosts, drifting in arcs over the trees and grass and hills. Lara couldn't see further than her front steps. She did have an umbrella. If anyone had said that she would find it a challenge to get two hundred feet from her residence to her place of work, she would have imagined she'd had to have broken a limb, or worse. How on earth was she going to make it down the river that the pathway had become, to the office?

Andrew had said it would be a busy day. She wasn't so sure. She anticipated a few cancellations.

The only way Lara could get down to the office in an appropriate way, was by dressing her top half smartly, (muslin shirt, necklace, silver watch) and folding her clean white cotton slacks small and wrapping them in a plastic bag. She hoped he wouldn't be there yet. Every minute spent away from him allowed his presence to swell in her imagination until the thought of encountering him turned her legs to jelly. She feared disappointing him.

Lara wrapped her shoes in a separate bag, and then set out barefoot, in shorts, with the umbrella clutched in her right hand.

Thunder still rumbled overhead. Sodden indigo clouds sat low to the ground and the rain fell straight down. Earlier, it was blown sideways by the wind and Lara wouldn't have made it to the office without getting soaked. She would never have imagined a job that came with this kind of stress. She walked blindly, taking tiny steps to avoid falling. A red river of mud ran all the way to the office. Her feet were completely red when she reached the parking area, and mud had splattered up her legs. She resolved this by sticking her legs out from under the shelter of the umbrella. The rain was as intense as a shower, and it did the job.

The office looked quiet. She could sneak in, change in the toilet and be there, ready to start at 9.00 am, but when she opened the door, the light in Andrew's consulting room was on. She could hear him washing his hands.

'Good morning,' Lara said cheerfully, and closed the umbrella.

'Lara,' he said, appearing in the doorway, drying his hands with a paper towel.

'Be just a minute,' she said and hurried past the reception desk with her clothes clutched to her chest, closing the toilet door behind her. His eyes following her and she knew he'd seen her ridiculous attire.

When she reappeared, she was properly dressed. She bundled her shorts into the plastic bag and put it out of sight in the storeroom behind the two now-empty cardboard boxes.

'You all right?' Andrew looked amused. Her heart faltered. She'd expected annoyance, coolness, not indulgent humour. His light khaki trousers were smooth pressed and his white collared shirt was open at the neck. His blue and brown flecked eyes sparkled.

'Oh, fine, fine. I, uh, just had to make it down the river of mud and didn't have a boat.'

'There's a pathway round the other side,' he said. 'It takes a little longer and it's a little overgrown but it's actually paved. I thought Valencia would have shown

214

you.'

'No, she didn't. I'll remember that,' Lara said. She hit the button on the answering machine avoiding his eyes. Already there were two cancellations.

'Ms McWilliam hasn't cancelled,' she said. 'But the next two have. She should be here any minute.'

'I'll come out myself to get the patients, if that's all right,' he said.

'Yes, yes of course.'

The rain was so heavy she didn't hear the slamming of a car door or footsteps coming up the stairs. The door burst open. A young woman, heavily pregnant, hair drenched and face flushed rushed up to the counter.

'Ms McWilliam?' Lara said.

'Melanie,' she said. 'Yes.'

Lara was about to tell her to have a seat, but she staggered up to the counter. 'I can't walk,' she said, panicked. 'Too much pain. Help me, please.'

Lara knew the look. 'One sec,' she said. She rapped on Andrew's door and opened it quickly. 'Andrew,' she said quietly. 'I'm sorry to burst in but your patient needs you immediately.'

He got up from his chair and was out in the waiting area in five seconds, just in time to catch Melanie as she crumpled to the floor.

'It was supposed to just be a check-up today,' she said, breathing hard. 'This started last night. The pain. But it wasn't this bad. I'm not due for a week.'

'Lara, help me get her onto the bed, will you?'

Lara and Andrew tried to lift Melanie, one of them on each side of her, but she pushed them away with surprising strength. 'Put me down, put me down!' she cried out.

'Her water's broken,' Andrew said, his voice calm. 'Bring me my black bag next to my chair, please Lara. And bring towels and sheets from the store-room. Then pick up the phone and call triple zero. We don't have time to get her to the hospital.'

Adrenalin rushed through Lara. When she got back to him, Andrew had taken one of the cushions from a chair and slipped it under Melanie's head. He'd managed to get her underwear off, and her dress up around her stomach. A wave of sympathetic nausea welled up in Lara as she watched the young woman's belly tighten. Melanie's legs were splayed and the doctor was between them. Lara remembered that while giving birth to her son Simon, she'd felt like she was being beaten across the back with a crow-bar every time she had a contraction.

'Ambulance and paramedics are on their way,' Lara said to Andrew.

'Thank you,' he said.

'Please help me,' Melanie whispered. Her legs shook violently.

'It's coming fast. Baby's head's crowning,' Andrew said to Melanie. 'When the next contraction comes, I want you to push as hard as you can.'

'I can't,' she moaned. 'I can't do it. I want to go home.'

A crack of thunder drowned out her moans and a rushing squall of rain bucketed down on the roof.

Lara got down on the floor beside Melanie, held her hand wiping the sweat from her forehead, and whispered into her ear. 'You can do this, Melanie. The next wave is going to do it — get your baby out, okay? Here it comes, get ready. Squeeze my hand. I don't care how hard. That's the way.'

'Hold on a second,' Andrew said. Lara looked up at him. His face was intently focused. She dared to look down. The baby's head was out, but the shoulders were wedged. Delivery looked as she remembered it felt: impossible.

Lara had never been this close to another woman giving birth and she almost couldn't stand it. Andrew didn't seem hurried or worried. She would never have imagined that anyone could grab a baby's head and pull the child out of the mother's body, but he did. The rest of the body slithered into his hands. A sob caught in her throat. Melanie turned her head into Lara's arms, her hair soaked, her body shivering.

'Melanie, you have a boy,' Andrew said, and held up the baby. He was still blue and white, his head misshapen, eyes black and open, like a tiny alien from an unknown planet. The baby sucked his fists.

'What's wrong with his head?' Melanie gasped.

'It's a bit squashed,' Andrew said, smiling. 'Give it a few days. He's beautiful and he looks fine. Congratulations.'

Lara was still on the floor next to Melanie. As Andrew placed the newborn on his mother's stomach, Lara wrapped her arms around mother and child and looked at Andrew, moved, admiring. His face, which had been so serious and focused, softened, emotion flickered in his eyes. Lara watched the tensing and relaxing of his jaw, as he delivered the placenta and cut the cord.

'There's been some tearing,' he said. 'I'll need your help, Lara. Keep them both as warm as possible.'

Lara covered mother and baby with sheets and towels. She stood up, light-headed and shaken and went to collect a small blanket off the foot of the bed

217

in his office.

When she got back, she wrapped the blanket over the top half of Melanie and tucked it around the baby.

The door opened and Valencia came in.

'There's ambulance arriving,' she said. Taking note of the scene in front of her, she clapped her hand over her mouth. 'My God, my God.' Lara saw the scene through her eyes. The floor was a mess of stained sheets and blood. Andrew had finished and straightened up. His neat clothes were bloodstained and he seemed not worried in the slightest. Lara looked down at herself and noticed for the first time that she was bloody too.

'Thanks, Lara,' Andrew said, with warmth. Their eyes met for a long second. A cascade of electrical flickers ran through her. He looked at Valencia. 'Does it look like the rain's going to stop?'

'No stopping.' she said. 'My God.'

'Valencia, if you could go and tell the ambos to come up here and bring the stretcher. Then if you don't mind getting a couple of umbrellas from the house we can get Melanie and her baby to the ambulance.'

When the paramedics arrived, Andrew briefed them. The two men and one woman looked relieved.

'What's happening?' Melanie asked. Lara was still by her side, her hand on Melanie's head. 'Is he all right, Doctor Roberts? I mean, his head and everything?' Melanie asked.

'He looks really fine, Melanie. Now these good folk are taking you to the hospital to ensure you recover properly. Anyone you want me to call?'

'My mother,' Melanie said. Her voice was completely changed, no longer distorted by pain. 'He's so perfect. Thank you, Doctor Roberts. Thank you ...' she looked at Lara.

'I'm Lara,' she said. 'Well done, Melanie. What a champion you are!'

★ ★ ★

An hour later, Melanie and the baby left with the paramedics. Melanie's mother had made it through the rain just in time. She drove behind the ambulance carrying her daughter and new grandson to the hospital.

Andrew, Valencia and Lara watched them drive away. Lara had a lump in her throat.

'You all right?' Andrew asked. She turned to face him.

A shiver of emotion went through her body. She nodded.'Fine. You were great,' she said. 'Melanie seems so young. It breaks my heart a little.' She thought of the young woman doing it all alone and felt for her. The experience had brought back painful long-buried memories of her own births, and of her lost youth.

She looked down at her stained clothes. Valencia looked with her.'Going to go clean up inside,' Valencia said.

'I'll go with you,' Lara said. She followed her to the house. Andrew wasn't far behind. The kitchen gleamed with state-of-theart stainless steel appliances and which had a stove in the centre so that the cook could talk easily with guests or family in the living room. The house was beautiful, with its polished wooden floors, high ceilings and wide windows. But it also seemed empty and sad. From the pantry cupboard, Valencia took bleach and other cleaning substances and equipment.

'You're welcome to use the shower,' Andrew said to Lara. Rainwater still dripped from his clothes and formed a puddle at his feet. 'At the end of the corridor there's a guest bedroom with a shower and clean towels.'

'Thanks,' Lara said.

The washing machine went on in the laundry with a beep and Valencia bustled into the kitchen.

'I get you clothes from me, from downstairs, Lara. You can fit my trousers, I think, and my shirts.'

'Thanks, that's lovely.'

Lara didn't realise how tired she felt until the warm water in the shower rushed over her head and embraced her. She opened a brand-new bottle of organic shampoo and conditioner. She used the homemade soap which had never been touched. Either Andrew Roberts was always ready for guests, or these had been here waiting a long time. She scrubbed her hair and body until her skin tingled.

Valencia's shirt felt wide and comforting, and she tied a knot at the top of the cotton knit pants to keep them up. She ran fingers through her hair and dared not look in the mirror. She did think briefly of her muddy shorts bundled into the storeroom in Andrew's office, and hoped he wouldn't get to them before she managed to collect them.

She followed delicious smells of garlic and butter to the kitchen and found Valencia at a wooden chopping board with at least fifteen different vegetables lined up to her left.

'I'm making lunch,' she said. 'You need some good food, and take a rest.'

'Only if …'

'I tell Andrew I make lunch for two and he say yes please, okay.'

'Okay. Goodness, Valencia, have you ever seen it rain like this?'

'Four years ago, we have big floods. We stuck here five days. No electricity, no water. No one can come in, no one get out.'

'I don't think I've ever seen rain like this.'

'Yes, I think this is a big one. Now, you can put your clothes in the washing machine. I make another load.'

'You sure? I can take it all to the laundry next week.'

'No no, do it here, please. All your laundry, okay?'

'Yes, all right. Now, put me to work. What can I chop?'

'Lara, what about you just go and have a cup of tea and a rest?'

'I think if I rest I'll fall asleep. Let me give you a hand here.'

'Okay,' she shrugged broad shoulders and smiled. 'You chop.' She pushed butternut and carrots to Lara's side and handed her a knife. 'You a midwife now, Lara, eh?'

'Not quite,' she said. 'I'm like the fathers who faint while watching their wives give birth. I couldn't do that on a regular basis. It takes a special kind of person. Someone like Andrew. He's excellent, isn't he?'

'Oh yes, he very good. Everyone love him and I think he do this a lot. In outback, everywhere. A lot of babies.' She chopped potatoes with terrifying precision, into tiny, equal-sized cubes.

They had to raise their voices because the thunder grew louder until it sounded like a continuous rumble. The rain fell harder and Lara glanced out of the

221

window. Rain swept across the lawn, gossamer curtains blown by a breeze. She had never seen nature so ferocious. Not even the winter storm of her early teens in England had matched this. Nonetheless, it mirrored to some degree what was happening in the region of her heart at that moment.

The noise of the storm drowned out any other sound. Lara didn't hear Andrew until he was right beside her.

'Now that's a storm!'

Startled, she turned her head. He too had changed. He was wearing shorts and a blue and grey striped t-shirt. What was it about him? Her heart turned over.

'I'm sorry, did I startle you?'

'Just a little,' she said and smiled. 'This storm's making me jumpy.'

'We haven't seen one like this for a while,' he said. 'I'm thinking how lucky we were with Melanie that things happened when they did. Any later and I don't want to know what might've happened.'

'Oh, what do you mean?'

'Well, look over there,' he said, pointing through the rain.

'Oh my gosh, is that the driveway?'

'It is.'

Lara watched the drive turning into several streams racing down towards the dirt road that was vanishing under water. 'Oh dear,' she said, and turned to look at him. 'I see what you mean.'

He turned away. 'Mmm, that smells delicious, Valencia,' he said. 'What are you making?'

'You not have breakfast, Dr Andrew. And then all that fuss. So now you must have a big lunch. Pumpkin salad, some other salads, your favourites.'

'That sounds excellent,' he said. A smile tugged at the corner of his mouth. 'I don't suppose you have this kind of rain in England, do you?' He looked at Lara. She shook her head.

'No. Funny though, we're so well known for our rain, but it has nothing on yours. In fact,' she said, borrowing a word from an elderly person they both knew, 'what we have in the UK could be said to be insipid by comparison.'

He smiled. 'Look out of the window there now. You'll see an interesting sight.'

He stood next to the sink and pointed to the bottom of the property. She walked over to stand next to him. What she saw took her breath away. The muddy drive had turned into a full stream, and where, a short while ago the drive had met the road, a roaring brown river at least three metres wide hurried over everything, whisking bits of broken branches and grasses and other debris into its foaming depth.

'Oh my goodness,' she said.

'I think we're all right with supplies, aren't we Valencia? And we know where the candles are?'

'Yes, sure,' she said.

'I also have a fridge full of food,' Lara offered.

'It might be better if you stay here Lara. It's not wise to brave this torrent, even walking up to the cottage. It's slippery and I haven't yet had some of those gums taken down next to it. I'd feel better if you stayed in the house, to be honest. Would that be agreeable? You can stay in the spare room. It's made, isn't it, Valencia?'

'Yes, bed's always made,' she said, chopping onions and wiping tears from her eyes.'

'Oh, surely the rain will pass by tonight?' She stared

at the walls of water pouring from the sky.

'I don't recommend it,' Andrew said. 'Please be my guest. It's safer that way.'

'Much safer,' Valencia said. 'This house is brick. That one, wood.'

'Like the three little pigs,' Andrew said.

Lara couldn't contain what she was feeling. She looked at his face, his hands. He'd just brought a new life into the world. It was hard not to feel twinges of deep affection for him, this man who was rubbing his chin and contemplating the roaring river at the bottom of his property. Watching Andrew's face as he delivered Melanie's baby — seeing his kindness, his expertise and knowing the truth of his own story — she had been overwhelmed with a feeling both new and incredible. It felt fast, but she'd been getting to know about him in his absence, inadvertently.

She looked away again, at the river. She did not want to give in to this strange wave of warmth, compassion and admiration breaking over her. She went back to making salad and Andrew went to a sideboard, opened a drawer and took out cutlery, crockery and a tablecloth. While she and Valencia worked, he set the dining room table and turned on two floor lamps. A short while later, she and Valencia sliced and buttered hot bread from the oven and brought food to the table.

'Listen to this, Valencia. I thought you'd like it. It's a CD from Bolivia … still Spanish, but a bit different. They're called the Aztecs,' Andrew said.

He took a remote control and pressed it, and in the living area, Lara heard a click, and they were surrounded by crystal clear stereo. Strains of Spanish guitar and flute floated through the air, a counterpoint to the thunder and rain that throbbed all around them.

Valencia smiled. 'I like it. Is good music.'

'It's yours,' Andrew said, and turned up the volume. 'I found the CD for you – some shop in Western Australia, of all places. Thought you might like it.'

'You don't have to,' she said, shaking her head. 'You too kind. Thank you.'

★ ★ ★

Lara hoped she was the only one feeling awkward at the table. Usually, she had enough words for three people in terms of making conversation. Between mouthfuls of salad and bread now, however, she found very few. Eventually she asked a question she had been contemplating.

'So, Andrew, how many babies have you delivered?'

Usually, she thought, when people talk to you, they make eye contact and then look away. What she found unnerving about Andrew was that he didn't look away.

'I've lost count,' he said, holding her gaze. 'But probably in the region of about fifteen hundred.'

'One thousand five hundred?'

'Over a twenty-five-year period, that is.'

'That's a lot.'

'Well it's one of the most common occurrences in remote areas.' He served himself more salad and crusty bread with roast pumpkin, and continued. 'Do you have children, Lara?'

'I do,' she said. 'Two. 'They're grown up. Simon and Rose. Fending for themselves, thank goodness.'

'Nice,' he said. 'They're in London, I presume?'

'Yes. They have their lives and are getting on very

well. Simon works in the music industry and Rose is studying art part-time and working as a curator at a gallery.'

'Impressive,' he said.

She felt uncomfortable. She didn't know what she might ask that wouldn't be seen as either prying into, or avoidance of the subject he didn't want mentioned. A pause too long for her comfort ensued.

'And Lara, what are your future plans?'

'That's a no-go area,' she laughed. 'Stay here until my visa runs out, I suppose. And then see what happens.'

Valencia had gone very quiet. She was even eating quietly. Lara noticed her glancing at Andrew. Then she looked at Lara. 'Finish eating, you two. I come back soon. I need to check something.' She bustled out of the kitchen.

Andrew and Lara continued to eat. He dipped his bread into his salad, and took a large bite. Lara was gratified to note that he was, after all imperfect. He got a crumb on the side of his mouth, which he did not notice, and which made him seem more approachable.

'Why did you choose Australia?' he asked.

Lara hadn't meant to reveal any deep personal details about her life, but somehow, the sight of him slightly unguarded, not noticing the crumb, allowed her to let down her own guard. 'I got on a plane to get as far away as possible from the tacky end of a twenty-plus-year-old marriage, and I wanted to go where the sun was shining. My husband left me.'

His look was unfathomable. 'I'm sorry to hear that,' he said. He took his napkin and dabbed the sides of his mouth. The crumb vanished.

It could have been the warmth of eating, or the cosiness of the house, but his cheeks seemed flushed.

Valencia walked slowly back into the kitchen.

'That was excellent,' he said to her. He looked at Lara. 'Thank you both for your culinary talents.'

'Welcome, welcome,' Valencia said. She smoothed her shirt down in front of her and said. 'You mind if I go downstairs now?'

'Not at all. I'll take care of this,' he said gesturing to the table. 'Thanks for all your help. Take the music with you, if you like.'

'No. I get it later.'

'Don't slip on the stairs,' Andrew said. Valencia smiled and walked past, patting his shoulder with a kind, broad hand. She disappeared out of the front door, closing it softly behind her, and Lara felt the vibration of her going down the steps.

'She going to be okay?' she asked.

'You mean the rain? Yes, of course, her flat is just below us here. She'll barely feel a drop unless the wind's blowing sideways.'

227

27

Andrew and Lara cleared the table to the sound of the Aztecs playing. Rain continued to pour, but the thunder had moved away into the distance. As a result of the morning's drama, Lara felt a sense of connectedness to Andrew, but she couldn't deny the tension. She was afraid of saying or doing anything that would go into territory that was carefully guarded. She watched him load the dishwasher: knives with knives, forks with forks, and so on; big plates carefully on one side, small on the other. He turned and caught her smiling.

'Something funny?' he raised an eyebrow.

'You're very well organised,' Lara said, aiming for politeness.

'It saves time on the other end,' he said.

'I wonder which way is actually faster.'

'The only way to find out is a timed experiment.'

'One day, if we're really bored at work, we could try it,' she said, hoisting Valencia's big pants up on her hips.

She caught a momentary smile on his face. A brilliant flash of lightning and clap of thunder made both of them jump. The lights flickered. Andrew turned on the dishwasher. He opened a kitchen drawer and took out some candles and matches and added a plastic hurricane lamp from the cupboard below. 'If the river ever flooded the house, this would stay alight and float on top of the water.'

'That's comforting to know,' she said.

'I'm sure the electricity's going to go,' he said. And

he was right. About thirty seconds later, there was another flicker of lightning, and all the lights in the house went out. The dishwasher and washing machine and fridge and everything that had been humming contentedly at ten amps, dropped to zero and the house was ghostly quiet.

'Does this happen often?' she said.

'During the storm season, it can.' He lit a candle. 'It's not even four thirty yet.' His face was unreadable in the late afternoon stormy candlelight.

'Funny, it feels like midnight. You said it would be a busy day.'

'Did I?'

'Yes. Just yesterday.'

'Oh right. My consulting room isn't usually a delivery room, though,' he said, carrying two candles into the lounge. 'Want to come and have a seat?'

Lara followed him. He sat down on a big, leather chair and placed the candles on a small table next to him. She sat down on the couch and tucked her feet under her, trying to relax.

'I should thank you, Lara, for your help. It was much appreciated.'

'No problem,' she said. 'Though I'm not sure I was much help. I'm not used to attending births ... especially on office floors.'

'You were very good,' he said, and she was grateful for the low lighting, because she felt embarrassed. 'Sometimes, when it happens so quickly, it's more traumatic for the body. It was good to have you there.'

'I could see how hard it was,' Lara said softly. 'Poor thing. No one really prepares you for what it's like.'

'If they did, no woman would give birth again,' he said, leaning back in his chair.

229

'Someone should tell every young woman, though. It's a conspiracy of silence,' she said. 'I always think of all those pregnancy and mothering magazines – so far removed from the uh, bloody situation that looked rather like a massacre — the one we had on our hands this morning. Which is the real thing.'

He smiled. 'True. I'll remember to keep you a safe distance from my pregnant patients so you don't break the conspiracy. On the other hand, I'll invite you in if I think anyone needs a bit of birth-control talk.' He grinned.

All she could hear was the rain. They talked for a while about England and Australia, and the advantages and disadvantages of growing up in either country. They stayed carefully on the surface of every topic, because every conversation could potentially have led to either one of them mentioning something about the recent past. He was masterful at burying it.

'I hope you'll excuse me, but I'm really tired,' she said eventually. 'I know it's only five thirty, but I think I'll go to bed if you don't mind. It's been quite an adventure for one day.'

He seemed almost relieved. 'Of course. Yeah, I'm pretty tired too. You take the hurricane lamp. Can you find your way to the spare room?'

'Yes, thanks. Down the corridor, next to the guest bathroom.'

'If you need anything … a drink, something to eat later …'

'No, thanks. I'm really fine.'

'Good. See you in the morning.'

She picked up the hurricane lamp. The corridor, without any diffuse light, felt close and heavy. The lamp cast long shadows. She passed the bathroom and opened the door to the spare room. A double bed, neatly made and ready for guests at any time, waited in the centre of the room. The curtains were already drawn. Lara closed the door, put the lamp on a bedside table and threw herself onto the bed. She contemplated taking off her clothes, but then thought better of it. What if lightning struck the house and they all had to run outside? Instead she pulled the covers back and crept, fully clothed, between soft cotton sheets.

She'd been sleeping for several hours, when a loud crack pulled her out of her dreams. She felt the noise vibrate through her body. She sat up. The storm still raged outside, but a strange orange glow lit up the curtains. That didn't seem right. She crept out of bed, pulled them open, and stared in disbelief. Lightning had hit a massive tree, which now lay across the driveway right next to Andrew's car. The tree had split clean down the middle. Orange and yellow flames licked and flickered along the sides of the gash in the trunk.

Lara realised she'd had no idea how dangerous storms could be. She felt grateful that she was in a solid brick house, away from the roaring flood, away from trees that could break in the wind, and with the ground so sodden, come crashing down on her cottage.

She switched on the hurricane lamp and opened the bedroom door. The corridor wasn't completely dark, so she stepped out into it, and followed the light. When she got to the kitchen, a single candle burned on the counter.

She looked around the room, but couldn't see Andrew. A burning candle left alight? Had he forgotten on his way to bed? She padded across the floor, placed the lamp down on the counter next to the candle and tried to see into the dark corners of the room.

'Andrew?' she whispered.

'Expecting someone else?'

The sound of his voice startled her. She put her hand on her heart to hold it in place. She saw his silhouette walking away from the window as her eyes adjusted fully to the light. 'Hope not,' she said. 'Though night monsters and scary housebreakers did come to mind.'

'Oh dear,' he said. She thought she heard a smile in his voice. He came into the kitchen, barefoot, wearing a dark dressing gown wrapped tightly around himself. 'Now that was quite a fireworks display.'

'Is it dangerous?'

'No. Well, I suppose it could have fallen on my car. And I could've been in it. That would have been it – but right now, no, the rain's already dousing the flames and it's going to be a job to get the tree removed, but you're in no danger.'

For another reason entirely, she felt very much in danger.

'That's a relief,' she said, not feeling at all relieved as they stood in the kitchen, shadows dancing between them.

She looked at the wall clock. Two minutes to midnight. He opened the quiet fridge and took out the milk. 'Like a glass?' he offered.

'No thanks.'

'It won't last long if the electricity stays off,' he said, and poured some for himself. He leaned against the dishwasher and drank it all in one gulp.

The knot on the pants she was wearing had come undone and they began to slip down. She fumbled,

232

trying to tie it again, while Andrew slowly put his glass down and watched her.

'Those clothes are a pretty bad fit,' he said, his eyes catching the light with an expression she hadn't seen before. It caught her completely unprepared. Was she dreaming or did his voice sound intimate, gentle – even seductive?

'What?'

'Those clothes. They don't fit you.'

'You're right. But they're better than the alternative.' She laughed softly.

'I'm not sure, about that,' he said.

'Pardon?' Lara swallowed. What was that supposed to mean? Her mouth dried. She shook. She tried to steer the conversation.

'I should have stayed in my own clothes covered in blood?'

He leaned casually against the dishwasher and smiled, hooking his hand into the belt loop on his dressing gown.

'No, I was thinking the other alternative.'

'Which is?'

'Well, nothing at all.'

His eyes were a glittering reflection of dancing candle flames and they held hers. Dark colour rose in his cheeks. Heat rose in Lara's.

'Are you flirting with me, Doctor Roberts?'

His bottom lip protruded slightly. 'Don't know,' he said with a half-smile. 'It's been a very long time.'

'Let me explain,' she said quietly, her body quaking, stunned at being exposed to this side of Andrew Roberts, 'that suggesting to a woman, alone in your kitchen at midnight that she should be wearing nothing at all, is more than flirty. I'd say you were coming

233

on to her.'

'Maybe I am,' he said.

Lara swallowed. 'Maybe?'

'If my attention's unwanted I could always retract it. Is it?'

'What?' Lara whispered, hearing her heartbeat thudding in her ears.

'Unwanted.'

The semi-dark protected her. She held his gaze and didn't move.

'No.'

Silence.

Neither of them moved. Her throat tightened. When she let go of the kitchen counter, and found she could hold herself up very well, she walked across and stood so close to him that she could feel his breath on her hair. He hadn't let go of the dishwasher. She raised her eyes to meet his and rested her hand on his chest.

'No,' she said again.

He wrapped his fingers around her wrist and brought her hand to his lips, pressing them into her palm. She leaned against him and he drew a long, uneven breath.

'This could be dangerous,' he said. She lifted her face and he touched her cheek, then tangled his fingers in her hair.

When Andrew's warm, soft lips touched Lara's, the effect on her was exactly like what happened when she drank Gin and Tonic – weak knees almost immediately, a desire to laugh, followed by the desire to cry, and quite quickly after that, the desire to go to bed.

'You don't know me,' she whispered against his mouth. 'I could be a psychopath. Or you could. We don't know much about each other. What if I'm not who you think I am?'

She felt him smile. 'If I could get Valencia's big bloomers off you, I think I'd be able to tell.'

'I don't know that she'll approve.'

'Oh, she will,' he said. 'I didn't imagine that finding out what lay inside Valencia's pants and shirt would be such a desperately attractive thought.'

'I might be half fish,' she said.

He laughed and stepped back. 'You might. Let's see, then.'

Lara had forgotten how quickly he'd managed to get Melanie's clothes off that morning. He was an expert at it. With the same deftness, he flipped through all the buttons on her shirt and it fell open. She wasn't wearing a bra, but didn't feel the same embarrassment she'd felt with Mario. The way he looked at her made her feel uplifted. She wondered, though whether there was any mystique about the human body for a man whose job was dealing with its malfunctions and sufferings. Andrew had no doubt, seen hundreds, if not thousands of breasts. Perhaps her half-naked state was nothing surprising to him.

He slipped his hands around her waist, and she felt her breath catch. 'You're beautiful,' he whispered.

Lara couldn't believe her ears. Or her hands. Or where she was standing, for that matter. Many things had been said to her over the years, but never, ever, that. Andrew looked at bodies all day long. That he'd said those words made her believe that he meant them.

Rain continued to lash the windows. A new squall rushed over the sky and the pounding on the roof reached a deafening roar. She slipped her hands under his dressing gown and ran them across the top of his chest. A tremor rippled through his body and he sucked in his breath. Then she pulled the gown open. He was wearing only a pair of cotton boxers. She leaned into him, skin to skin and he drew a deep breath. 'I have to admit I don't really know what I'm doing,' he said. 'Something's come over me.' She could feel it — his need, but also his hesitance. 'Lara, I have a fortress around my heart, to use the words of an old song.'

She hugged him closer. Both of them trembled. Something with the emotional consistency of molten lava filled Lara's heart and made her eyes burn. 'Why don't we just see what happens?'

'Maybe we should get out of the kitchen, then,' he said.

He flipped off the hurricane lamp and picked up the candle. He took her hand and she held up her pants, stumbling after him towards his bedroom.

Flashes of lightning briefly illuminated his face. She thought he looked like a sculpture. His proportions were aesthetically perfect. She had never appreciated anyone quite in this way before. When they reached the bedroom, he put the candle on a small table at the foot of the bed and pulled her close. 'Like I may have said, it's been a long time,' he said against her lips.

They both looked out of the window. They could see the lightning-struck tree and the last flames flickering. As if that were a cue, Andrew blew out the candle. And the fire that smouldered between them ignited. They stepped hurriedly, easily out of clothing that had already almost fallen off them. He ran his hands up the entire length of her body and inhaled a staccato breath. 'I'm not sure how to do this,' he said, laughing, nervous.

'Give me your hand,' she said in the darkness.

They sank down onto the softness of pillows that smelled of fabric softener and ironing. Lara felt like never before — open, her soul awash with emotions and sensations she'd only ever dreamed of. Thank you, tantric Mario, she thought, for the tutorial. She led and Andrew followed. He sucked in his breath. 'This what they teach you in England?' he whispered.

Against his lips she said, 'no, this is completely Australian as far as I know.' Her body and hands knew what to do as she brought the doc back from a distant place where he'd filed away the part of him that had sensual sexual appetites. After a while he found his bearings and Lara's whole body felt like it was singing. He gathered her close and they became one with the thunder and rain. The rumpled bedding was the sea on which they burned and tumbled, and their sweat-drenched bodies rose and fell with the tide, buffeted by the waves, crashing finally together onto a faraway shore.

28

Slowly, Lara opened her eyes. The sky was almost light. A faint drizzle still pattered down on the roof, but the dramatic storm had travelled up the coast. Lara turned her head. Andrew wasn't there, but she was in his room, and those were his closets, and she could see herself in the mirrors and wished she couldn't, because she thought she looked like a train wreck. She feared that the night had brought up painful memories for him. His wife was the last person he'd made love to, and that had been more than three years ago. He was still wearing his wedding ring. Lara buried her head back under the bed covers.

Then, through the closed door, she heard the piano. The piece was something classical. Soft and sweet. She sat up and looked for her clothes as she recognised the piece. Bach's Prelude in C Major had been one of Simon's exam pieces. She found Valencia's pants crumpled in a heap on the floor, and the shirt lying there like an old snake skin, and she put them on, pulled them tight around herself and tiptoed to the door, opening it quietly and walking down the corridor to the waterfalls of sound that drifted through the house.

The prelude came to an end. She stood rooted to the floor at the entrance to the lounge. She was afraid that if she walked another step she'd break the spell, and the man, the house and the music would all vanish into the mist like a fairytale.

Andrew was bent over the piano, deep in thought,

unaware of Lara, his dressing gown loosely open at the front, his naked chest visible. He lifted his hands, put them sensuously down on the keys, and played Elton John's *Yellow Brick Road*.

From Bach to Elton John, quite a versatile repertoire, Lara thought. She stood transfixed. Outside, the sky grew light. Through the big windows she could see the burnt tree trunk lying blackly on the misty grass, like a gigantic serpent guarding the entrance to the house. The music grew louder, and Andrew's whole body moved. She watched his fingers and understood with her heart what he couldn't express in words.

Bloody hell, something was happening to her. She wanted him to heal, to feel joy. To not feel pain any more. What was going on, she wondered? Andrew looked up and noticed her, but he was mid-song and didn't stop playing. He kept his eyes on her and played the last chord.

'She is awake, then,' he said.

'That's lovely, Elton.'

'Pretty rusty, really. I hardly touch this thing anymore.' He ran his hand through tousled hair. 'I play for some old folks once a month where my mother lives in a care home. That's about it.'

'I don't think you sound rusty.'

'I made you a cup of tea,' he said, nodding at the coffee table. 'It's probably cold by now. You were still asleep.'

'Thank you,' Lara said, touched. 'That's sweet. I thought you'd left.'

He looked at her. Her feet unglued themselves from the floor and she shuffled towards him, trying to keep the shirt on and the pants up.

He opened his arms wide, and she walked into

239

them. His fingers played with the elastic of her big pants. 'I thought I got rid of these,' he said and gave them a tug.

'Andrew!' she laughed as they fell in a pool at her feet.

'What?'

'What if someone walks in?'

'Who would?'

'Valencia.'

'She won't mind.' He smiled and swung his legs over the piano seat. 'Come here.'

Doctor Andrew was not only a good doctor, nor only a good piano player — he was — and this was a shock for Lara to discover — despite the reservoir of grief which sat in some sealed compartment of his soul, funny, flirtatious and disarming. She found this combination irresistible and wondered whether she should be resisting. This was happening so fast she felt like she had jet-lag. Zero to a hundred in three metaphorical seconds. Or something like it.

His touch on her skin felt fiery and she gave up the idea of slowing things down. His lips and tongue blazed indelible trails across her naked flesh. They stumbled away from the piano and onto the softness of a rug in front of his couch.

★ ★ ★

This time, when she woke, she had no idea where she was. She thought the rain had started again, but it was the roar of the kettle. She'd been tucked under a sheet.

She watched him moving about the kitchen. Graceful, velvet and steel, fire and ice. He walked to the

240

living room from the kitchen carrying two cups of tea. 'I hope you like milk and sugar because that's how it comes around here.'

She smiled and took the cup. 'Thank you. Wow, the rain finally stopped,' she said, 'and obviously the electricity's back on. I can do some laundry today.'

'Laundry,' he teased. 'So that's at the front of your mind after wild sex? I like your priorities.'

She laughed and sipped the sweet tea, and he climbed under the sheet beside her.

She smiled. 'To be honest, it's actually just me making meaningless conversation to stop me from saying things I might regret.'

His shining blue eyes stared at her over the top of his tea cup. 'Like what?'

'Well, if I said them, I'd regret them, wouldn't I? You already have a fortress around your heart and I know that if I say anything, you'll just reinforce it with fences and barbed wire.'

'Walls do serve a purpose. I don't want you to get hurt,' he said, and rested his hand on her thigh. 'You're wonderful. Perfect. Thank you for last night. And this morning.'

Lara wanted to dissolve into him. Instead she crossed her arms in front of her.

'Thanks,' she said. 'Though I could think of at least one man who'd disagree,' she said

'He must be insane.'

'Nice of you to say.'

'It's true.'

'Thanks, Andrew.'

'I have to tell you something though.'

'I'm all ears.'

'I find it hard to let people in. I can be crusty.'

241

'Crusty?'

'Like a crustacean.'

'I love crabs,' she said.

He laughed. 'You know what I mean.'

'So?' Lara said.

'What we did has left me a bit stripped. Pardon the pun.'

'You can tell me about that.'

'I can tell you that I couldn't live through being hurt in any way, ever again. When Gabrielle died, something in me died. I don't want you to feel hurt by my behaviour. I can be quite shut off.'

Lara realised she hadn't breathed.

'Okay,' she said. 'Thanks, doctor. I'll keep that in mind. By the way, how old are you?' she asked.

'Fifty,' he said.

'Ancient,' she said and laughed. 'And I'm forty-four, heading for ancientness. But what if we're only half way through our lives? I have no idea how we circumvent suffering. Even the sun will eventually go out. There's no happily-ever-after for anyone, not in the way we imagine it to be. So where does that leave us now?'

'I don't know,' he said. 'She was your age, Lara. Bone cancer got her. It took her in a year and a day. After she died, I took everything of hers out of the house. Out of my life. And I shut down my heart so I could survive.'

Lara felt terrified and honoured that all of a sudden, Andrew had broken the code of silence.

'I get it,' she said. She put her cup down and turned to him. Then she took his cup and put it down at his side. She slid over him and breathed in the warmth, the presence of his body. And then she kissed him slowly, for a long time.

When she stopped and looked into his eyes, they shimmered.

'Are you some kind of a witch?' he whispered.

'Maybe,' she said. 'But I thought, as a doctor, making love might be devoid of mystique. You know so much about the workings of the body. Does it spoil it?'

'No,' he said.

'Aren't you thinking about everything in a more sort of mechanical, physical-process kind of way — like oo, there's a rush of oxytocin – heart-rate is increasing …?'

He laughed. 'No, hardly,' he said. 'I'm human too. I'm probably more in awe of the body, more struck by its ability to maintain health, to heal itself, experience pleasure and to become whole. When it does, it seems like a miracle.' He slid his hands down and held her hips. 'For example, that birth you saw did quite a bit of damage to that young mother. But Melanie will heal from her tears. Her body will come back to its original shape, able to experience pleasure and even give birth again. That to me, is a miracle.'

'I've been there,' she said.

'I know you have,' he said, and she felt she was beginning to drown in the blue-brown of his flecked eyes. 'But I will confess that there was a time, a short time, when I saw things differently. After Gabrielle died, all my patients suddenly seemed to be in varying degrees of decay. I can't explain it. It's not how it seems anymore.'

'That's good to hear,' she said.

They held each other, Lara admiring how one head fit under another; how pelvises matched, how convex shapes fitted neatly into concave, and how skin pressed together became warm and moist. She realised she'd never experienced the world or another human being this way, and it felt as though this was finally her, seeing reality as herself, feeling herself to be at the centre of her own narrative, not waiting for a road-map, a request or a need that came from somewhere else to tell her where to go next, what to feel, what to think.

The sun made a valiant attempt to break through the clouds, and when it did, the world shone back a luminous green, and birds shrieked joyfully from the trees.

* * *

Valencia widened her eyes the moment she walked in. The washing machine hummed and thunked, Andrew, dressed in shorts and his striped t-shirt, was cooking breakfast, whistling a tune, and Lara stood next to him in his blue dressing gown.

Valencia looked sideways at Andrew.'Good morning,' she said, and stood there, hands on hips.

'Got the washing going,' Lara said, unable to meet her eye.

'You see fire last night?' she asked.

'Yeah,' Andrew said, flipping a perfect fried egg. 'Entertaining, at least.'

Valencia walked over to Lara and gave her a half-believing onceover.'You sleep well?'

Lara had to look Valencia in the eye and nod, but could not hide the flush she felt creeping up her neck all the way to her cheeks. 'Valencia,' she said and grinned at her,'I did. I spent fourteen hours in bed, thanks.'

Valencia put her hand over her mouth. She looked like she wanted to smile, but didn't trust herself to do so. Instead, shaking her head and sneaking a look at Andrew, she said, 'You two?'

Lara grinned.

'Now, go you go and sit down,' she said suddenly, bustling into the kitchen and bossing Andrew out of the way so that he held the spatula up in mock surrender. Her mouth twitched sideways into a smile, which she tried to hide. She grabbed the spatula from him and wagged it threateningly. 'I make these eggs. Go!'

★ ★ ★

That afternoon, Lara made it back to her abode. Everything was intact. She'd snuck by the office on the way up and retrieved her muddy shorts from the storeroom, stashed there before all the craziness set in. She'd left Andrew and Valencia to organise the tree service to come and deal with the massive burnt log in front of the house. The property was still sealed off from the road, and the Internet was down.

Lara sat down on her bed. More had happened in the last several weeks of her life than in the previous twenty years. She had done more life-affirming things than she'd ever imagined possible. This included paying a sex god to take her places she'd never been, modelling for a French photographer, humiliating her unfaithful former spouse and his lover and most recently, making love to a doctor she'd only recently met, with wild abandon. She'd also forgotten about the amount of cellulite on her thighs, and had not stopped even once to consider eye-bags, wrinkles, or breasts that might be tempted to head south in the middle of the night while no one was watching. Nor had she given a thought to legs that were unwaxed or whether the small mole on her cheek had recently sprouted an insulting dark hair. She hadn't said fuck for a while, except in direct reference to its actual meaning and she had stopped feeling self-critical. She wondered whether she was healed.

29

It took two days for the mud and sodden pathways to dry out slightly, for the road to reappear, and the Internet to be put back into action, and another day before the trucks arrived with saws to cut through the fallen tree, and remove the debris. During that time the household ate all the food in Andrew's fridge and in Lara's.

Once the phone lines were back, Lara and Andrew went to the office and worked to retrieve messages.

'Look at this,' Andrew said.

Thankyou Dr Roberts, and thankyou Lara so much. Dr Roberts, I don't know what I would have done without you. Lara, thank you. You should be a midwife. ☺ Baby Zack and I are doing well. You were right about his head, too. It looks perfect now. By the way, a big tree fell across our drive after we got back from hospital so the timing couldn't have been better. Thank you both. Love, Melanie

'That's sweet of her,' Lara said. Andrew took her hand. It felt good to have this letter of appreciation to them both, treating her and Andrew as a team.

Lara acknowledged to herself that everything that had seemed foreign and unfamiliar in Australia had become intimately familiar.

When Andrew went back to the house to fetch his phone, Lara made a call to Carremere to let them know that the storm had prevented her visit. She asked after Dot, and Debbie said she was fine. As for the lieutenant, Debbie said, he was ill and frail, and no longer eating anything at all.

The next day, Lara found herself alone for a few hours in the afternoon. The weather warm and steamy, relaxed her. Andrew had gone into town. She made a late afternoon cup of tea and sat on her veranda.

Valencia appeared on the mud path.

'You should go the other way,' Lara called out.

'Too long,' she said. 'I came to say hello and sit with you.'

'Let me get you a cuppa,' Lara said. 'Water's still hot.'

Valencia looked like she had something to say. She seemed to have included Lara in her own personal space. After it was obvious that Lara and Andrew had been together, Valencia acted like the parent of the lonely child who finally brings home a friend. There was an underlying attitude of gratitude mixed with concern that Lara could detect in Valencia's demeanor.

Valencia felt comfortable in Lara's presence and sat herself down on the other chair, while Lara went to make her a cup of tea.

'I like English tea,' Valencia said. 'Is very good. Thank you, Lara.'

'My favourite too. So, Valencia, what can I do for you?'

'For me?'

'Yes, you know, you look like you want to ask me something?'

'You are clever Lara.' She looked down at her feet, embarrassed.

'Not to ask. But to tell.'

'Perfect,' Lara said, sipping her tea. 'Tell me then.'

'Doctor Andrew. You make him happy. I been hearing him play piano. I never hear music before. Not like this. I want to say thanks to you.'

'Tell me more.' Valencia looked at Lara quickly and then looked out at the bush.

'This man,' she said, 'Andrew. He lose everything. God take away everything he love. And he still stay so kind. Is why, Lara, I take care of him, and pray for him, and bring you here in my prayers.'

Lara looked at her and saw a person whose big heart was devoted to people other than herself. Lara realised, quite suddenly, that there were people in Australia, after a few short months, whom she loved. She didn't know what to say for a moment.

'You know, I tell him lot of times to find a nice woman, you know, just for companion … eh, man cannot go without for such a long time, is not good. He say he not right and not ready.' She looked at Lara as if asking a question,. Like a prying mother, Lara thought, and smiled gently.

'He was ready, Valencia. And everything was good. You don't have to worry.'

'No, no,' she said, and smiled. 'I'm not worried. You are good for him. I come to say please stay here, Lara. Don't go away back to your country.'

When Valencia left, Lara put on shorts, a tank top and hiking shoes and went for a stroll down to the river's edge. Crows complained from a Poinciana tree. Doves cooed. Corellas shrieked from their places high up in a blue gum. The air was rich with the smells of earth and blossoms. Lara took in a deep breath and felt that she finally belonged somewhere.

In the evening, Andrew returned. She saw his car from her kitchen window, and forced herself not to run out to him, to stay, tidying up her fridge, sweeping the floor, and scrubbing the bathroom. When she heard footsteps striding up the wooden stairs, she couldn't stop her heart from racing. He appeared in the doorway, and she felt nervous and happy. She wrapped her hair into a bun.

'Hello.' He smiled, standing without moving.

'Would you like to come in?'

'That would be nice, thank you.' He walked into his own cottage, ran his hand through his hair and stood in front of her.

'How are you?'

'I'm feeling great,' she said and smiled. 'Are you okay?'

'Yes, thanks. I have been having a hard time concentrating on anything.' He smiled, looked at her. His cheeks had a touch more colour than usual.

'Would you like something to drink?' she asked.

'Maybe later. I, uh, Lara, I actually came here to ask you something.'

'Ask away. I hope I can help.'

'Well, this is a work-related question. You've been working so hard and it's really starting to shape up in there, and, well, what I want to say is, I need you full time. Would you consider it?'

'Working for you full-time?'

'Uh, yes, exactly.'

'Well,' Lara said, and sat down on her bed. 'Aside from the small issue of my status in this country, and my ineligibility to be legal here and work and get paid, yes, of course I can do that.'

'Really?'

'Except for Tuesdays.'

'Tuesdays?'

'Yes — I have a prior commitment most Tuesdays.'

'A commitment?'

'Yes.' She felt guilty. Why didn't she just tell him?

He didn't pry. 'All right. Tuesdays are yours.'

'Good,' she said. He didn't ask further questions but she could see he had several. 'Listen,' she said. 'Would you like to, um, stay here for some supper? I could make a quick curry and it'd be ready in about twenty minutes.'

She looked at his face. He seemed poised to decline. 'That sounds very nice. Give me ten minutes and I'll be back.'

He strode out of the cottage and down the veranda stairs. She fell back on the bed, stared at the ceiling, elated. She noted the large Huntsman spider making its way to the centre of the room. Her previous self would have passed out at the mere sight of such an enormous arachnid. Now she just watched it as if she were watching the sunlight fall through a gap in the leaves. The past few days had done something to her; she felt changed, and she felt like she could wait for whatever slow magic was unraveling in her life. She could feel the walls of Andrew's fortress, evident in how he seemed to be able to sever the soft, romantic part of himself which she'd seen miraculous evidence of, from the everyday business-like aspect of himself, the doctor persona, attractive and kind, and yet subtly out of reach.

Lara sat up. She got off the bed and began to select spices out of her cupboards, vegetables out of her fridge and put the pan on the small stove with oil and garlic and soon she had the whole place smelling like a southern Indian restaurant. She opened all the windows to let the night air in, found two candles and lit them, and went outside to place them on a small table.

251

An incongruous sound reached her: glasses tinkling in the bushes. Footsteps followed.

'This looks nice.'

'Hi,' she said, feeling as though this was a first date. Andrew took the stairs two at a time. She saw he held two thinly stemmed wine glasses in one hand, and a bottle of wine in the other.

'A South African special,' he said. 'From a colleague who used to live there.'

'Oh, that looks amazing,' Lara said. The glasses caught the candlelight as he set them down.

'I've never been here at night,' he said. 'You've made the place feel cosy and inviting, Lara.'

'Thank you,' she said. 'I really like it here.'

'It's nice be asked to dinner on my own property. Smells good. What is it?'

'You know how curry is the national dish in England?'

'No,' he laughed. 'I didn't.'

'Consider I'm making a traditional British meal tonight. Madras curry. Medium. Hope you like it.'

'Great,' he said. 'I do kind of like the idea that India colonised Britain back, in at least one subtle way.'

'Absolutely,' she said. His eyes twinkled in the candlelight. He was wearing a soft light blue t-shirt and denim shorts. She was still in her shorts and tank top, unconcerned about her appearance. She wondered what it was about him that made her feel so comfortable.

When they sat down to eat, Lara looked up and saw that above them, the canopy of the Milky Way blazed from horizon to horizon.

'This is incredible,' she said.

'A display I organised just for you,' he said.

'Very kind,' she said, and took a sip of wine. 'And, nice wine.'

'The meal's delicious,' he said. 'Thank you.'

Small talk masked the big questions that were growing in her heart and they ate in silence for a few minutes punctuated by scratches and scuttlings in the bush, and the pulse of frogs and crickets.

'So, what's going to happen,' he asked, 'when your visa runs out? We might need to try and get you a proper work visa. I have no idea how hard that could be.'

'There are probably ways for me to overstay my welcome and not be noticed, but it's likely I'm going to have to go back to the UK, much as that pains me, although it will be good to see my kids.'

'What if,' he said, his gaze looking almost fierce in the flickering candle light. 'What if I didn't want to let you go, for non-workrelated reasons.'

'I don't know,' she said. 'I had not planned anything beyond getting away from England when I left.'

He smiled, took a sip of wine. 'There are probably a few ways for you to stay in this country. We could explore those, if you like.'

'I'd love to be able to stay longer if I could,' she said. 'It would be nice to spend time getting to know you more.'

They stared at each other. Lara felt her temperature rise.

'What more would you like to know?' He briefly looked down to contemplate his wine glass, the way the last drops swirled at the bottom near the stem. Then he looked at her.

'Anything you want to reveal,' she said, her voice soft.

'I think I've been quite revealed already,' he said.

She smiled and twirled her wine glass by its stem, as if it were a rare flower, remembering the last time she'd had anything to drink, courtesy of Brock & Co. She thought of what she knew about Andrew now, and felt warm from her head to her feet.

'It's a little unnerving when you smile like that,' he said.

'Why's that, Doc?'

He stared her down, but his eyes were kind. 'Because I start to feel things that I don't know what to do about.' He leaned across the table and took her hands in his. Then he blew out both candles. Lara looked up at the sky and felt closer to the millions of brilliant spinning galaxies out in the universe than she'd ever felt before. Her heart skipped beats and she allowed herself to tumble down an Alice-in-Wonderland-like spiral of emotions. 'Wow,' she whispered.

'It feels good here now,' he said. 'This place used to be gloomy, but your presence has changed things. It definitely feels different.'

'Really? Valencia said something similar.'

'So, you two talked, did you?'

'A little.'

'I'm glad. I like how you've made everything feel new. Renewed.'

'Speaking of new,' she said, mischievous. 'My bed has a brand new very comfortable mattress.'

He leaned further across the table and Lara thought her heart might be in danger of bursting at the look on his face. Their lips touched. His kiss felt like it was designed to extract her soul from her body – and she allowed it to happen.

'How about I clean all this up later?' he said.

'Love that idea.'

They got up and by starlight, made their way inside.

At her bedside, Lara wrapped her arms around him. He whispered her name into her hair and in that second, she felt she could sense everything about him; his grief, his hunger and his fortress walls, though at this moment those walls felt more like holograms she could move through right into the secret chamber where whatever he guarded was exposed.

'I hope you know what you're doing,' he whispered. Meaning, you might get hurt, she thought.

His kiss burned. He stripped flimsy clothes from her and his hands trailed heat across her skin. She sank into the softness of her bed and his body, outlined in the faint starlight through the window, was a sculpted work of art. He slid his hands beneath her hips and pulled her towards him.

Sheet and bodies tangled. Pillows lay strewn. The currents that took them, shook them and tumbled them. What Lara had learned from her gifted buddy Mario was priceless. Without him, she wouldn't have had this much to give to Andrew. She watched his confidence grow, felt him take hold of the masculine power that she had seen in him all along, as he carried her to where he wanted them both to go.

She knew, as her body sang, that she'd fallen in love with the doctor who didn't want to love anyone again.

Afterwards, she lay in his arms.

'Lost for words,' he said.

She had her head on his chest, listening to his heart. Lost my mind, she thought.

They stared out of the open door at the moist cricket-filled night air.

'What are those stars?' she asked.

255

'That's Orion, the hunter, low in the sky, see his elbow? It's drawn back ready to shoot his bow and arrow into the universe,' he said.

Her hand crept onto his taut abdomen and she left it there.

'You alright?' he said.

She smiled. 'Yes.'

'You know, I had a thought. We could tell the immigration authorities that you're Australian by injection,' he said. 'What do you think?'

'You're *bad*,' she said and laughed.

He kissed her lips. 'Allow me. I've been good for so long,' he said.

She wanted to show that she understood – the past, his fear.

'I wish we'd met before life did so much bloody damage,' she said. 'But then I suppose we wouldn't have met.'

'No,' he said. 'We wouldn't have.'

The walls were still there beneath his skin. She could feel them.

They fell asleep with the door open to the night, and woke with the sun pouring onto their faces, their arms wrapped around each other.

'Good morning,' he said.

'Hmmm.'

She struggled to an upright sitting position. He stroked tendrils of hair from her forehead.

'Want some tea?'

'That'd be lovely,' she said. 'Are you always the tea-man?'

'Always,' he said. 'Milk and sugar?'

She cast an eye over the beautiful man in her bed — beautiful and not thirty-one-and-a-half like Mario, nor sunken into middle-of-life disinterest and dishonesty like Brock. She reached up and ran fingers through his unruly greying hair. She loved that his hand wandered across her skin and she didn't want to move in case the moment vanished.

'It's seven,' he said. 'I'll make tea and then should get back, shower and get some proper clothes on,' he said. 'Valencia will be wondering where I am.'

'I'll write you an excuse,' she said. 'Dr Andrew Roberts is late for work because his exercise routine went a little overtime.'

'If it wasn't a working day, I'd stay here with you and perfect that exercise routine. You've brought a part of me back to life, Lara. I thought that could never happen.'

He bent, kissed her lips and stood up. She wrinkled her nose and smiled. He put on the kettle.

30

Friday morning. Lara had spent the night on her own because Andrew had a business dinner with a colleague. She thought it might be a good thing, since she'd barely left his side night or day, for days now. She'd had time to text Joanne, tell her what had happened, to speak to Simon and Rose and to send an update to Ruby.

Ruby's return text made her laugh.

Ruby: *Do you think our days of paying for sex are over now?*

Lara: *What a thought!* ☺

The next morning, Lara got dressed and went down the drive to the mailbox to retrieve the mail, before heading up to the office. She pulled out two white envelopes addressed to Andrew, and a large brown one addressed to her. The only person she'd ever given her physical address to was Jean-Luc.

On the way back to the house, she tore open her envelope. Staring back at her was a black and white version of *The Kiss*. Also, a proof-copy of the magazine page where it would appear, with a little note, 'love and thinking of you, J.L.' Lara did a double take. It was, objectively speaking, a rather sexy and awesome shot. She admired the photo for its artistic merit yet again, but oddly, the sight of Mario now made her feel slightly embarrassed. Had she actually felt jealous of this youngster? She smiled. Honestly, Lara, she thought. Of all the crazy things she'd done since she arrived in Australia, by far the most ridiculous was running away from Ruby's house. And yet, without that, this would never have happened, she thought, looking around her.

Though Andrew had shared some of his past with her and she'd told him about her children, he'd said nothing more about his loss and Lara couldn't bring herself as yet to spare many details about what had happened with Brock. She had not spoken about her super Mario adventures either. She thought it best to put photo evidence of the Mario episode in a place where it wouldn't appear by accident until the time was right to talk about it. She looked at the photo again, and then slid it and the magazine page back into the envelope which she pushed under her bed.

Not seeing Andrew for eighteen hours felt like forever. She jogged towards the practice.

He was behind the counter on the phone and her heart flooded with warmth when she saw him. He smiled and the room lit up. When he finished his conversation, he came around to the front of reception and lifted her into a hug, kissing her hard. 'I've missed you,' he said, smoothing back hair from her forehead.' Don't ever go away for so long again.'

She laughed. 'You're the one out for dinner dates with business partners. You should be more mindful of your priorities.'

'It's good to hold you again,' he said. 'And we do have a busy day today. But only until noon. I blocked out the afternoon.'

'You did?' She leaned back in the circle of his arms.

'I'd like to have a bit of an uninterrupted long weekend with you — if that suits you Ms Winters?'

'What do you have in mind?'

'More than one thing,' he said. 'And Valencia has

some well-deserved time off too. She's gone up to Brisbane to see her son. You know, some time I'd like for you to meet my mother. She's a bit caustic, but I think you'd like her, and she, you.'

'I'm sure I would,' Lara said, and felt blood rise to her cheeks.

'What are you looking so mischievous about?' he said.

'Nothing,' she said and laughed. 'I'd love to … meet your mother.'

Thankfully the phone rang and he let her go. 'That's your job,' he said. 'We close here at one.'

'Of course Doc Roberts.'

★ ★ ★

They were busy for the next five hours without pause. Lara enjoyed observing Andrew at work. He came out to greet his patients himself and though she looked like she was busy at work, she listened and watched. She saw him with frightened children, with grumpy old men, and with anxious young women, and to all of them he offered the same gentle, patient, but no-nonsense compassion. If it were at all possible, her admiration for him grew until she could barely contain her emotions. She busied herself to keep her feelings in check and had just taken down the medicare number of the last patient, and was seeing her out, when he popped his head around the door.

'Tired?'

'Whacked,' she said. 'That was crazy.'

She closed the sliding door to the outside and locked it. 'We're closed now,' she said.

'I thought I might have a slower start, but it looks

260

like everyone's been saving their ailments for me. Mrs Slatter, to name one. They know they can see my colleague in town any time when I'm away, but some patients don't like change.'

'You were so gracious with her,' Lara said, clearing the desk of everything but pens and clean notepaper. 'I thought she was going to make you accountable for all the new pains she told me she's added to her list since you went away.'

'Yes, well,' he said. 'She's not an easy one, but I don't suppose being short with her would make her feel any better.'

'I don't know how you do it. I think I would have shown her the opening to my secret trapdoor and let her fall in.'

He smiled. 'You do not have a secret trapdoor. You're the epitome of empathy and grace.'

'Oh, I do,' she said and smiled. 'And I'm not. I actually have put people in there.'

'I have to pity anyone who falls through,' he said.

'Don't worry, I use it only in emergencies,' she said. 'Very few have fallen in, and those who have, they earned it.'

'Come here,' he said.

'Now?'

'Right now.'

He slid his arms around her and kissed her softly on the lips. Then he looked at her, all playfulness gone from his eyes. 'Great job this morning,' he said. 'Thank you.'

'It was my pleasure as always doc.'

'Do you need food? I need food.'

'That would be nice.'

'I want to, need to show you something,' he said.

261

'Sure.'

'You'll probably want to get changed though, so why don't I make us a snack and you head off and get changed. Wear comfy clothes, some walking shoes, and I'll see you back here?'

'Sounds fine,' she said and stood on tiptoes kissing his cheek. 'Adios for now. I'll be back.'

She picked up her phone from the counter, and slipped out of the door.

Twenty minutes later, she hurried back, smelling bread toasting. She went up through the front door into the kitchen. Andrew had cooked salmon in lemon and thrown together a salad garnished with sesame seeds and avocado. He'd also made them fresh juice and a large juicer stood on the table with the residue of carrot, beets, kale, and lemon. She almost said, wow, that looks like immortality juice, and was grateful she caught her words, remembering why he would have such healthy food set out.

'That looks thoroughly like what the doctor ordered,' she said instead. 'You can be my cook any day.'

'At your service,' he said.

By the time they sat down at the large dining table to eat, she was ravenous.

'Where are we going?'

'For a walk. I don't know how much of the property you've seen?'

'Not much,' she said, sipping the juice. 'This is so good,' she said.

'Glad you approve. When we've finished, we'll head up the back.'

'Are we going anywhere specific?'

'I'll show you. It might explain a bit more.'

'Okay,' she said.

After lunch, she followed Andrew out of the house and up into the bush behind. The path was still sodden and barely visible, but there was a track, and he followed it sure-footed.

'How big is this property?'

'Forty acres.'

'Are we still on it?'

'Absolutely. It includes this whole mountain.'

Vines and eucalyptus trees grew so profusely it was hard to see anything else. Andrew's demeanor had changed. He seemed to have gone somewhere inside himself. His steps grew larger, more fervent. Lara did her best to keep up with what became a punishing pace. He was fit and she wondered how. Since they'd been together they'd done not much more than eat, make love, work and sleep. The undergrowth changed, grew sparse, and then tall waving green grass appeared as they arrived at the top of a hill. Far on either side, the Pacific stretched out to the sky. Below them the green unfolded in different shades, and the clouds in the distance let golden sunrays stream down into the sea.

A sea breeze guested up from the valley. Andrew stopped a few steps ahead of her. He thrust his hands deep into his pockets and kicked at something on the ground. Then he got down on his haunches, and looked at her, reaching out and pulling out a few weeds, smoothing the ground with his hand.

Lara's hair had blown into her mouth and she had to wrestle it back from her face. 'What is it?' she asked. Andrew didn't say anything. Her eyes followed his hands. They rested on a small, rectangular stone, the size of a baby bath, pressed into the ground. It was engraved with something.

She knelt down next to him. Her first thought was:

he's taking me to his wife's grave. But the name on the stone wasn't Gabrielle's.

'Eli Roberts.' She read the name so softly she thought the wind took the words from her mouth and blew them away. 'Too precious for this world. Died, aged seventeen months. Loved for ever and ever. Mum and Dad.' She looked up at Andrew. He stared far out towards the end of the world. His eyes shone and his stony countenance stopped her breath.

'You never get over it,' he said. 'Gabrielle never got over it. The grief went right to her bones.'

'Oh, Andrew.' Lara's chest heaved at the full realisation. She could not imagine living beyond her own children's lives. She crept over to him and put her arms around him. His hand closed over hers, cold. His in-breath was a shudder. She wet his shoulder with tears and held him tightly in her arms.

'He was bitten by a brown snake. And I didn't know it until it was too late. He was playing next to his paddling pool. I was watching him and did not see the snake. The bite itself can feel just like a scratch. By the time we found the marks, he'd gone into cardiac arrest. I'm a doctor, and I couldn't save my own baby son.'

Lara couldn't speak. He was silent too. After long moments he said: 'And I couldn't save Gabrielle either.'

The full force of his words, knocked any response out of her as she comprehended what that meant to Andrew.

'So, you see, after a certain amount of pain, of loss or damage, it was hard to imagine that anything could ever resemble normality in my world again. I've been so taken by surprise with you – but I don't want to pretend that I'm someone I'm not. My heart is buried with him, Lara, and with her, and I don't know if I have anything to give that isn't tainted with this tragedy.'

Lara knew that she wanted more than anything for this man to be okay. And it was beyond anything to do with her. She felt love. She felt what he'd been through. They sat, looking out at the horizon. There were no words, only silence and the sound of wind through the trees. Low clouds raced beneath the higher ones, blocking the sun. Far out to sea, dark patches of indigo and streaks of light and dark marked where storms fell. Although it was summer, Lara shivered. She kept her hands on his, and felt each finger, its shape, its strength, the smooth, gold wedding band on his left hand. These hands had held his newborn son, and carried him through life for seventeen months, and loved him, and tried to save him, and then had buried him. They'd held and loved his wife, and nursed her, and cared for her, and then buried her too. She couldn't bear his grief. It went through her and she understood the fortress, and why.

'I'm sorry,' he said. 'I've never brought anyone up here. I don't mean to burden you.'

'No burden,' she said. 'Thanks for sharing this with me.'

'We should go down,' he said.

'We can stay here a while,' she said. 'If you like.'

'You sure?'

'It's beautiful up here.'

He looked surprised. She kept her body close to his, gazed out at the distant ocean, and understood life as a journey of love and loss, of laughter and tragedy, a journey far too short for so many. She brought his hand to her lips and kissed it and dared not look at his face.

After half an hour, Andrew stood and helped Lara to her feet. In silence, they started to walk down the hill. Halfway down, he took her hand and held it tightly all the way home.

Later in the afternoon they made love. His arms carried her into a world of desire that made her ache for what she could not reach. Their passion was wordless, flesh against flesh. She showed him what she felt, and realised she loved him irrevocably and that she did not want to do anything to stop the rushing emotions that made the world around them dissolve into photons.

Rain came again in the late afternoon, and she lay on his chest and heard the rumble as he spoke. 'I've been having therapy on and off for, let's see, over two years now. None of it has moved me forward an inch. And you arrive and blast me out of the water. But I feel guilty, you know, for these moments of joy for feeling lust, desire. Can you get that?'

'Yep,' she said. 'Just go with the flow. Okay? We have no idea about anything else except here and now.'

He turned to look at her. 'You dazzle me,' he said. 'Why does everything you say make me come undone? What shall I do with you?'

'Not sure, but I can think of a few things, some of which you've already done. I don't mind if you do them again.'

They spent the weekend like a couple on honeymoon. They mapped out places along the coast that had significance for one reason or another and ticked them off on a list. They climbed to the lighthouse and ate chocolate ice-cream together, and when she got chocolate on her chin, he licked it off. 'Now the memory of you eating ice-cream alone in a new country is overlayed with this one,' he said.

They walked hand-in-hand along the beach in Byron. 'And now, your arrival here, watching all those young happy couples holding hands and feeling like life had passed you by has a new chapter,' he said.

They went to Tallow beach in the evening and dug a hole and made a fire.

'Doc Roberts, your memories of this beach and evenings spent alone with a fire, have a new story,' and she kissed him. Because there was no one there, she stripped off her clothes slowly and lay on the towel they'd brought and watched him look at her with disbelief.

'You're really going to make sure I don't forget this,' he said. She smiled. One day she would take him to the cave on the remote beach where she'd been with Mario, and ensuring no one was using the space in the vagina cavern, she had a plan for making new memories there. She was happy to wait, though. For now, she realised she'd stopped trying to be anything except herself and in the moment.

When Monday morning came, Lara woke up in Andrew's bed, looked over at him sleeping and had a thought; if she could see her kids several times a year, she would have no reason to want to be anywhere but with the doctor. His face and every expression in his eyes were imprinted in her heart. She was getting to know his body as well as she knew her own. She held his pain as she held her own, carefully, understanding it seeped up to the surface at times in odd ways. She whispered to his sleeping self, 'I don't want to let you go.'

* * *

Monday was another busy day in the practice. Andrew had an evening out with some old friends, which she encouraged him to go to. As they closed the clinic, she reminded him about Tuesdays.

'Just so you don't forget, I'll be off tomorrow to make my Tuesday appointment.'

It seemed ridiculous now to be keeping her friendship with his mother a secret from him. She would have to break that silence, but she couldn't figure out the best way. He'd said he wanted them to meet, but evidently that time wasn't quite right yet. It could go very smoothly, she hoped. She'd pretend they'd never met, be introduced to Dot at some point in the near future, and then down the track they'd reveal their secret and everyone would laugh and live happily ever after.

'What's the secret appointment?' he asked, his tone intimate.

'I'll tell you soon,' she said. 'I have this little bit of stuff to attend to, and then I'm free. You wouldn't be able to meet me for lunch tomorrow, would you?'

'I'll see what I can do,' he said. She detected distance in his voice and felt slightly sick, but she couldn't reveal the truth.

'You pick the place,' she said. 'Can you get an hour or so free?'

Again, his voice sounded cooler than she wanted it to be.

'Fine,' he said. 'Do your stuff. There's not much happening here after one. There's a nice organic restaurant overlooking the sea in Byron. We can meet there around one fifteen.'

Lara did a hasty calculation. She needed to get to Carremere but guessed she could get away from there by twelve and in be Byron by one.

'I think that could work.'

'You think?'

She wished she could just tell him. 'It's fine. One fifteen sounds great. You have my mobile number.'

'Yes, I do,' he said.

The mood in the practice felt taut. Lara could see a struggle on his face. On the one hand, the increasingly deep and trusting intimacy and ecstasy meant that they were beginning to feel like a couple, welded at the lips and hips. On the other, there was his need to hold onto the safety of his boundaries and her need to find a way out of the pickle she'd made for herself.

'It'll be great,' she said, breaking the stiffness around them. She smiled at him. 'I'll see you there. You can go. I'll clear up and lock up.'

He smiled, relaxing slightly. 'Thanks Lara,' he said.

'See you tomorrow in Byron. Have fun tonight.'

When he left, Lara felt her heart go out the door with him, and she wanted to run after him to get it back.

269

31

Lara arrived at Carremere just after ten in the morning. As she went into the reception area, she saw by the look on Debbie's face that all was not right with the world.

'Deb — everything okay?'

She put her hand on Lara's arm. 'Come with me.' They walked into the communal sitting area. 'The old lieutenant passed away yesterday.'

A few residents were there,in their wheelchairs, sitting like statues. Two bedridden residents had been wheeled in on elevated beds and had fallen asleep in front of a television set. No wonder Dot was so full of spicy attitude, Lara thought. She really didn't fit. And there she sat, in the far corner, looking out at the greenery. She seemed oblivious to Lara's entrance, and Lara had an insane desire to take Dot out of the place forever. Why was she here anyway, she wondered? Did Andrew find the burden of looking after his mother too much? Did she need such significant care?

'Hey Deb, do you mind if I switch off this mindless TV? The only awake and conscious resident in the room doesn't seem to be watching it.'

'That's fine,' Debbie said. 'I'll do it, but if anyone wants it back on again, we'll need to oblige.'

'Sure,' Lara said. Debbie went to turn off the TV. Lara turned to her.

'I hope he didn't suffer too much.'

'I hope not too. We tried to make him as comfortable as possible. He went into a coma two days ago. I brought Dot to see him before he died. I think she liked him,' she said.

'She knew his mind was still sharp even though his functions had all but deserted him. I'll go say hello to her now, Deb, if that's okay. Thanks for switching off the TV.'

Lara's shoes squeaked across the shiny floor and she came around to the front of Dot's wheelchair.

'Hi Dot.'

She looked up. 'He died. They tell you?'

'Yes.'

'I think we need to get out of here. Now isn't soon enough. Take me to the swamp. Anywhere.'

Dot's mood was dark blue, like the sky just before a storm. Lara grabbed the back of the wheelchair. 'Okay, sure.'

'Lara, you know, I'm beginning to be of the mind that I'd rather die somewhere else. In my own bed. I was the one who insisted on coming here because I thought it was a good idea, but now I'm changing my mind. I made an error of judgment and now I want the hell out of here. If Andrew can manage it. I haven't spoken to him yet, but I will.'

Lara wheeled Dot outside and was careful over the bumps and gaps in the paving.

'Faster. In fact, you go as fast as you like. I just need to feel some air moving past my face and remember that outside this place, life goes on. Tell me how work is these days. Tell me about my son. Is he behaving? Do his patients like him? Is he treating you well? He came to visit me last week. And I've said nothing about you, by the way. But sometime soon perhaps it might be time to let our cat out of the bag.'

Lara sighed. 'Dot, I have to tell you something.'

'Well, go on, spit it out.'

'Dot, I think I'm … no, I actually am hopelessly in love with your son.'

'What? Stop this bloody thing. Come around, I want to see your face.'

Lara brought the wheelchair to a halt in front of the pond. Mosquitoes rose out of it like so many evil spirits and began to land on the two women and feast on their flesh. Lara knelt at Dot's feet and placed her hands on the old woman's knees. There was something about Dot's mouth, a vulnerability, a softness that her son had inherited, that Lara loved.

'He's the kindest, sexiest, most intelligent man I've ever met. But I know it's a hard one. He's had too much pain, as he says, too much loss to ever trust, to ever love …'

'And you've told him all this, have you?'

'Told him what?'

'That you love him and he's the kindest … et cetera?'

'No! God no. He would run a thousand miles.'

'Oh, for God's sakes! Get off your bloody arse, and tell him like it is,' Dot said. 'What's to lose? I thought you were a straight talker!'

'I am … it's just that …'

'Bollocks. You're wasting time,' she said. 'My son has had his fair share of heartbreak in the world, as have we all. There's no doubt about that. But emotions, dear girl, are not set in stone. They evolve and breathe and move, trust me, even when the body is old and wrinkled and unattractive. So don't tell me that he's beyond ever feeling anything again.'

Lara swallowed. Her legs trembled. Dot put her hands over Lara's, and said, 'What's got into you?'

'I don't know,' she said. 'He doesn't know I'm here, for one, so I'm keeping this a secret from him. Also, I'm afraid of hurting him, and of being barely over a horrible divorce and on the rebound myself. I've hidden pictures of Mr Erotic Mario under my bed and haven't told Andrew about that interlude yet. I'm afraid of doing things prematurely, or too late. I don't know, and this is all so hasty.'

'Now you listen here.' Dot tried to pat Lara's hands with her shaking ones.

Lara saw the mother in her and in that moment, she felt ready to listen to whatever she said.

'My son has surely survived worse than confessions of love from a beautiful woman, you understand?'

'Yes ma'am.' Lara smiled.

'So you get yourself to him now, ASAP, and tell him everything. And if you don't, mind you, I'll be doing it for you.'

'That sounds like an order,' Lara said.

'It's a command,' Dot said.

'I would never want to go against that,' Lara said.

'Wise choice,' Dot said.

Lara took in a deep breath. 'I'm meeting him for lunch today. I think it'll be a good time. I'll confess everything, including how I feel. Because you're right, there's always something to lose in this life. And you should tell him that you want to come home.'

'Oh yes, I will. Now that's my girl,' she said. 'Time is of the essence. Rush me back, and get going, or I'll have to call him and tell him everything myself — and that would ruin the romance of the moment.'

'That's for sure,' Lara laughed, and began to wheel

273

the impatient resident back to the communal room where now no TV blared and a new kind of peace pervaded the atmosphere.

32

Lara's palms were as sweaty as they'd ever been as she drove into town. Byron Bay was known as *the meeting place*. For tens of thousands of years, the first people of Australia had been coming to gather here, and she found this incredible. Aboriginal Australians were the oldest continuous culture in the world. And, she was on their continent. Lara felt the power of this land and wished she could stay for always, learn more and be part of its story.

She pondered this as she edged into the only free parking space she could find, behind a row of shops. She was forty-five minutes early, happy that she had plenty of time to gather her courage to tell Andrew the truth. She tried to imagine his reaction. He might withdraw. It might ruin everything. She might seem too forward. He might look at her with kindness and pity and treat her like one of his patients. Maybe he would tell her that while he enjoyed making love to her, his fortress and gold wedding ring were forever. She ran a few more scenarios through her head and decided that most of them were possible, and that she would have to risk it anyway.

She locked the car, put on her sunglasses, and was fumbling, trying to get the keys into her handbag, when a familiar voice took her by surprise.

'Hey Lara!'

She looked up. 'Mario?'

'So happy to see you. I thought you'd vanished off the face of the earth.'

'How are you?'

'Really good. And you?'

'I'm good.'

'You look wonderful,' he said.

'Thanks. You do too.'

And he did. In a purely aesthetic and artistic way. She appreciated his brown locks, his sculpted body, his chiseled jaw, but didn't feel any surge of electric attraction towards him.

'Hey, I heard from Jean-Luc the other day,' she said.

'You did?'

'Yes, he sent some of those pics. Have you seen them in print?'

'I have. They're great – I'm proud of him. He's going to be back here some time and maybe we can all get together then. He's got a job here.'

'I did hear that,' she said, 'though my visa may have run out by then.'

'Oh no! Listen, I've been thinking about you so much and I have things I want to say to you. Do you have a minute, or are you in a hurry?'

'I'm not in a hurry, but I do have to be somewhere in exactly forty minutes.'

'Alright. A twenty-minute coffee?'

'Fine.'

'Thank you. Let's go here.'

'You're welcome,' she said. Was this the man who took her to the cave by the sea? Was this the person whose actions caused her to be so distressed when he went upstairs to give Ruby her money's worth? Oh my God, she thought, I must have been feeling very small and insecure.

They sat down at a coffee table right on the pavement. 'Lara, I've tried to call you so many times. I'm sorry about what happened, you know, with Ruby. Very unfortunate.'

His warm eyes looked soft, sincere. He reached out and placed his hands over hers.

She smiled. 'Forget about it, Mario. It's really fine. I harbor no anger or anything. I was in the middle of a crisis. You didn't do anything wrong. Let it go.'

He looked up, and blinked, squeezing her hands. 'That's a relief. I thought I'd done major damage.'

'Not at all. You know, like I said, I tried to be a Room Two person but I wasn't cut out for the role. No hard feelings, Mario. You're great at what you do.'

He pressed his hands harder over hers. 'Thank you. You're very kind. By the way, I've taken my ad out of the paper.'

'Oh, why's that?'

'Would you like me to get you a flat white? They're quick about it.'

'Alright. Thank you.'

'I'll be back to tell you my news in a second.'

He went to stand in line.

Lara sat at the wrought iron table, looked at the couples sitting at the others, noted the smell of sunscreen and fresh coffee, She mused at how llama-walking, tantric sex-working, and nude modelling were just a drop in the ocean of occupations possible in Byron. She looked at her watch. It wouldn't take more than five minutes to walk from there to the restaurant to meet Andrew, she thought.

She had plenty of time.

Mario came back to the table with their coffees and sat down.

'I'm off to Tasmania,' he said. 'Leaving on Sunday.

277

'What? Tell me more.' Lara thought he looked different, more open. She felt a wave of kindness towards him, understanding in that moment that he wasn't the cocky stud she'd once assumed him to be. 'Does this have anything to do with you taking your ad down?'

'It does.'

Lara took her latte and sat on the edge of her seat. 'I can't wait to hear,' she said.

Mario looked at his cup and then up at her. His cheeks coloured.

'Lara, I feel bad. Embarrassed. Before I say anything else, please accept my apologies. For everything I put you through. Regardless of what you say, I need to say that.'

'Thanks, Mario,' she said. 'Apology accepted. Now, moving on. Since our last encounter I've found myself, a life, a path. I've reconnected with Ruby, and you were right about one thing: my ex came running back for an arse-kicking which he received, I'm proud to say. Also, I've met a lovely man.'

'That's awesome,' Mario said. 'Hearing that makes my day.'

'Really?' She grinned. 'Thanks. I'm happy. Now tell me about you.'

'Well, I've been doing some deep reflection. Long story short, I realised that in my idealistic attempts to love women and make them feel whole, I'd hurt a few. You helped me in that department, in a few ways I don't want to ignore.'

'That's interesting.'

'I made lots of assumptions.'

'Like what?'

'Well, as you pointed out some time back, I just assumed being honest and open would take care of any pain, dissolve any possibility of anyone feeling betrayed.'

'But?'

'Well, life's not like that.'

'No?' She smiled.

'No. Much as I hate to admit this, loving people means being jealous sometimes, because we do need to attach. That's a human need I never considered as being different to enmeshment. I've been getting some counseling. I never imagined me doing that.'

'That's fabulous,' Lara said. 'If only because it made me nervous that some young stud seemed to have the world completely figured out.'

He laughed. 'Ah, the arrogance of youth, right?'

'Right. So now that you're all grown up,' she said, 'what are your plans?'

'Let's go back to that day when you talked to me about Sophie. That got weirdly under my skin. Recently, because I've been feeling, I don't know, like being more authentic and admitting things I hadn't, and after talking this through with my psychologist, I set myself the challenge to summon the courage and write Sophie an email.' He paused and rubbed his forehead. 'You were right, Lara, I broke her heart. I was a bastard. Like so many other men.'

'Don't be so hard on yourself,' she found herself saying. 'You were trying to be the best person you knew how to be. Like most of us. Just not all of us.'

He took a sip of his coffee and then put his cup down, taking both her hands in his again. 'I realised, Lara, that in trying to avoid doing to women what my dad did to my mum, I'd gone right up the same street.' He shook his head. 'Anyway, you were the one who showed me the inside of a broken heart. I'd thought

279

I could heal you, take away your pain. How's that for arrogance?'

Lara smiled.'It's been replaced by humility, so I can't fault you, Mario. So now what happens?'

'I go back to Tasmania next week. Sophie agreed to meet me for a meal. I've no idea what will happen. But at the very least I owe her a face-to-face and an apology. I'm ready to hear whatever she wants to throw at me.'

'Wonderful,' Lara said.'You need to let me know what happens, okay?'

'You bet,' he said.

'Listen Mario, I've got to get going. It was really great to run into you and with all my heart, I wish you good luck in the far south with Sophie.'

He let go of her hands and they stood to say goodbye. He hugged her tight, then looked into her eyes, and then he bent his head, and pressed his lips to hers.

It wasn't an especially chaste kiss. She could feel the conversation between them: *Thank you. This was great. We learned a lot. We shared a lot.* His lips captured hers and held them for a little too long, and she didn't push him away. It was a sweet kiss, and when she finally stepped back, his eyes shimmered.

'Take care,' she said, holding onto his arms affectionately.

'Good bye Lara. Thanks.' He kissed her cheek and turned away.

Lara got up and began to walk, not thinking that the loud footsteps behind her were following her until the presence of the person was almost on top of her. She turned. Her breath caught and she looked right into Andrew's face. His countenance was ashen, his lips drawn in a thin line, and his demeanour unrecognisable.

'I've been here for a while watching you. I didn't want to interrupt your Tuesday *appointment*.'

The blood drained from her face. Fight-or-flight; her body pushed blood to her extremities so she could outrun approaching danger, but the danger wasn't physical. Her body didn't know this, though, and she felt instantly lightheaded. She thought she might faint. Andrew faced her like a stranger. His eyes had turned to ice.

'I would never want to intrude on your freedom,' he said, lips visibly dry, face hard and cold and far away.

How long had he been there? Lara was desperate to say, *it's not what you think*! But the words died in her throat. He turned away and began to walk down the hill.

She found her voice and leapt into action, flying after him.

'Wait, Andrew! It's not what you think!' She caught up with him.

He was striding away, a full metre at a time. 'I'm not sure what I think, Lara,' he said. 'It's what I saw that really bothers me.'

'Listen to me, Andrew, please. I was just saying goodbye. Mario is well in the past. Honestly, you have to believe me. It's not what it may have looked like to you. He was … he was …'

'Forgive me if I don't have the stomach to discuss the details of your farewells to former or perhaps current boyfriends.' His eyes were aflame.

'Mario's no one to me, Andrew. You're reading this as something it's not. You have to believe me!'

He turned. His stride increased rapidly and Lara ran, desperate, losing him with every passing second.

'If you don't mind, Lara, for the sake of self-preservation, and because I'm not in the habit of sharing women with other men, and probably never will be, would you do me a favour, and make sure that by tonight, you've moved yourself and everything you own, right off my property? I'll plan on returning home after midnight.'

He turned away from her. The fortress was impenetrable. Hot tears closed Lara's throat as she jogged alongside him. 'Please listen to me,' she sobbed.

'I'm sorry. Whatever it was between us is over. It's obvious to me that neither of us is ready for any kind of commitment. Don't come to work tomorrow. Valencia will take on my administration at the clinic until we find a suitable replacement.'

Lara stopped. Andrew kept going as fast as he could.

He was gone. Out of her space, around the corner, out of her sight, and out of her life. Lara went into shock. The after image of Andrew's vanishing figure convinced her that the last five minutes had actually taken place.

She didn't move. Then, like someone moving through thick gelatin, she took slow, uneven steps back towards her car, and collapsed on the bonnet. No lunch. No afternoon date at the organic restaurant. No Andrew. Nothing. Nowhere to go. The end. Impossible to believe. He had broken away forever.

She had to go back to the cottage because everything was there. Food filled the fridge and cupboard. Her clean clothes were hanging at the back of the cottage on a make-shift line. Her chest burned, and her throat too.

After lying over the car in stunned disbelief for what seemed like an eternity, she stood up, head reeling. She got into the car and drove. Tears blurred her vision. If she'd seen anyone driving like this, she'd have called them a maniac. Fuck! She thought. Bloody, fucking hell! She hit a hundred on the small back roads and flew over potholes on the dirt road up to Andrew's house. She had ruined her last chance at happiness in one, ridiculous, completely unforeseen moment. *It's not what you think, it just isn't,* her insistent internal voice kept saying. But the universe knew that it was a useless, fucking pathetic response to the situation.

Andrew's car wasn't there. She didn't want to see Valencia. She tore up the drive, parked the car, and ran blindly up through the forest to the cottage.

Crying, she threw the entire contents of the fridge and cupboard into the big, outside bin. Within minutes she'd packed the bathroom and all her clothes into her suitcase. Anything that wasn't essential she tossed out. She left the bed as it was, pulled out the envelope with the pictures of *The Kiss*, of her and Mario, and then with a permanent marker she found on the kitchen counter she wrote, angry, heart broken, and nihilistic, on the back of The Kiss:

Andrew this is what you would not let me SAY:

1) I paid this stud of a man to shag me when I first arrived here broken and yes it HELPED! He is a SEX-WORKER and he was GOOD!

2) I modelled with him – his gay friend who took the photos has a JOB because of these pictures and they will soon be PUBLISHED.

3) I did not kiss him, HE kissed ME in the coffee shop. It was a GOODBYE from HIM. If you want further details ask your MOTHER.

4) I only wanted one person after I met you and it was NOT HIM.

5) Goodbye FOREVER.

In another seven minutes Lara was in her car with her suitcase, her handbag and her open return ticket to London Heathrow on Singapore Airlines. There was no sign of Valencia and she thanked God for that small mercy.

It had taken thirty-five minutes for her to be on her shell-shocked way out of the doctor's property.

The drive to Brisbane Airport was the longest two hours of Lara's life. She could have gone to Ruby's again and started the whole story over, but she decided that enough was enough. This was life, unfair, cruel and absurd. She cried all the way to the long-stay car-park. She had a car plan in place already. She would leave the Toyota for Ruby to inherit. Lara would write her a letter, put the keys in an envelope and pay for a week of parking so that it might stay there until she found a way to get it. They would do change of ownership paperwork by mail.

Free of everything now except her suitcase and thoroughly shattered heart, she went to the check-in desk to enquire about the next flight to London.

'Our next flight leaves tonight at seven,' the sweet lady said. 'But it's fully booked to Singapore. You'll have to wait until tomorrow.'

'Can you can put me on an urgent waiting list? I really need to get back to the UK.'

'We can't promise anything.'

'I'll just wait,' Lara said. It wasn't as if she had any choice.

'We'll page you if a seat becomes available. I can get you on tomorrow's flight. You can come back in twenty-four hours.'

'No. I'll wait here in case,' Lara said. The woman shrugged, immune to all the emotion Lara was generating.

Lara walked away from the desk, dragging her belongings behind her. She considered going to the nearest bar and attempting to drink herself to death. She settled for a hot chocolate and slumped into a heap on the cafe's cushioned-leather booth.

Sometimes, you have to admit defeat, Lara told herself. Complete and utter defeat. She'd bloody brought this on herself. The message hit her with such clarity and she couldn't deny it. No more escapes. She had to go back to where she'd come from and face the fact that she was a lonely, pathetic, and for now actually homeless almost-divorcee with a back pocket full of crushed dreams. She'd lost everything: the old, the new, and the future. She'd hurt some-one she would never have dreamed of hurting. And the worst of it was, he would not ever believe her, he would forever see her as someone she wasn't. He had retreated to a cold, faraway place and he detested her. He would shut himself off and never find love or trust anyone ever again. Nor would she. She'd gone numb. Her delicate dreams, her potential would never be fulfilled. She could see herself becoming obsolete and invisible to everyone but Joanne and Simon and Rose, but they'd all have their own lives anyway. Decades from now she'd eventually die a lonely and miserable death in some putrid old-age home smelling of piss and three people would come to her funeral.

Lara couldn't bear it, but this was the only reality she could see. Her life lay in front of her, an endless stretch of grey, heartbroken days and deadend stories.

She cried some more, ordered another hot choco-late, and fell asleep at the table.

33

Lara woke with a jolt. Her name was being broadcast by the airline, asking Lara Winters to come to the service desk. She looked at her watch. Was it possible that she'd slept for three hours and no one had bothered to wake her, or worried that she'd died?

With a leaden heart she walked to the counter. She guessed there was now space on the outbound flight.

She pulled her suitcase to the line. There was only one person in front of her talking to the Singapore Airlines employee and he was taking his time. She looked at her watch and at him. Perhaps since losing Andrew she was going to be seeing shadows of him everywhere she went. The man looked just like him from the back. The way he held his body seemed achingly similar.

When he turned around, Lara saw to her amazement that it was Andrew.

Shock does strange things to the brain, she realised later. Thoughts raced through her mind: he'd followed her to make sure she got on the plane and got out of his life. She stepped up and found herself staring at Andrew's flushed cheeks. Her body shook.

'Lara Winters?' the airline clerk said.

'Yes,' she said, still staring at Andrew. 'You have a seat for me on the flight to Singapore?'

'No. I'm afraid we don't. But this gentleman urgently needs to see you.'

'No seats yet to London via Singapore?' she asked dumbly, still looking at Andrew.

'None yet. We'll let you know.'

She stepped to the side. Andrew cleared his throat. When he spoke, his voice was so gentle she felt her tears returning.

'Lara?'

'What?' In her mind's eye Lara still saw him in Byron Bay striding forever away from her. 'Why are you here?' Her voice shook.

'Have I lost you?' he said, and although she could not believe what she was seeing, tears shimmered in his eyes. 'Have I?'

'You told me never to come back again.'

'Oh Lara,' his voice broke. 'I … I can't believe I've been such an idiot.'

'What?' Her legs were on the verge of giving in. She needed to sit down.

'Can we go somewhere?' he asked. 'I need to talk to you. Please do not think of getting on that plane. Can I take your suitcase?'

'What?'

'I got your note. The pictures …'

'Oh, right.'

'Where can we go?'

'There's a cafe over there,' she said, and pointed to the place where she'd just been for the past three hours.

'Okay.'

'What happened?' she asked again, her voice rough now, her head clearing. 'Why are you at the airport?'

He stopped. 'Because I almost let you go, and … and I can't let you go,' he said.

Small butterflies of hope were beginning to flex their wings somewhere deep in Lara's solar plexus. 'Why not?' she whispered.

He let go of her suitcase.

'Because I don't want to be without you. Ever. I'm a hot-headed idiot, Lara. After I left you, I came home. I rushed into the cottage, thinking maybe you'd still be there and I could say go on, tell me what happened, really, and then I found the pictures and your note. Good God, I'm stupid. I'm so sorry. I called my mother and she gave me a lecture.'

Tears were slipping down Lara's cheeks.

'You're not angry with me for having a secret friendship with her?'

'No! I'm confused and I'm angry with myself for my ridiculous behaviour. No, Lara, I am mystified by you, by your relationship with my mother and that you told my mother everything but not me,' he said.

'Yes,' she said. 'Your mother is a legend.'

'Why, please explain, couldn't you tell me? About the secret friendship? About that tantric guy?'

'I just didn't get the chance. I was waiting. I was afraid that somehow you wouldn't trust me. That you'd shut me out.'

He took a step towards her and opened his arms. She hesitated for a moment, seeing the distress on his face and stepped forward as he folded his arms around her. 'I do get it,' he said. 'I'm so sorry. Your secret Tuesday meetings were not with the fellow who kissed you, but with the octogenarian with the sharp tongue.'

'Exactly,' Lara said into his shirt. 'I was concerned you'd be upset with me for muscling in on your personal territory. I couldn't find the right way to tell you.'

'Oh Lara,' he said. 'What have I done?'

'Broken my heart,' she said, her voice cracking.

His bottom lip trembled and he fought back tears.

'But also shown me something,' she said.

'What?'

'That I love you, and that you haven't done anything that can't be undone,' she said. Lara took Andrew's hands, feeling how soft they were, and how strong. She noticed with a start, that the ring was gone from his left hand. Her heart filled with something that felt like red gold. She lived. She loved. She hoped. And she said, 'can I explain something to you now?'

'Of course.'

'I was a passive recipient, not a participant, in that lingering kiss you saw. I believe the extent of it was accidental. I want you to believe me.'

Andrew nodded. His lips opened as if he meant to speak. Lara continued, without waiting for what he was going to say.

'Mario is a good human. He helped me over a rough time. He did his job well back then, when I needed to experiment with new things. And about the pictures? I modeled with him for a French buddy of his. We're ending up in a magazine, as I said. At the time it gave me a boost. That kiss you saw was an emotional thank-you. On his part. He's on his way back to revisit the love of his life. He's just discovered that he is capable of loving someone, a girl he'd left in Tasmania. He's credited me with helping him understand that love between two people exclusively, is possible. He was hopeful and emotional and nervous and he wanted to apologise for his previous flippancy about love, and how love can make two people want to be with each other for life. I'm glad for him. The kiss was not what you thought it was.'

'I'm sorry,' Andrew said softly. 'Can you forgive me?'

'If you can forgive me for keeping Tuesday's dates from you.'

'You mean my mother?'

'Yes.'

'She adores you. Dot Roberts. What a woman my mother is. If I had come here and found you'd left already, I would have followed you to London. For her sake as well as mine. Please tell me you're not still planning to get on the next plane?'

She hesitated.

Andrew's face flickered with concern.

'I'm about to overstay my welcome in this country.'

'I see,' he said and considered something for a moment. 'Well then,' he continued, 'it seems there is only one good solution.'

He took her hand and kissed it.

'Lara,' he said.

'Yes, Andrew.'

'In the name of pragmatism, and because neither of us has cause to believe in happily-ever-after …' He paused.

'Yes?'

'… And with the understanding that I'm sometimes boring, often insecure, and frequently away …' He paused again.

'Yes?'

'… And we're both still dealing with fallout from the past that is messy and sometimes painful. And because life is short and we never know what will happen …'

'Yes.'

'I hope I've covered all bases. Lara, with all that in mind, and for purely pragmatic purposes, would you consider marrying me?'

Lara couldn't help the shock.

'Pardon?'

'I can't ask that again.'

'I mean. Just. Give me a moment.' She closed her eyes. She felt the pulse in their fingers where they touched and opened her eyes again and squeezed his hand.

'So, let's see; for purely pragmatic purposes, and knowing all that … and because my visa is going to expire soon, and life is too short, I think, yes, I have to say in honour of Carpe Diem, I would consider marrying you.'

Andrew pulled Lara into his chest again. She lifted her head and they stared into each other's eyes and smiled. His lips touched hers. Her heart raced as she responded, and pressing her body against his, she made sure that the kiss they shared was as far from chaste as any kiss ever exchanged between two souls.

'Forget the coffee shop. Let's get a hotel room,' he said roughly as he pulled away.

Lara became aware that a few passersby had stopped to stare. Some people applauded. Andrew looked at her and they both smiled.

'Yes, let's,' she said. They held hands and stumbled, drunk with emotion, towards the exit signs. She didn't return to the check-in counter, to tell the clerk not to worry about getting her onto a plane.

They left the Brisbane airport lights far behind and raced north on the highway.

'Where are we going? My car is still parked in the long-term parking. I haven't ditched it yet.'

'I'm not sure,' he said. 'It'll come to me.'

Andrew's hand rested on Lara's knee and she looked

291

at him again and again, to make sure that this reality, was indeed, reality, and not a dream, or a figment of her overactive imagination.

'Did you say hotel room?' she said.

'I did. I just have to find the right one. I don't mean just any hotel room. I want a room with a view.'

'Oh, really? What kind of a view, sir?'

'A spectacular view. A seaview. And a mountain view. And perhaps a waterfall view, thrown in for good measure. We need a day or two to recover.'

'That's a bit of a tall order, your three views.'

'Maybe. But I know something like it exists. A little patience and we'll find it.'

★   ★   ★

They didn't find a hotel room. They found a whole resort as evening descended. It was in the middle of the rainforest on the Sunshine Coast, about an hour north of the city. The bedroom overlooked a small pool and beyond that, the deep blue of the sea glowed in the dying light of the day. Behind the resort, but not quite within view, through rainforest undergrowth, was a thundering waterfall that tumbled like so many white ghosts over a sheer rock face.

Lara put her suitcase down and opened the window. Kookaburras laughed. 'How did you know about this place?'

'A patient recommended it once, long ago. I've never been here,' he said. 'But I kept it in mind.' Lara sat down next to him on the bed, shoulder to shoulder. For a moment they looked at each other. She took his hand.

'It's amazing,' she said.'

292

'Let's go for a walk,' he said. 'There's a path to the sea.'

They walked in darkness from the room through the dense bush to the ocean. But then as they felt soft sand beneath their toes the seascape opened up in front of them, illuminated by an orange moon that hung almost full over the water. The hills on either side reflected in blue shadows along the shoreline. The moon lit the waves as they strolled on the water's edge, and in the west a few streaks of cloud still remained.

Andrew bent down to roll up his trousers. Neither of them had changed since their airport encounter.

'I haven't had so much happen in one day since Brock left me,' Lara said.

'I'm sorry for everything you've had to go through,' he replied. 'Including my hot-headed mistrust.'

'It's okay,' she said. 'If I saw what you saw, I wouldn't trust me either.'

'Yes, but you would have stopped to listen.'

'True,' she said. 'But your heart's been tested more than mine has.'

He was quiet. 'People die of broken hearts,' he said.

'I know,' she said.

'I know that's what happened to Gabrielle. I think I felt bad for living on.'

It was Lara's turn for silence.

'I can't believe you'd want to be with me,' he said. 'Knowing everything you know about me.'

'You're not that bad,' she said and smiled. 'But, more seriously, I'll not intrude on your space, on your memories and love for Gabrielle and Eli,' she said. 'Take the space you need, okay?'

He squeezed her hand. 'It's time to move on,' he said. 'Be in the land of the living. It's what both of them would have wanted.'

As they walked, the hills ahead of them at the end of the beach loomed up like sleeping giants. At the edge of the bay, waves thundered onto rocks and sent moon-lit spray into the air.

'I noticed you're not wearing your wedding ring anymore,' Lara said.

'I was married to a ghost. It's time to let the past go.'

'We don't have to do rings,' she said.

'Only if we want to,' he said.

'Because our arrangement is purely pragmatic,' she said.

'Precisely,' he said. 'Whatever you want.'

'I used to think romance was synonymous with roses and cards at the right time, and rings and poetry.'

'And now?'

'None of that has the power to generate this,' she said, and indicated the night sky, Venus over the sea, the moon sliding higher into the heavens. Andrew slipped his arm about her waist. They could have been any couple, Lara thought, in the middle of their lives, strolling along a moonlit beach.

'We're a cliché,' she said. 'Don't you think?'

'What's wrong with that anyway?'

'Don't know. I used to think it was something terrible. Maybe when you think your experience is unique and then realise it's a copy of a million other lives, it makes that experience cheap, not precious enough. Brock leaving me was a cliché. Millions of bored men desert millions of tired women. I was one of them. It depressed me.'

'I know. It takes a bit of an effort to rise above the ordinary. If we ever do. I think we can, though some people are more susceptible to typical primate behaviours than others.'

'Are we exhibiting typical primate behaviours now?'

He grinned. 'No. But later we will be.'

'I won't want to make any effort to rise above that,' she said.

'Me neither,' he said. They made it to the dark rocks at the end of the beach. There was no one around. They turned around and began the walk back again. 'I promised Dot I'd bring her home,' Andrew said. 'I didn't know she wasn't happy. I'm so glad she told me.'

'Oh, Andrew, now that makes me glad. Where will she stay? What will she need?'

'I thought she could stay with us, in the house. We'll set up the cottage as a comfy guest room for when your kids come and visit, and let's plan to get that happening soon. We'll look after Dot, and get help as and when and if needed. What do you think?'

We, us, my kids, she thought, and nodded.

She smiled and watched their feet leave momentary marks in the sand, indentations that were swallowed up by the waves over and over as they went.

'I think it's wonderful. What did Dot think of that?' she asked quietly.

'Dot commands it.'

'Obviously. I'll wait on her night and day.'

'What about me?' he said.

'I'll fit you in somewhere,' she said.

Andrew stopped. A late flock of gulls flew overhead and landed on the shore in front of them. He pulled her close and whispered, 'when I saw you kissing that bloke it actually drove me crazy. I could have killed him.'

She laughed and put her hands on his chest. 'He didn't even put his tongue in my mouth. He just clung on with his lips a little too long.'

'Whatever. I couldn't stand it. It made me crazy.'

'No one's ever been driven crazy on my account,' she said. 'Not that I know of. In all my life.'

'Well that has changed,' he said, and began to kiss Lara so passionately that she had to pull back and explain something to him.

'There's a very comfy bed a fifteen minute walk from here.'

'I know,' he said.

'And there are problems with sand,' she explained. His response was to take off his shirt and throw it on the ground at her feet.

'We're covered,' he said, sliding his hands up her shirt sleeves so that she shivered.

'We could be arrested,' she said against his mouth.

'Exciting!' he said.

★ ★ ★

If the universe had given her a picture of the romantic scene that unfolded on the beach, Lara wouldn't have dared to believe it. In the morning she sent Joanne, her kids and Ruby, a photo of a heart-shaped stone on the beach sand, and a selfie of Andrew and her.

34

They collected her car and headed back to Byron Bay in convoy.

Driving ahead of Andrew, she felt his presence behind her all the way. It felt good to be tailed like that, knowing if she broke down, or went the wrong way, he'd be there, at her back. When they arrived in Byron, tears sprang up behind her eyelids. She realised she thought she'd never see the place again. She drove to a familiar property and parked outside as Andrew drove up behind her. They both got out. Emotions ran through her, all the colours of the rainbow, from indigo to bright yellow.

He walked over and took her hand.'This is the house where you first stayed when you got here?'

'This is it. See that cottage on stilts up in the trees? That was my first home on the continent. I loved it up there.'

They walked through the back-garden gate and headed up the path to Ruby's front door. Lara had sent a text, but wasn't sure it had been received. She knocked.

Ruby appeared at the door, and when she saw Lara, and then Lara with Andrew, she put her hand over her mouth.'Holy Smokes!' she said.

After hugging her friend tight, Ruby looked at Andrew. 'And you are?'

'Andrew,' Lara said.'Dr Andrew Roberts.'

'Well, nice to meet you Doc Roberts. Now, you're going to have to tell me what's going on here before

I jump to conclusions. But first, come in, come in. Nigel? Honey, we have guests!'

Nigel. Mr Long Schlong. Nigel came down stairs and Ruby made tea. They all sat together in her living room.

'To what occasion do we owe this wonderful visit?' Ruby asked.

'Ruby well, firstly, sorry for my silences. There's been a lot going on. The news I'm here to announce is I'm going to make this place my permanent home, and this man ...' she looked at Andrew, 'we're getting married.'

'Blow me down!' Ruby said, and ran to Nigel to kiss him full on the lips. Then she kissed Lara and then, to his awkward surprise, Andrew.

'Love is all around us. Heck, yeah! It's morning, but let's have a drink. My darl, that is the best goddamn news in forever — since Nige came on the scene,' she added, giggling. 'Now, before we all get drunk, listen to this, Doc Roberts. When your lovely Lara first got here, I took her to a psychic. And the psychic said — yes, she did — Divine Deborah said that the one Lara would meet, would have grey hair and glasses. You look about exactly like the man she was talking about. Remember Lara?'

'I do,' Lara said and smiled. 'She also said not to worry about my kids when I wasn't worried. I hate to point out that it's a bit of a no-brainer, more than her innate psychic abilities. I'm forty-four. It's likely that any man I meet at this stage of my life will be either grey or have glasses or both.' She smiled at Andrew.

'You can think what you like, darl, but she said it, and it's true. And what about Brock? Did he not try to grovel his way back to you?'

'Oh, all right, he did.'

'So, was the psychic right, or was she right?' Ruby insisted.

'I'll give her seventy per cent,' Lara said generously.

'Thank you! Have a seat Andrew. Nigel, be a doll and get the whipped cream, will you? I left it in the fridge.'

★ ★ ★

At the end of the visit, on their way back to their cars, Lara said, 'here's a test for you.'

'Yes?'

'I'm going to tell you something. Don't jump to conclusions.'

'Okay. Go.'

'When I first met Nigel, neither of us had any clothes on.'

Andrew's face was immobile.

'Good.' She laughed.'You're not even wincing.'

She told him about the nude beach, and Ruby and her and Mr Long Schlong.

'Truth is, though,' Lara said,'I'm a prude and I managed to avoid seeing what was right in front of my nose, by staring intently at his face.'

Andrew squeezed her hand.'Your trust test.Did I pass?' he asked.

'I'll give you about a ninety per cent,' she said.

'I'm happy with that if you are.'

'I get it,' she said. 'I know what it is to lose trust. But one day when I've loved you for years and years, I want to believe you'll score a hundred per cent on the 'do you still trust me?' test.'

Andrew looked at her, bemused, as a smile spread

across his face. She saw that he couldn't say anything. She took his hand and said, 'let's go home.'

They arrived back at Andrew's house and parked their cars on the grass. Lara felt tired, but when she saw Valencia came running out of the house, the blood began to flow back to her legs.

'Two and a half days ago I packed everything away,' Lara said to Andrew. 'I thought I was leaving forever. There's nothing in the cottage to go back to.'

'I know,' he said. 'Let's start out the next leg of the journey together. From scratch. Stay with me from this moment on?'

'Yes please,' she said.

'Oh, thanks God,' Valencia cried out as she came up to Andrew and Lara.

'Doctor Andrew, you find her? At the airport?'

'Yeah,' he said. 'I caught her just in time.'

'He not let you go,' Valencia said to Lara, dabbing her eyes with the corner of her shirt, and then embracing her. 'He go to find you, and bring you home.'

'Always,' Andrew said. 'I'll always come and find you and bring you home.'

'Doctor Andrew. Your mother. She call. She very cross. She say, when in hell you going to come get her out of the shit hole.'

Lara couldn't wait to see Dot.

'Tomorrow,' he said. 'Tomorrow first thing we'll bring her home and take care of her here for the rest of her life.'

'You tell Mrs Roberts, okay?' Valencia said to him.

'Okay, Valencia, I'll give her a call in a minute. Thanks.'

Lara moved in with Andrew. Wryly she thought, there was nothing to move, except a suitcase and herself, along with her recent past, her recent history. It was remarkable how easily and comfortably they all fitted into her side of the king-size bed.

They slept with the windows open, and the night wrapped itself around them and held them there in the darkness. Somewhere just before dawn, Lara woke up. The bed was empty.

She got up and crept out of the bedroom. The front door stood open and swung in a late wind. She stepped out onto the veranda and saw Andrew there, leaning against the railing, staring out at the hills, at the stars. When he turned to her his face was wet and shiny and she was afraid to come close.

'What is it?' she whispered.

He didn't say anything for a moment. Then he sighed. His face was full of emotion. He took three steps towards her and held Lara against his heart.

'It's love,' he said.

Acknowledgements

Thanks to the wonderful team at Journeys to Words Publishing and especially to publisher Jen Hutchison. My gratitude too, to the wounded women warriors in the world who have shared their stories with me of loss, betrayal and finding hope again.

Other titles published by Ulverscroft:

ALCHEMY AND ROSE

Sarah Maine

1866. Will Stewart is one of many who have left their old lives behind to seek their fortunes in New Zealand's last great gold rush. Rose is about to arrive on the shores of South Island when a storm hits and her ship is wrecked. She is snatched from the jaws of death by Will. Drawn together by circumstance, they stay together. But after a terrible misunderstanding they are cruelly separated, and their new-found happiness is shattered. As Will chases Rose across oceans and continents, he must come to terms with the possibility that he might never see her again. And if he does, he will have to face the man who took her ...

WHERE THE DEAD MEN GO

Liam McIlvanney

After three years in the wilderness, hardboiled reporter Gerry Conway is back at his desk at the *Glasgow Tribune*. Once the paper's star reporter, Conway now plays second fiddle to his former protégé, crime reporter Martin Moir.

But when Moir goes AWOL as a big story breaks, Conway is dispatched to cover a gangland shooting. And when Moir's body turns up in a flooded quarry, Conway is drawn deeper into the city's criminal underworld as he looks for the truth about his colleague's death. Braving the hostility of gangsters, ambitious politicians and his own newspaper bosses, Conway discovers he still has what it takes to break a big story. But this is a story not everyone wants to hear as the city prepares to host the Commonwealth Games and the country gears up for a make-or-break referendum on independence.

THE GREAT ESCAPE FROM WOODLANDS NURSING HOME

Joanna Nell

At nearly ninety, retired nature writer Hattie Bloom prefers the company of birds to people, but when a fall lands her in a nursing home she struggles to cope with the loss of independence and privacy. From the confines of her 'room with a view' — of the car park! — she dreams of escape. Fellow 'inmate', the gregarious, would-be comedian Walter Clements also plans on returning home as soon as he is fit and able to take charge of his mobility scooter. When Hattie and Walter officially meet at The Night Owls, a clandestine club run by Sister Bronwyn and her dog, Queenie, they seem at odds. But when Sister Bronwyn is dismissed over her unconventional approach to aged care, they must join forces — and very slowly, an unlikely, unexpected friendship begins to grow.